A VERY MERRY ALPHA CHRISTMAS

LOGAN CHANCE

Liz —
Enjoy this
holiday gift
Logan Chance

Copyright © 2019 by Logan Chance
All rights reserved. No part of this publication may be reproduced, distributed, or transmitted in any form or by any means, including photocopying, recording, or other electronic or mechanical methods, without the prior written permission of the publisher, except in the case of brief quotations embodied in critical reviews and certain other noncommercial uses permitted by copyright law.

To obtain permissions, please contact Loganchanceauthor@gmail.com

There is nothing I would not do for those who are really my friends. I have no notion of loving people by halves, it is not my nature.

JANE AUSTEN, NORTHANGER ABBEY

A girl should be two things: classy and fabulous

COCO CHANEL

INTRODUCTION

**A Very Merry Alpha Christmas
(A Holiday Romance Collection)**

Is there anything hotter than getting your very own alpha under the Christmas tree? How about three filthy alphas instead?

This is a fun and steamy holiday collection filled with not one, but three sexy alphas just for you.

NORTH:
North Caspian, a very successful alpha boss and his lively employee, Holly Winterbourne, will heat up your holiday and kindles. North owns a store for the celebrity babies of Hollywood. When Holly accepts a job there, she is immediately intrigued by her Scrooge of a boss. THIS BOOK

IS FUN. (No celebrities were harmed in the making of this book)

EVEREST:

Ginger Darling hates her boss. Meredith Taylor is a mean, overbearing tyrant controlling Ginger's holiday plans in the palm of her greedy hands. Ginger decides her boss needs to get laid, and the stranger she met in the elevator earlier this morning is the perfect choice to stuff Meredith's stockings. He was handsome enough. Not that she noticed.

Everest Snow has a secret, and a mission. He won't let some redhead angel ruin his plans. Date her boss? Gladly, it only helps him achieve his goal...but why can't he get his little matchmaker out of his head? And why is he going along with her ridiculous ideas instead of making a move on her under the mistletoe? Everest and Ginger will liven up your holiday. Get ready.

GRAHAM:

Graham Steele is the owner of the Mountain Goat Resort and Zoe would love nothing more than to get her handmade soaps in every room. "It was only supposed to be one night of bliss before my big meeting. But, I never expected to run into my one-night stand the next morning as I pitched my proposal. And I never expected his counter proposal...a fake engagement."

(Graham is a Holiday Novella previously published in 2018 and will include new bonus material.)

Keep in touch with Logan.
Join The Logang
Get a special gift from Logan!
Hang out with Logan on Facebook
Like Logan
Visit Logan on Goodreads
Follow Logan on Amazon
Follow Logan on Instagram
Follow Logan on Bookbub

***

Want more sexy fun romantic reads?
Sign up for Logan's List and receive a copy of RENDEZVOUS, a steamy spring fling novella.
CLICK HERE to claim your book.

EVEREST

Ginger Darling hates her boss. Meredith Taylor is a mean, overbearing tyrant controlling Ginger's holiday plans in the palm of her greedy hands. Ginger decides her boss needs to get laid, and the stranger she met in the elevator earlier this morning is the perfect choice to stuff Meredith's stockings. He was handsome enough. Not that she noticed.

Everest Snow has a secret, and a mission. He won't let some redhead angel ruin his plans. Date her boss? Gladly, it only helps him achieve his goal...but why can't he get his little matchmaker out of his head? And why is he going along with her ridiculous ideas instead of making a move on her under the mistletoe? Everest and Ginger will liven up your holiday. Get ready.

ONE

Ginger

AH, Christmas. The time of year that warms your heart. Makes you sing sweet songs of joy and peace, and browse online for the perfect gift. Something that truly speaks of a person near and dear to you. Well, in most cases. In my case, it would be shopping for something that speaks to how big of a bitch my boss is. And not a cool bitch in the way that most women aspire to be a bad-ass boss bitch. No. I'm talking epic she-devil type of bitch. Wanna throat-punch a bitch type of bitch. But, that will never happen, because she is also a mob boss. Allow me to clarify. She owns one of the most successful cosmetic companies in the country. Same difference.

"Miss Pennywise Wannabe is honestly making you work late on your birthday, G?" my friend, Bianca, asks, even though she should already know the answer to that question.

When do I not work late? I'm practically living at my place of employment these days.

I blow out an exasperated breath. "It's fine, really," I lie. "I can celebrate my birthday tomorrow. Or you know...never. Keeps me younger this way. Gotta look at the bright side, Bianca, I guess."

Bianca huffs into the phone, rather loudly. "Do not tell me the twenty or so people I have here waiting to surprise you when you get off work to help ring in your twenty-second birthday is all a figment of my imagination."

"Bianca, I don't know what to say. I mean, maybe I can skip out..." I can't even finish my words before Meredith Taylor, the queen bee of her beauty company, Guru Girl, pages me on the intercom.

She's one of those mediocre social media influencers turned pro, now prominently legitimized on Forbes richest under thirty list and everything.

It's inspiring to a girl like me. We're close in age, and I have dreamed of launching my own line since I was a kid fooling around with my mom's Covergirl lipsticks.

I have a decent following of people I teach makeup tutorials to online, for my channel Red Hot Beauty Looks, but who doesn't these days? It's like everyone is practically a model or a guru of some sort, when really the bulk of us are just dreamers working nine-to-fives we despise. Like me. Like right now. But, I want to do something special to separate myself from the crowd. Working for Meredith gives me a little bit of clout. And I try to keep my eyes open to everything she teaches me, even the little things. So, yeah, my days are long, sometimes never ending, and I have to cancel plans with my friends regularly and I have no real social life. Let's not even discuss romance.

That is DOA. I haven't had sex with anything bearing a pulse in months. Thank goodness for vibrators and *Magic Mike* being streamed on Netflix. At least there's that small blessing.

The trade is worth all the sacrifice. You get nowhere in life just sitting back and watching as a spectator. You have to be down in the field getting your knees dirty if you want to win the game. And damn it, I want to grab life by its muddy balls.

Unfortunately, working here at a beauty company isn't all about glam. I also have to put up with a lot of mundane tasks, too, from my hellish boss. Like getting her coffee, booking her mani/pedi appointments, and sometimes giving her hair a blow-out. I actually don't mind she asks me to do that, to be honest. It's one of the closest things she asks me to do for the industry I love. And it also makes me feel like perhaps she views me as someone who isn't a horrible flop of fashion.

I mean, you wouldn't ask someone to style your hair for important meetings and networking parties if you didn't think they looked good, right?

But, there are things about me she's not impressed with, including my coffee fetching skills, phone answering skills, and overall office duties. I'm honestly surprised I have this job at all. It was a longshot to even get an interview, but for some reason, I'm here.

Maybe she sees potential in me. And that is my hope which keeps me coming back day in and day out, putting up with such a tyrant.

The only thing bothering me about working today is the fact there's a beauty guru, Trinity Sykes, who's launching a new mystery product for her Holy Trinity company and I want to buy it so badly. I'm a huge raging fan girl of Trinity. But, there's absolutely zero way I can buy it from work. And the hype and demand for her products are so great that you have to basically refresh her web page every thirty seconds until launch to even stand a chance at buying something.

I don't dare log onto Trinity's website from Guru Girl's computers. And I double don't dare even looking it up on my phone.

Trinity Sykes is Meredith's biggest competition. I'd be slaughtered for showing her support. They've been at war for two years, though no one really knows why. Meredith chalks it up to jealousy, but others whisper about a cheating scandal.

Who really knows.

Not my circus, not my monkeys. Ya know?

Suddenly, a familiar sound fills the quiet space of our offices and I know exactly what it is. Despite rumors on page six of the *Gossip Daily*, it's not a cat being skinned alive.

This sound happens about once every three months when a new product of Guru Girl is getting ready to launch. It's the sound of Meredith going insane. Seriously. It also sounds like a cat being skinned alive, hence the speculation and random PETA undercover jobs. Nails on a chalkboard would sound perfectly angelic, like a harp being artfully strummed, compared to Meredith Taylor in a fit of rage. She's a fucking rusty fork screeching across a dinner plate. I'd trade that sound over her screaming through the office any day of the week.

"Bianca, I have to go," I whisper into the phone before hanging up as Bianca tries to get in one last rebuttal on the 'whys' of how I need to be home right now.

After a small prayer to the cosmetic gods, I roll my chair back and take a deep breath. Why does twenty five steps toward her office feel like walking the plank?

Right before I reach the threshold of her doorway, painted

hot pink, mind you, she screeches, "and you better have my Quad Grande, non-fat, extra hot caramel macchiato upside-down when your late little ass walks in here."

Ugh. Her coffee. How did I forget? Oh, right. My bestie was guilt tripping me for not celebrating my own birthday. There's no way in hell I'm walking in there without steamed caffeine perfection as a peace offering.

"Oohh I...spilled it, um, tripping over a...Versace model. They're all over the place today, thanks to the winter ads." I need to learn to lie better. And faster. "I'll be right back." As fast as I can trot on four-inch heels, I move my ass to the hallway with two sets of elevator doors.

It's a gamble, but the set of doors on the right hardly ever come down in less than two minutes of waiting. I jab the button on the left set of golden doors and bounce impatiently as time crawls. The building's pretty busy today, thanks to the winter collections and last minute details everyone is working on for the new product line's campaign. There's also a crap load of security. There's always a few guys undercover that you get used to seeing day in and day out when you spend as much time here as I do, but with the holiday rush there must be extra personnel on the books to ensure nothing gets fucked up.

Remember earlier when I said Meredith was a mob boss? Yeah. About that...the beauty community is kind of like the mafia. There's this hierarchy. There's these unspoken rules. And there's an endless game of sabotage.

It's survival of the fittest when big money is involved. And the beauty industry is a multi-billion dollar game. There's going to be some serious foul-play. And there's always some major drama to go along with it. Welcome to my life.

"Oh, come on. Move you stupid elevator."

Is kicking the door a bit too much? I don't feel bad about it. In fact, I'd like to Hulk Smash the door right now.

Why does this always happen to me? I swear, I need a refund in life for my bad luck. I have a list of things that hate me. Technology, money, and elevator doors.

But, I'm also not a huge fan of elevators back. So the feeling is mutual there. I just don't like the feeling of being trapped in confined spaces, and I *really* don't trust them. I mean, it's basically a rope connected to an anvil. Whoever invented elevators was some kind of evil genius. It solved a problem, sure, but at what cost? I'll tell you—my sanity.

When I was six, I was trapped inside of an elevator for two hours during an epic blackout in New York. While it made me have a greater appreciation for firefighters, it also manifested severe anxiety for riding inside of elevators.

My office in this building is eight floors up and in my apartment a few blocks north it's ten. Unfortunately, it's a necessary evil for living and working in the city.

"Oh, for the love of lipstick," I groan. "Work you damn demonic thing."

Someone behind me laughs. I don't dare turn around because I might be willing to Hulk Smash them too. I am in a no mascara-smudging mood.

Instead, I chance creeping on my phone to see if Trinity Sykes's mystery box has gone live yet.

Of course, it has.

And it's already sold out.

I stab at the elevator button again.

"Calm down, Killer. It's a busy day around here. You have

to be patient," a deep voice says from behind me. "You're only going to break it."

Don't turn around, Ginger...
Don't turn around, Ginger...
Don't turn around, Ginger...
Don't turn around, Ginger...
I turn around.
Holy dream touch blush, Ginger.

He's *not* what I was expecting. Mainly, because I have to look up. Way up. The man is like a skyscraper. My eyes are level with his chest when I face him, planted right in the center of his charcoal grey tie. It's a long, painfully slow haul all the way up to his eyes. I gulp once I reach his top floor. The man's eyes are like brilliant gems in his sockets. All twinkling and marvelous. A celestial canvas of emerald stars. I'm a bit lost as I stare at him, unabashedly gawking, until he cracks a playful grin.

That too, folks, is equally as marvelous.

His teeth are as white as the Milky Way and bone straight. Full pout too pretty for a man but perfect for him. His neck is thick and has those muscular handles across his shoulders that turn even the smartest of women into inept drooling zombies, but instead of craving to eat brains, I really just want to wrap my lips around his dick.

There.

I said it.

Even though it's so out of line.

He's a stranger...beautiful, but still.

I feel myself quaking. And that is just not normal. But neither is this mystery man. He is otherworldly. A beautiful alien waiting for a ride.

From the elevator.
I need to calm down.
Or lie down.
With him.
He can invade my Area 51 anytime.
Stop it.
I clear my throat and scrape a little bravery together.

"It's already broken, sir, in case you can't tell by the fact that it isn't coming down." I tap my painted blood-red nail to the button as proof.

He grins wider. "So why did *you* press it so many times, Killer?"

"I..." My brows knit together as I try to trudge up a lie. And fail miserably. "Look," I sigh, "I'm just trying to get out of here. I have enough on my plate without dealing with this too. So, please, don't harass me when I'm already up to my eyeballs —that are not as spectacular as yours, mind you—with drama and trouble. Thanks and Merry Christmas."

He blinks, rapidly. "You must work for Guru Girl."

I blow out an exasperated breath. "Did the extra wrinkles on my face or my non-stop ranting give it away?"

He smiles. "You don't have any wrinkles. You're pretty flawless to be honest."

Is it hot in here? Asking for a friend.

Play it cool, G. "Oh. Well, aren't you self-redeeming."

"I try." He smiles and something in his features changes. Becomes a bit warmer? The man sticks out his hand and offers a shake. His wrist dons a watch as sparkly as his eyes, complete with teeny-tiny diamonds around the face and banding making it look like freshly fallen snow sparkling under moonlight. It's got to be stupid expensive. Who is this guy?

"Let's start again, shall we?"

"Ok. Sure."

"I'm Everest Snow." I shake his hand. It's warm and strong, and a real good grip, too. He clears his throat. "Annnnd you are?"

"Oh." I break myself from his hold and snap back to reality. "I'm Ginger Darling. And yes, I work for Meredith Taylor at Guru Girl. I'm her assistant, actually." I feel a bit taller standing next to him now.

His eyes sparkle impossibly brighter, but his smile turns fiercely menacing. It also turns me fiercely the hell on.

"Do you really, now? Well, how about that. I never would have thought she'd hire someone like...*you*."

What the heck does that mean?

I'm not gonna go lose my cool for this guy. I stand taller in my heels.

"I do," I tell him proudly.

"And how does a girl all of...twenty years old?... land a job like that?"

"Twenty-*two*, actually. Thank you."

"Didn't answer my question, Darling."

"Well, I guess I must've had an impressive resume."

"I bet." He smiles tight.

What the hell does *that* mean?

Shut up, Ginger. Turn around and shut your face-hole.

Instead, I put my hand on my hip. "I happen to know a boatload about the cosmetics industry and even more importantly have a deep passion for all things beauty related. I live for this stuff. How dare you. You don't even know me."

His eyes do the magical little twinkling thing again. "Trust me when I say, *you* weren't the one I was doubting."

"Nice save, Mr. Sparkle Pants, but I think I'll just wait in silence for the elevator from here on out, if you don't mind, sir."

His shoulder lifts and falls nonchalantly. "Just speaking the truth. That's kind of *my* passion."

"Really? I would have guessed something more along the lines of standing in front of a camera while you get endless pictures snapped of you and your— " I wave my hand up and down his tall frame. "Well, all of this goodness."

Everest laughs. "Thank you, but no. I prefer being on the other side of the camera, actually."

"So you take pictures? You're a photographer? Is that why you're here today? For the campaign?"

Everest's thick brows pull tight for a moment and then I try to keep track of how many brain cells I lose while he glosses his bottom lip with the tip of his tongue.

Stay on planet Earth, Ginger. Keep it together, sister.

"You ask a lot of questions, Ginger Darling." He leans in, his good smelling suit wafting his delectable scent toward my face. It's an instant turn on. I love a man who knows how to properly perfume himself. What the hell am I saying? But, it's true. Couple that with his good looks, budding charm, and fabulous fashion sense, and I need to sound the alarm: Bitch down. Send help now.

"Why are *you* pressing the button if it doesn't help, Mr. Snow?" Our eyes meet in a brief challenge of wits. Everest jabs the button a couple more times. "Just being thorough, Miss Darling."

"I *bet*." There. That felt nice, throwing his own words back at him. My high doesn't last very long though, because the elevator doors suddenly ding and spread wide.

We both rush inside, stumbling a bit as we catch our ride and then stupidly, really stupidly, fight to press our respective floor levels. Everest has the advantage because of his Adonis like height, but thankfully, I have cat-like reflexes. I press the button for the lobby and he presses the number two. I wonder why. That's the legal department. What does he want to do there? He has to be a photographer. But why dodge the question earlier? That's some serious bragging rights, not something to recoil away from. Color me intrigued. Oh, *and* really effing late.

"Back off, Hercules. I was at the elevator first." I jab the button, rapidly.

He tugs on his thick locks. "I told you if it's lit don't press it again. You'll only end up..." We suddenly whir to a halt. Everest groans, pinching the bridge of his nose. "...breaking it."

And then everything goes black.

"Oops."

Emergency lights click on, leaving us in a pale-greyish light, surrounded by the mirror behind us and gold paneling.

Now, I'm not a big fan of freaking the fuck out in times of emergencies or disasters. In fact, I'd like to think I'm a pretty good Girl Scout, but this sends me heaving. I mean, full on clutching the railing and praying for my life type of meltdown.

And the prick laughs. "It will be back up and running soon. Calm down, Killer."

I can't even form a comeback because I'm frozen with fear.

He must notice, because he rushes to where I am and kneels down beside me.

Yeah, I'm on the floor as I hug the railing above my head.

His strong hand lands on my back, and he rubs soothing circle patterns across my spine.

"I'm sorry," he says in a hushed voice. "I wasn't trying to be a dick. I didn't know this was real."

"I just hate elevators," I manage to squeak out. "Oh God, this is the worst birthday in the history of all birthdays."

"Not true," Everest says, still rubbing my back, and then he sits next to me on the floor of the elevator. "You haven't heard about my fifteenth birthday when I lost a game of truth or dare. I had to streak butt ass naked down my block in front of the girl of my dreams house—Nicola Whitney—only to have her laugh at me, right to my face."

I try to laugh but it sounds more like a donkey with asthma. "That's pretty bad."

"Yeah."

"I guess, jokes on her now."

"What do you mean?"

He seems so innocent when he says it. Does he honestly not know he's hotter than the hood of a car in the middle of summertime?

Scorching. Blazing. Hot liquid magma. This guy is a walking volcano on the verge of an eruption.

And he has zero effing clue? Only adds to the hotness factor, in my opinion.

"Well, I don't know what you looked like in highschool, but I'll confess to you in this horrible coffin of an elevator, since we might never see the light of day again, that you are by far the hottest man I've ever laid eyes on. And I have seen some serious men in this place. I'm talking like . . ." My lips are suddenly locked by a thumb pressed firmly to my mouth.

"You ramble when you get nervous." He grins. "You know that?"

I shake out of his hold. "I'm not nervous. I'm petrified."

Everest hums and then looks around the space. "Oh, see that?" There's a piece of mistletoe hanging from the top of the elevator. Ha, what prankster put that there? Above people's heads so even strangers who happen to be trapped together for two minutes would have the very uncomfortable moment of should we or should we not. Oh, damn. I am now that person.

Everest throws his hands in the air. "I'm just saying it's there. I read once that focusing on an object or having a good distraction helps in this kind of situation. Honestly."

"I'm not kissing you."

"Of course not."

"I'm being serious."

"I'm sure you are." His eyes do that twinkling thing again. "We might be stuck in here for a while."

I gasp. "You said it would be up and running quickly."

"I was mostly trying to comfort you." He chuckles. "I honestly have zero idea how long this might take. But, I would suggest getting comfy. Like perhaps, just resting your head back and staring up at that wonderful little token in the ceiling kind of comfy."

Do not look up, Ginger . . .

Do not look up, Ginger . . .

Do not look up, Ginger . . .

Listen, hear me out...not only do I look up, but I also grab him by his luxurious suit lapels and tug with all my might to smack his fabulously sexy kisser on mine. And holy crap he tastes like a candy store. His mouth is Peppermint Patty mint-a-licious and his tongue is an expert sugar plum fairy dancer. Everest groans as he claims my face in his palms, framing my cheeks as he deepens our kiss.

I forget about the elevator as he kisses me. I forget about

my birthday. And disappointingly, my bestie Bianca. I don't even care about how late I am to deliver Meredith's ridiculously over-the-top latte. All I care about is this kiss. It's leg-shaking, heartbreaking, spin me on my axle type of good. I want to drink down how he smells and the groans he exhales from his mouth into mine.

His kiss is the only thing convincing me to not be afraid and shove a fistful of fingers into his thick quaft of locks. He pulls me in close to him, chest to chest and I'm lost inside his big strong arms, my breasts heaving against his rugged torso. We're like a tornado spinning out of control as he swoops me up into his lap and I can't help but to grind on him, feeling every bit of desire he has underneath those thin black dress pants.

"Damn," he says on a groan, moving his mouth from my lips to my throat.

Happy birthday to me...

I roam the muscles of his back as he claims the pulse point under my ear with his hot wet lips. The tips of his fingers skirt up my thigh, stopping just at the hem of my dress as if he's not sure how much further to take this.

I scrape my nails down his back completely loving how it feels to be wrapped around him. I don't do things like this. Ever. But holy eyeshadow, it's so hot and it feels so, *so* incredibly good. I'm about to give him the green light to keep going, to have me anyway he pleases, but suddenly, the lights flicker back on full blaze and the doors pry open.

On the other side of the elevator doors there's a firefighter dressed in his dark signature FDNY shirt and yellow pants. His mouth pinches as he tries not to smile at what he finds.

us. Two grown ass adults grinding and making out like feral teenagers unsupervised. Oh, the scandal.

I nearly laugh at myself.

I'm a bit surprised at myself. I usually would be bright red, blazing with embarrassment, but something about this, something about Everest makes me feel right. It almost makes me feel safe.

"You two ok in here? I could uh," he says with a little snicker. "I could close the door if you wish. Go get a slice, and come back later?" There's a group behind him that laughs, too. I'm guessing it's the rest of the firehouse.

Ok, now I'm freaking scarlet all over. The heat flares up in my cheeks and ears. And it's not because the fireman is also a big hottie. Chandler it says on his shirt.

What the hell is today? National Hot Guy Day? National Bitch Down, Send Help Day?

Well, folks, the help ain't helping because they're just as lethal as the culprit.

I fan my face and try to climb to my feet but my legs are all wobbly like a baby doe.

Everest rises up and keeps hold of me with his strong arms until Bambi gets her shit together on the only pair of red-bottom heels she owns.

"Thank you," I say to him.

Everest nods, something lingering in his eyes as he walks me to the door, allowing the fireman to pull me up.

We're not very far from the door, only a good foot difference from where it should line up perfectly, but I still need help getting free. As soon as I reach the floor and can breath the fresh air of the hallway, I feel so much better.

Another fireman asks me a slew of questions about

wanting to go get checked out at the hospital and if he can offer me a blanket or water or something, and in my midst of being so distracted, I don't get a chance to turn around in time and see Everest leave.

Which is odd in itself. Who makes out with a person and then just hauls ass? Maybe he has a girlfriend? Ugh. Shittiest birthday ever.

I sling my purse back on my shoulder and thank the men again as I try to focus. I still need to get Meredith her ridiculous coffee.

I take a deep breath. I'm about to storm the stairs so I can finally get out of this hell pit when I feel someone tap me on the shoulder. It's the hotty fireman. Chandler.

"Does this belong to you?" he asks.

He's holding out the mistletoe.

"Um ..." I pluck it from his fingers. "Yes. Thank you."

"Sure thing."

"Hey, you didn't see where he went, did you?"

"Who?"

I blink. "The guy that was in the elevator with me."

Chandler shakes his head. "There was just you."

"Are you joking?"

"I'm a fireman. We don't ever joke, sweetheart." He spins around and I swear I hear him laugh.

Ladies and gentlemen, I present to you a big ass case of what in the actual fuck?

TWO

Ginger

"OH, YOU WHORE." The only thing worse than getting ditched after an epic make-out session and grind-fest is your BFF laughing at you after you tell her all about it. "When you come home, you better spill the tea, the whole tea, and nothing but the tea."

"Bianca," I say lowly into the phone as I try to balance Meredith's latte in one hand, my macchiato quad in the other, and also hold my cell. I'm sure I'm already fired and will return to find my shit boxed up and waiting by the front door, if I'm lucky, but on the off chance Meredith doesn't fire me, I definitely don't want to return empty handed. "I'm begging you to please stop saying 'spill the tea.' Do you even know what you're saying?"

"You have changed Ginger Darling," she huffs, but it's playfully dramatic. "Just remember who stood by you through

Ramen noodles and dollar store makeup when MT starts making you the face of her empire."

"Oh, please. I'm nobody."

"You're amazing, G. Call me later?"

"Totes ma' goats."

She laughs at my lameness. I roll my eyes at it too. How could I not?

The line goes dead, and I shove my iPhone back into my purse and walk a little easier with only two objects to balance versus three.

I hustle to get back to Guru Girl, both dreading and anxious to discover my fate. Trinity Sykes's face beams across an epic billboard in Times Square showing off her new mystery box line of products. Finally the items are revealed. And when I see each product slowly bloom on the screen to reveal itself, I'm shocked, to say the least.

Forever Frost is the name and each item is almost an exact copy of what we've been working on at Guru Girl.

What the hell?

The name is even the same. Her collection is called Forever Frost and Meredith's is named Forever Frostbitten. Meredith has to be losing her shit, for real.

I move as quickly as possible back to the office. My chest heaves as I reach the floor, having climbed eight flights of stairs to reach her office, complete with coffee.

Meredith sits there at her hot-pink desk, complete with a faux fur hot-pink desk chair with the name of the company Guru Girl etched into the fabric. Everything in her office drips in hot-pink and monogramming and what isn't flashy and pink is flashy and gold. It's her signature look and styling.

Meredith acts like she can't hear me. She's lost in whatever she's staring at on her computer screen.

"Um . . ." I clear my throat and she blinks to life. It's like she slips a mask back on as she pays attention to me standing here, but instead of being a major bitch she just snaps her fingers for the coffee in my hand. "Sorry. There was a major elevator issue and we got stuck inside."

She sips greedily at her latte and I hold my breath hoping it's perfect. I didn't even have time to double check the order like I normally do.

"We?" is all she returns to me.

"Oh, yes. I got stuck with one of the models from Versace. Or at least he looked that good. I honestly don't know what he does. Photographer maybe? But, he was amazingly hot. Anywho, he broke the elevator and we were stuck inside."

She stares at me for a moment like I've lost my mind. And maybe I have. "There aren't any models shooting past three, Jennifer."

Oh, right. Yeah, she does that sometimes, too. Calls me by the wrong name. I've stopped correcting her because honestly, I've seen her do it to others too, and I think it's just her way of being extra bitchy. I don't want her to know it bothers me.

"Oh."

"Do you have any idea what's happening right now?"

"I um...I saw Trinity's billboard reveal. Yes. I'm so sorry, Meredith."

She scoffs. "You think I care? You have any idea what this scandal will do for our sales?"

What? "You don't care that she stole our idea?"

"*My* idea," she corrects, and it makes me want to vomit a little. Maybe I'm not some big shot company owner but damn it, I was there helping with the creation. I even named two of the shade colors in her liquid lipstick line. Big Red Bow. And Silver Bells.

Is she serious? Ugh. I can't take it anymore.

"I just thought maybe you would be angry she stole from us. And that she'll get credit for what we *all* worked so hard on."

She smiles wickedly, just like Cheshire Cat from *Alice in Wonderland*. "Jennifer, the only thing that matters at the end of the day is who kills it in sales. Don't be so naive. You're too nice and nice girls always finish last."

I swallow down the truck load of things I'd love to say to her, starting with my name not being fucking Jennifer. This lady needs a serious wake up call on how to treat people. No tact. None.

But like any good worker bee, I just nod and smile and let her be right. "Yes, ma'am. Uh, is there anything else you need for the day?"

Say no. Please say no.

"Actually there is." She hands me a stack of color swatches. "Go through these and pick out five shades. We're launching a new lip line immediately in response to Trinity's theft."

"Another winter collection? And I get to put it together?" What in the merry Christmas is this?

Meredith shrugs casually. "It's no big deal. Just a little in your face moment to throw some daggers back at Trinity. It will make us look good." She squints. "Unless you can't handle it, Jennifer?"

"Oh, no. I can. Truly, I can. I'm just a bit surprised, that's all."

"Well, head down to legal and sign some forms, then start brainstorming. Happy birthday, Jennifer."

I'm practically speechless. "Th-thank you. So much. Truly." She may have the name wrong, but she has the birthday right. I'm shocked.

She waves me off and goes back to staring at her screen.

I hustle my ass down to the company lawyer's office feeling like I'm floating on air. I'll get to pick and choose colors and names and everything kickass about an actual line of products? Are you kidding me? I'm soaring above the clouds. Getting locked in an elevator was honestly the greatest thing to ever happen to me. I don't even care if I was blown off by old what's his face. Everest Snow. Hottest man on planet Earth with a mouth like a poet and a body like a brick.

I knock on the door to Mr. Watson's office, and then push it wide open. And to my shock and surprise, inside the tight office is a face staring back at me that makes me weak in the knees.

He grins that menacing smile of his that could stop a freight train dead in its tracks from its power.

Everything about him is uber masculine and dripping with sex appeal. From the way his crisp white button-up shirt clings to his well-defined arms, to the way he has his hair swept up in a chaotic artful wave.

"Well," Everest rumbles, giving me a taste of that heart-stopping gaze he hones so darn well, "if it isn't the elevator killer herself." He pushes out a chair beside him. "Have a seat, Ginger Darling. We've been expecting you."

THREE

Everest

I CAN STILL TASTE her on my lips. Ginger leaves me with an unquenched thirst for more of her as I lick the flavor of her gloss from my mouth. She's a gingerbread and mint type of girl. I like that about her. It surprised me. Although it shouldn't have.

Speaking of which...

What the fuck was that in the elevator? I mean, I was honestly trying to distract the poor girl from having a panic attack. It scared me to see her like that. The same girl that kicked the crap out of the elevator frame just minutes prior was clutching the railing, looking pale as fuck and breathing hard. I didn't know what to do other than try to soothe her in that kind of situation. The mistletoe seemed like a good joke, a good way to do that. But the kiss? That kiss was something I wasn't banking on at all. And after she planted her sweet lips on mine, I was so fucking gone. I've never in my life had a feeling in my gut like that feeling I had while kissing Ginger Darling.

Her breath, her taste, her touch. How she clung onto me like I held all the answers. It was like kismet. And my brain had to get out. Because I'm not allowed to have *feelings* for Ginger Darling. I'm not really allowed to be fucking kissing her.

I have a job to do. I have a goal and I never stray from a plan. It's how I got to this level in my life. My reputation would never live down being seen consorting with Ginger outside of what my true plans for her are. People wouldn't understand, and I'm not about to get my world twisted in a knot over having some kind of masochistic urge to claim her.

First chance I took, I hauled ass out of the elevator, tossing the mistletoe at the fireman who saved our asses. I didn't look back. I didn't think about it again. I can't risk getting caught. I needed to disappear before she could see where I was really headed off to. And thankfully, I got lucky. Until, I didn't.

Until she walked her sweet little ass into Watson's office and turned white as a ghost seeing me sitting here at his desk, as a client. At least, that's how it looks. That's how I want it to look.

Ginger is still wearing her sexy as fuck red dress. The fabric clings to her curvy frame accentuating her hips and firm ass. Those tits could win awards. But none of it has anything on her strikingly beautiful face. Full lips and cobalt eyes. Her red hair flames atop her head like the goddess she is, even when it's all over the place, messily swept into a bun. Her skin is peaches and cream, but her lips are bright with the red-colored gloss.

I could nearly come just looking at her. She's like a naughty elf's wet dream. I try not to be so obvious but she's so fucking hot it's hard. Quite literally. I have to shift in my seat and tug on the tails of my button-down just to keep quiet about the situation happening under my designer threads.

Also, don't get me twisted. I'm not this guy. I'm not the guy walking around in a suit that costs more than most people's annual salaries. Not at fucking all. But for this week? This week I'll be this guy. Even though my closet at home is full of jeans and Chucks. Humorous screen tees and casual duds are my thing. I like to be comfortable. It speaks more of my person than my bank account and that's how I prefer shit in my life to run.

If Ginger walked in wearing worn out jeans and a scrappy tee, I'd happily still want her. She's beautiful beyond her clothes and that's something to aspire for, isn't it? The real kind of beauty you can't buy or fake. That's what gets me hard. That's something I'd champion. But, that's for another day. Today, I don't let her affect me. Today, I play it smooth.

"Have a seat, Ginger Darling. We've been expecting you."

She glances wearily between Watson and me.

"You are?"

"Yes. Of course." I have no clue what the fuck I'm talking about, by the way. But I need an excuse to get out of here before I blow my cover.

"Yes, we have, Miss Darling," Watson pipes up and I'm honestly shocked at his words because...*we* are?

I try not to laugh. I have zero fucking clue why Ginger is in his office, but I'm more than willing to roll with it.

"Who wouldn't wait for you, Ginger." I hop up. "Here, take my seat. I was just on my way out."

She stares up at me, a bit in my way of fleeing as she stands between the doorway and my freedom. "You have a habit of doing that, don't you?" She seems pissed. She hides it well, but I'm a pro at reading faces and body language. Plus, why wouldn't she be? I practically mauled her and then fled without so much as a 'thank you' and any man who has been blessed to put his lips on her mouth should most definitely be bowing at her feet.

I pretend not to notice as I reply, "Doing what?"

"Leaving rather abruptly." Oh, yeah. She's pissed.

I grin. "Maybe you just need to catch up, Ginger. Move a little faster to keep up with me."

She huffs. "In your dreams, Sparkly Pants."

I feign being burned. "On that note, I'll leave you two to your business." I try to slide by Ginger and make my way out, but now there are two people in my way. And the second person is much more pissed than the first.

Meredith "Hell on Heels" Taylor fumes as she blinks between us.

"Excuse me," she demands. "Move please, giant man in my way."

I chuckle a bit. "I was here first."

She steps up to me. "I own most of this damn building, bucko."

She's a spitfire, I'll admit that much. "Well, I didn't know that," I tell her. "But now that I do, by all means." I move and wave my hand for her to pass me by.

But, she just stands there, assessing me up and down for a moment until she hooks her neck around to question Watson about me. "Who is this man in my office?" And that is *so* Meredith Taylor. She could have just asked *me* my name. But no, that would be too respectful. She's a woman that loves to degrade people. Especially, the important ones. At least, that's her reputation.

"I'm just leaving." I have to get out of here. I move past her but then I'm anchored down by Ginger grabbing at my shirt sleeve.

"Oh, but you just got here, Mr. Snow." Her eyes are doing something. They grow a bit larger than normal and wait for me to say something in return as her lips smile tightly. "You should meet my boss. This is *Miss* Meredith Taylor. You know, the woman you could not believe would hire a girl *like* me. Remember?" She faces Meredith. "This is the guy who got me stuck in the elevator. The reason why your coffee was so late."

I laugh. "That's why you were so angry? Because you had to fetch coffee? And I didn't break the elevator, Ginger. You're the one who kicked it."

She straightens her spine. "I only kicked the outside doors."

"Yes." I grin. "But then you violated the inside, too, didn't you?"

She's gone from pissed to fuming. She gives Taylor a good run for her money.

I smile bigger as she grows impossibly cuter. I only like razzing her because her nose wrinkles up in this adorable way. And then I notice she has a beautiful dusting of light freckles across the bridge of her nose. And if her fury didn't turn me on, the freckles definitely fucking hit the mark. God damn. Does she get any sweeter?

Meredith pushes between us. "Jennifer, did you sign the documents I requested, yet? Winter won't wait forever. We need to get to work on this right away if you want your chance."

Did she just call her Jennifer? What the fuck? She doesn't even know her name? Her own employee?

Ginger smirks a little, glancing at me, but shies away when she stares back at Meredith, which is completely understandable. The woman is a tyrant.

"I was just about to. If I can get a moment with Watson, that is. Alone."

Was that a dig at me or 'Hell On Heels'?

Don't care. This is getting interesting, either way.

What is Meredith talking about? Has she offered a deal to Ginger? Hell no. Not on my watch. The lady doesn't even know her name. There's no way she'll respect anything Ginger does for her. And that just isn't fucking happening. Not on my watch.

"I actually interview people," I interrupt, angling myself more toward Meredith than Ginger, acting like a wall to block her. "I'd love to interview you. Such an interesting woman. Powerful. Smart." I put out my hand so she'll notice my expensive watch.

And she takes the bait. "Oh, are you one of those horrid tabloid bloggers?"

Ok, maybe not.

I laugh in a way that says *are you shitting me lady?* "Not even close."

Meredith eyes me like she's picking out a new handbag. "In that case," she purrs, "sign me up."

Bingo.

FOUR

Ginger

I'M WATCHING a horror film happen right before my eyes. Everest is flirting with Meredith? At least, that's what it looks like to me. But why? Is he some clout chasing whore disguised in a nice suit and heartbreaking smile?

What's even worse is that Meredith appears to be smitten with him, like honestly taken by his charms. It's an easy thing to do because he's so disgustingly handsome and coy, but it still irks me. By the time he's done whittling his way into her world, she walks away like a high school girl experiencing her first crush. I think it's honestly the only time I've ever seen her actually happy. If you can even call it that.

Everest has this shit-eating grin on his face when he emerges from Watson's office. He shoves his hands deep into his pockets. I try not to pay attention to the fact he has a very narrow tapered waist that probably resembles a washboard when he disrobes. Fuck. Now I'm picturing him naked and how it would feel to rub myself like a dirty distressed shirt all over his ripped abs.

That is, of course, when he decides to turn my way.

With a shake of my head, I turn to go back into Watson's office to sign my name away on the project Meredith has planned for me, but Everest jumps in front of me as a line of defense between me and the door.

"Where do you think you're going, Killer?"

"Get out of my way, Everest. I have actual work to do."

"No, you really don't." He gently lays his hands on my shoulders and ushers me away, but I shake him off.

"You're going to get me in trouble again. I was actually starting to have a good birthday until you showed up. Things were on the upswing." I face him. "But now it's all jumbled up again."

Everest's eyes soften and he gazes down at me. "What exactly are you so eager to sign in that office, Ginger Darling?"

"It's none of your business."

"Ok, let me propose this in a different way. Don't think the person you're making a deal with, a legally binding deal, should at least know your name?"

"She knows my name," I scoff.

"She called you Jennifer."

"It's just her way of being a jerk. Some people trap you in elevators. Others call you by the wrong name. You know?"

"I didn't trap you." He smiles. "But I damn sure don't regret getting trapped with you."

"Really? Because it looked a lot like you'd rather be

trapped with my boss than me, the way you acted in Watson's office."

Everest shrugs. "Would that be so bad?"

"What?"

"Meredith being a little distracted. Would that be so bad?"

I swallow. "You're asking me if it's ok that you interview her?"

"Maybe I should do more than that," he muses. "Maybe she needs a good man in her life to get off your back and not be so "hell on heels" all of the time, Ginger."

I baulk at him, and then die of laughter. "This has to be a joke. You're joking with me right? Pulling my leg? You don't honestly want to date my boss. Not Meredith Taylor."

"Why not? It damn sure couldn't hurt."

Is he going insane? He's too damn charming and good looking for someone like Meredith. She will eat him alive. If she were a mother lion she'd be the one who eats her cubs. That's the kind of woman he wants to date? Why? Hm.

"And what do you get out of it, Everest?"

"Does it matter?" He shrugs and that twinkling comes back into his eyes. I've come to observe that usually leads to some kind of trouble where Everest is concerned.

My thinking cap tightens as I stare him down. I cross my arms and give more serious thought to his idea. "Why are you telling me this?"

"Because it seems like you have an issue with it after our little...moment."

Stab me in the chest with a spoon. "Is that what you call it?"

"What would you like to call it, Ginger?"

"Something that is never, ever, *ever* happening again. That's what it's called, Snow." I tug the mistletoe from my bag and extend it to him. "Here you are. You're gonna need this back to even have one single iota of a shot at landing Meredith Taylor as your date, let alone whatever else you have up your designer sleeve."

"Oh damn. You've been walking around with this all this time, baby?" He grins, staring at the mistletoe. "Oh, Ginger, you were just waiting to see me again, weren't you?"

"In your dreams."

Everest smiles, and then takes the mistletoe from me. He gazes down at it for a long moment. "Ginger."

But he doesn't say anything else.

"Yes?"

"Just making sure you're aware that I remember your name."

"What? Why?" I ask.

Everest snaps his eyes back up at me. They deepen and smolder. "Because I want you to think about that before you sign your life away. Meredith's the kind of woman that would trade one of her own children for a good headline. I'm the guy who knows who you are. I'm the guy, at the end of the day, who will remember your name."

Everest softly caresses the bottom of my chin and then turns away. I stare at his back as he heads for the elevator.

This is crazy. I don't even know this man. How can he be so all-encompassing when I don't even know a single thing about him other than his name? He could be a serial killer or some creepy stalker for all I know. Just a few short hours ago, he was an annoying pest at the elevator doors, and then my secret crush as we locked lips. And now? Now, I want to run after him. It's like he has some kind of magnetic pull embedded in me after our kiss. I can still taste him all minty and manly on my lips.

But, I have no real reason to trust him, other than the fact, in my moment of feeling terrified he came to my rescue and rather than mock me he comforted me. He found a way to make me feel safe.

Maybe that's a good reason to follow someone. To trust someone. When the truths of life come knocking, they are the ones who are on the other side, waiting to offer you a safe place to shelter, and let you in.

Or, maybe he's just an epic jerk, trying to use my vulnerability to get at something else. Something I haven't quite figured out yet.

But I will.

BIANCA RUSHES me as soon as I walk through the door. I'm exhausted and in desperate need of a drink. A really strong drink.

She's wiggling something I recognize right away in her hand, all bright cobalt blue and shimmering with glitter.

"G." She beams, holding up the box. "Look at who sent you a PR package."

What?

I grab the box from her hands. "You have to be kidding me. What is going on with this day? It's like one weird event after the next."

She laughs. "Well, it's your birthday."

She's right. I can't even be mad at her. My birth was not normal. I came into this world feet first, what they call a breech baby. I broke my clavicle during birth and needed to stay in the hospital all pinned up like an injured baby bird. It's like I have no ability to do things normally.

But you're not here for that story, and frankly I'm not drunk enough to rehash history.

My present reality is I don't get many PR packages from companies that want me to review their products on my vlog tutorials and I damn sure never ever, *ever* get anything from someone as big and incredible, or as well-known as Trinity Sykes.

But here it is.

Her collection that she ripped off from Meredith and Guru Girl. I marvel at how stunning it is because, damn it, the thing is like a fine piece of art. It's more than makeup, it's more than just stuff to put on my face, it's everything. It's perfect. It's what I get off on as an artist, seeing this beautiful box full of ideas and colors brought to life, complete with a story that is clearly defined.

Holy candy cane lip gloss.

"Why does this look so incredible?" I mumble, pulling the palette out of the box.

Bianca smooths her hand over the glossy ice-blue box embedded with white glittery flakes of fake snow.

"Looks better than Meredith's Frostbitten." That was Bianca. She's bold like that. "I'm just saying, Ginger. You know I have to keep it real."

"She stole this idea, Bianca. But...how the hell is it so much better? Like everything is just better quality, better looking, better feeling. Damn it, feel the paper alone she used to wrap everything in. This is custom for this kit. This isn't what something knock-off feels like. Every piece would take months to design and put together."

"What are you suggesting?" Bianca holds her hands over her mouth. And then squeals like a little pig. "This is piping hot tea!"

"Please stop saying that." I roll my eyes and laugh a little. "I'm probably just sleep deprived and not thinking clearly. There is no way Meredith would ever copy someone. She's a legend. An icon."

I slide the package back to Bianca. "Merry early Christmas, Bianca."

"Really?" This makes her day. She even leaves me alone about the whole birthday party thing.

But, there's still booze and cake. Thankfully. We dive into both at warp speed. I'm shoveling huge bites of cake into my mouth letting the vanilla frosting swirl across my taste buds as she asks about Everest. I nearly choke.

"That good, huh?" She giggles.

I clear my throat and sip a long swig of wine. "Doesn't matter. He wants to date my boss."

Her eyes widen like saucers. "Are you shitting me?"

"I wish." Wait, what? I shake my head. "I mean... it's whatever. I don't even know him."

She hops up on her knees and faces me on the couch. She's applied the blue frosty color of Trinity's winter collection to her lids and that color mixed with her platinum blonde hair gives me serious Elsa from *Frozen* vibes, which only makes me laugh as she tries to have a serious convo with me about this whole Everest ordeal. And yes, it's an ordeal.

"G, you can't just make out with some random guy in an elevator and then say it's no big deal."

"Why the hell not? It's my life. It was a moment and now it's over. I'm good. I am *soooo gooood*."

She lights up like a Christmas tree. "Because this is everything. You haven't even talked about a guy, let alone made out with one, in months."

"Thank you for reminding me of my desolate and uber depressing life." I swig directly from the wine bottle. "God, he was so damn hot. And hard."

She bursts out laughing. And so do I.

"I knew you loved it."

"His mouth, his hands, his eyes...oh my gosh. His eyes are amazing. Green gemstones. And his smile is like a dream come true. Like a badass version of a Ken doll with an actual dick."

"But he wants Meredith? Ew. Why? I mean, she's pretty and all, and I get the whole she's rich thing, but yuck, is he just a gold digger or something?"

I slap my forehead. "Thank you, Bianca, for reminding me of my poorness."

"I just don't get it. That's all I'm saying. And why make out with you first?"

"I...I don't know." My head hurts.

"Maybe, it'll be good though. I mean, she's such a bitch."

"Are you suggesting I let this guy try to date her and whatever else, just to have a better, nicer boss?"

She nods with a smile. "We can always do a background check." She hops up and sprints for her laptop. "We'll make sure he's not a serial killer or something horrible, and then we'll decide."

I roll off the couch right onto the floor where she parks her little detective self. "What has my life become?"

"Epic." She laughs, typing at warp speed as she finds a place to do this thing. "Now. . .what's his full name?"

Fuck.

I take a swig of wine and stare at the blinking cursor on the screen, waiting for me to give up the goods.

FIVE

Everest

BREATHE. That's my motto for today. Breathe.

I stand outside the office doors of Guru Girl, waiting to make my move. Inside of my black dress pant's pocket my phone keeps vibrating, because my boss Hunter wants to know what the fuck is up. I've been avoiding him on purpose. I need to stay focused, and I really need to stay in character. This week's going to be hell.

The door to Meredith's office is hot pink and emblazoned with her signature logo for Guru Girl with the same double G's right in the middle. Which makes me twelve again, and inside my head thinks of every dirty joke regarding double D's and G's and well...you get it. I'll spare you the rest. Besides, I'm much more refined than my teenage self these days, with one exception—I feel like I've got a serious crush on a certain redheaded beauty. Unfortunately, she's also behind this door.

Doubly (no pun intended) unfortunately, she's not the person I'm here for today. Although, once I open the door, I wish I was.

Damn. Ginger sits at her hot pink desk looking like a goddess. A fucking goddess. She's undeniable. A ten. A girl with a great body is all good and everything, but damn I love a girl with a great set of eyes. Stop it. I'm not telling more juvenile jokes. I told you.

Ginger Darling has an incredible set of electric blue eyes that scream and demand attention. The fact she's also this amazing little make-up artist that knows exactly how to frame them in warm caramel tones that really make them...just fucking amazing. I'm honestly a bit in awe and it's unsettling. I'm never in awe. So, I breathe.

Fucking *breeeeathe.*

She spots me as she looks up to take a sip of her iced coffee. For a moment, there's something in her features that shifts, almost like she's happy to see me, but it quickly fades and turns into the all business route. "Can I help you?"

I play it cool. "I'm here to pick up Meredith for our lunch meeting."

"Oh." Ginger fumbles around her desk and it's then that I notice what she's up to. The pantone color swatch books. Storyboards. Ugh. She's creating something for Meredith.

I step closer as she swoops everything up into a neat pile and tries to act casual about it.

I lean on the desk a little, tapping my finger against the wood. Ginger glances up at me with her wide-eyed gaze, all innocent and sexy. Her lips could light a fire. My dick goes hard just thinking about those full glossy lips wrapped around it. The sounds she makes when she's turned on. Her breath on my face panting in ecstasy. Fuck. Breathe.

"Busy little bee, aren't you?"

She blinks her long lashes. "Um, Meredith should be out soon if you have an appointment." She holds my attention as she flicks her eyes from mine to my mouth. Fuck. Did she just moan?

I lean a little closer and lower my voice.

"You really think I give a damn about seeing her right now?"

"Um..." She rises from her desk and gathers up a bunch of papers.

I still her hands and then say to her, "What's wrong, Ginger?"

"Nothing. I'm just busy. You guessed it right. I'm just a busy little bee."

"Your smile isn't real."

"What?"

"It doesn't reach your eyes. What's really going on in that beautiful mind of yours?"

"I told you. I'm...just busy."

"Still thinking about us in the elevator?"

"Look," she says with a little sigh, "I don't want to make things awkward. In fact, I think it's great that you're interested in Meredith. She needs a good man in her life."

"Really?" I nearly laugh at her words. What would ever make her assume I am a good man? And why the hell would she want her boss to be happy after all the hell she has put everyone through?

"Yes, really. So please don't make lunch weird. Let's just get through it. Ok?"

"What do you mean?"

"I'm her assistant. And that means I tag along on most of these kinds of things."

"You've got to be shitting me."

"I wish."

My brow arches. "Do you?"

"Everest," she says, but doesn't continue.

We're locked in each other's eyes as time ticks on. What I wouldn't give to just lift her on this desk and fuck her senselessly. Those long legs wrapped around my waist. Her sweet voice in my ear as I make her come. There would be no better Christmas gift than that. Dear Santa, I've been naughty, yes I know, but I'm trying to make up for it. Please leave Ginger Darling under my tree. Naked. With a big red bow. Sincerely, Everest Snow.

I put my hand under her chin and it's all bets are off. We crash into each other and spiral out of control with a heated kiss that shoots straight to my dick. I'm so hard. My hands grab her ass, loving that she's wearing a tight-fitting jumpsuit that feels like a second skin under my touch.

Ginger tastes like a candy cane today. It only heightens my Christmas fantasy to the next level.

I picture her in my mind sucking on the candy, taking a long piece of the stick into her mouth and slowly pulling it away, and then humming at the taste of it. I could nearly come just picturing it in my head as she roams her hands across my expensive suit jacket and moans in my mouth.

Her hot breath is across my face and all over me and I cannot handle this shit. I want her so fucking bad. I'm seconds away from tossing her tight little body on this messy desk of hers when I hear the creaking of a door.

We immediately pull apart and turn away, respectively trying to recover and hide the evidence of what we've just done.

It's so naughty. Neither of us is getting shit from Santa. Let's be real.

But fuck, her kiss is so worth being bad for.

SIX

Ginger

I SHOULD BE PAYING attention to what's happening at lunch, but instead, I'm lost remembering what just happened in my office. Holy crap.

I nearly had sex with Everest on my desk. In my mind, all I wanted was for him to swipe his strong hand across the papers, send my work flying to the ground, and take me on that desk. I'm still wet thinking about it. And the worst part is, he's here with us, smiling that perfect smile of his with all his glimmering super perfect white teeth and charm.

And instead of staring at me, challenging me to not want him with his eyes and sexy tone, he's smiling that sexy ass smile at Meredith and acting very interested in everything she has to say, even though she's mainly talking about herself.

Ugh, of course she is. He's interviewing her.

Bianca and I found out that the name "Everest Snow" is a nothing burger. Yes, you heard me right. Nada. There's literally not a damn thing on the internet about him. So, I'm highly suspicious about why he's so interested in my boss. And me.

Or am I just a bar to leap over to get to her? I don't know. But, holy nail polish, he turns me on so badly. And honestly? There isn't anything about him that gives me bad vibes. I'm still drawn to him. I still crave him and fantasize about him.

What does he want with Guru Girl?

I made sure Meredith invited me to this meeting to keep an eye on him. That's an easy enough task. He looks fucking amazing. He's dressed in an expensive dark jacket and matching pants, looking dashing as ever with his dark hair in a chaotic mess that somehow he makes looks like a piece of art. And super sexy. He's aggressively masculine from his sharp jawline to his broad shoulders and even with his jacket on, you can see what a killer body he has under those clothes.

I've felt his strength and power as we tangled ourselves up in those two hot moments we've shared. And now, thinking about them all over again is making me want to bite down on my linen napkin because I'm about to moan his name if I don't.

I opt for filling my mouth with more wine instead. And as I take a sip, my eyes meet with Everest's for a moment.

He keeps stealing glimpses of me every now and then, but turns all his charm back to Meredith, who seems pretty smitten with him. I mean, how could she not be?

I'm not going to get upset about this. I'm not going to let it ruin the fact that I will have my own collection soon. There are more important things in the world than hot sex, charming men, and love. Right? Right. So, I keep my chin high and smile as I drown myself in wine. Which is dumb. Because I'm now beyond tipsy.

The good news though? There's now two Everests. And both of them look incredible.

"Jennifer, is the car waiting?" Meredith asks.

"*Youuuuu* bet your sweet ass it is." I put my cell to my ear because I have not in fact remembered to call for the car. But I am now. Or was.

Everest leans across the table and carefully snatches my phone out of my hands.

"What the heck, snowman?"

"I'll call for a car, *Ginger*."

"Sure, steal my job too." I swig another sip, but the glass is sadly empty. "Fitting."

"Jennifer," Meredith says, smoothing her hair back behind her ear in that pompous ass way she does things. "Watson tells me you haven't signed our deal yet. Is there a problem?"

"Nope. No problem. No problemo. None. *Nada*. Zip. *Zilch*. Holy shimmering highlighter, there's so many words that mean no. *Wow*."

"Then maybe you should sign them now?" She ruffles through her Louis Vuitton, and then slides over a folder.

Everest's hand tugs the folder away.

I glare up at him. "What's with you stealing *everything*? This is Christmas. A time for giving."

He hides a smirk. "I don't think you're in any kind of shape to be signing anything. Let's just wait on that."

"It's not your business, snowman."

Meredith backs me up. "She's a big girl. She can do what she wants. Men don't tell women like us what to do. Do they, Jennifer?"

"It's Ginger." Oh. The way Everest says my name sounds like an exclamation, a claim, a territory she should not cross. His eyes are heated when I stare at him. His nostrils just slightly flaring in annoyance and defiance and I'm beyond turned the hell on.

Who is this man? I don't know.

But I'll take two of them.

"I'M FINE. REALLY."

"You're walking like a newborn baby deer."

"Don't mock deers. It's politically incorrect."

Everest cracks a grin. "I doubt it is, and I'm not mocking them anyhow. It's a fact. They walk horribly as newborns."

"How do you know that?"

"Discovery Channel." He shrugs and then searches around. "Uh, your keys?"

"In my purse."

I can't let go of him, because if I let go, I'll fall down. We're outside my apartment door and I pray that Bianca's not home because this will be the "piping hot tea" she lives for. Me failing on my first ever attempt to conduct an investigation, and not only did I fail, but I brought home the main suspect. And now I'm telling him to take my keys and bring me into my apartment.

Everest roots around for the keys and then lets out this sexy sounding "ah-ha" once he finds them. Only he could make something like that sound good, I don't know why.

He carries me over the threshold and then closes the door with his foot, upping his appeal with how coordinated he is.

Might not sound like much, but I've dated a man who didn't know how to walk and chew gum at the same time before, so, you know, I have little to no experience with a man this well equipped, seemingly in every aspect.

He even knows how to handle Meredith. I mean, she wasn't even pissed that I had to take off early. Old Meredith Taylor would have had my head for a stunt like this. She barely even blinked at me as I got into a cab with Everest.

He sets me carefully down on the couch and I can't help but to snuggle into my sofa cushions. I'm so tired and the wine is not helping with that. There's no sign of Bianca.

Everest glances around for a moment, and then pulls a blanket off the back of the loveseat. That makes him laugh. Hard.

"It was a gift," I say in my own defense. "And it was an amazing gift."

"It's a burrito blanket. You honestly look like a little old lady all wrapped up like a burrito."

"I told you—*amazing*."

He's quiet for a moment. "It is."

I peek at him. "You were totally thinking of making a joke about eating me or something in that range of thought, weren't you?"

"Maybe."

"Don't play, Everest."

"Ok. Absolutely." He laughs.

"I knew it."

Everest smiles and then turns away. He pulls a chair away from my dining room table, and sets himself up close to me.

"What are you doing?" I ask.

He swipes a gossip magazine from my coffee table. "Just

making sure you get some sleep." He grins. "And don't do anything stupid like drunk dial an ex or your boss."

"You just want to sit there and imagine me as a Fourth Meal."

He laughs and it's real. And cute. And everything I desire. I have to snuggle myself deeper into my burrito blanket so I don't try to do something dumb. No, not like drunk dial an ex, but more like hop up from this couch and tackle this hottie with all my might.

I can't have feelings like that though, because this man is now dating my boss. Taking her to lunch. Smiling at her and calling the car to make sure she's taken home safely. Ugh. I close my eyes. It's safer this way if I can't see him. But, his presence being in the room follows me into my dreams where I'm swept away by the feeling of him never leaving my side.

And my mind replays us in the elevator all over again, except this time, the roles change a bit. Instead of that hottie firefighter Chandler being the one rescuing me, it's now Everest. I'm trapped inside of the hellish ride and calling for help only to have him open the doors with his bare hands, his skin glistening in manly sweat. Did I mention he's shirtless? Because, oh my eyeliner, he is. And it's a spectacular sight. Everest has a chiseled body that would make any of the Greek gods feel less than worthy, with his hair all swept up in chaos, those white teeth shimmering like diamonds. I nearly die from how gorgeous he is when he smiles.

"Are you ok?" he asks.

"I'm stuck in this elevator. Help me, please."

"Don't worry," he assures, "I'm here now, you're going to be just fine." Everest hops down from the landing and is swiftly on his feet, right before me in the darkened elevator. In this close proximity, the heat of his body rolls off him and I instantly get wet. His eyes are on fire as he takes in my appearance all disheveled and helpless, sweaty, and dying to be free.

"Trust me?" he asks, moving closer.

"Yes," I nearly moan. "God, yes."

He hums and then touches the underside of my chin. "Fuck, you're beautiful," he says, lifting my chin a little. "And so brave. I bet you were so scared, being trapped in here all alone."

"I'm not alone now."

"No." He nods. "You sure aren't."

"How will we get out?" I try to glance around but I'm stuck in the vortex of his gorgeous green eyes as he stares at me.

Everest caresses my face. "Trust me, Ginger. I just need you to trust me."

I wrap my arms around his neck and bring his face to mine, crashing our lips together. And this time it's so much hotter than the first time. Our clothes seem to dissingrate from the heat between us and I feel him hot and hard as we cling to each other, lost in a tornado of a kiss that whirls and spins out of control. Everest backs me up into the glass mirror of the elevator walls, deepening our kiss as he hoists me onto his hips, pinning me there without mercy. His hard cock grinds against my wet center and he pumps against me, breathing hard into my mouth as we break for the tiniest moment.

"I want you so bad, Ginger Darling."

"Mmm, Everest."

"Baby, oh, please, let me fuck you."

"Yes," I cry out. "I need you so much."

"Fuck yeah, you do. I need to know what that tight pussy is

like wrapped around me. Think you can take all of me, Ginger?"

"Give it to me. Yes."

Everest kisses the column of my neck until he reaches my collarbone. His hands knead my breasts and he sucks on my nipples. I quake under him, begging with my grinding hips for him to give me more. His body's so hard and muscular as I feel him under my own needful hands. It keeps me from remembering the danger we're in, as we hang in the elevator without power. Only a sex god like Everest Snow could keep me from thinking about how scared elevators make me. And he does it so damn well.

"You like getting fucked like this, baby, don't you?" he asks all huskily. "How many fingers can you take, Ginger Darling?"

"Ohh, yes. Mmm. More."

He plunges two fingers inside my wet pussy and I cry out.

"Yes, let me make you come."

"Oh, Everest."

"Say my name, baby. When you come, say my motherfucking name."

He pumps his fingers inside me, circling my pulsing clit with the pad of his thumb. His mouth attacks mine, his tongue a viper as he expertly laps at me giving me open mouth kisses so I can pant against his lips.

"Mmm, fuck me," I beg. "Please."

He takes me up high, like ascending on an epic rollercoaster. Until it comes crashing down. And not in a good way. In the way that I hear serious laughter and I'm shaken until I groggily open my eyes.

And there he is. All smiles and hotness staring back at me. For a minute I try to cling on to the dream, the feeling.

"Ginger..." he's calling me back to reality. "Open your eyes."

No. Let me stay here in my dreams for a while. Let me have my happy place. Let me have an orgasm.

He laughs again. I blink. I see him. Oh, shit.

"I'd be happy to, Ginger." He grins all cocky and smart...assy. "But I need to leave, Darling."

Did I say 'fuck me' out loud? "I didn't mean to say that. I was still dreaming."

"Yeah?" He toys with me, curling a section of my hair around his finger. His eyes stare adoringly at me which does weird things to my heart. "About who?"

"Mr. Clean," I lie.

He bursts out laughing. "Yeah, that sounds totally believable, Ginger."

"I was. He happens to be quite sexy."

"He's an animated drawing."

"That I'm sure is based off an actual person. Or at least, some kind of fantasy women have about a man not only being willing to clean their house, but also really freaking good at it."

Everest's eyes brighten. "I'm sure the marketing department had that very same thought in mind."

"Of course they did." I wrap the burrito blanket tighter around me because it feels like it will hold me together rather than turn me into the pile of mulch I feel like becoming when he smiles like that.

"Is that your fantasy?" he asks. "A man cleaning up your house? Doesn't sound too scandalous to me."

"You don't get it. It's not just any man. It's a very muscular man that you'd assume does something more manly—

according to what society has dictated is a man's job and a woman's job. It's breaking the stereotype."

He nods like he believes me, but also has a tug of laughter poking him in the cheek that he's really trying hard not to give in to. "So, you have social justice as part of your bedroom fantasies?"

"What could turn a girl on more than being empowered?"

His eyes flare. Boom. Got him. He tugs the burrito blanket around me like he needs a shield, too. That makes me smile. Big time.

"You're quite something, aren't you, Ginger?"

"Depends who you ask. Meredith can't even get my name right. My bestie thinks I'm an artist. People I don't know on the internet look to me to give them advice on how they should look. Life is weird. Life is so random. How does anyone trust it?"

He nods. "This we can agree on."

"What about you?"

"What do you mean?" he asks. Everest sits next to me on the couch, cupping his hands over his knees.

"Well, who are you? I feel like I know nothing about you. Other than the fact that you know my boss and kiss really good."

"That right?"

"Shut up. You know you do."

"Maybe I need to know more. What was your favorite part?"

"I said shut it."

He laughs a little. "Fine."

"Waiting on the info here, Mr. Snow. Is that even your real name?"

Everest looks away for a moment and then turns back to me. "Do you really like working for Meredith? That's something you've dreamt about your whole life? Working for a lady like that?"

"Listen..." I sigh a little. "She's not the friendliest, that's for sure, but you know she's in an industry that demands having a spine."

And while I feel like shrugging it off, Everest doesn't let it go.

"So you think she really has the talent to be where she's at?"

"What are you suggesting? I thought you had a thing for Meredith?"

"I have a...thing for the truth...let's just put it that way."

"I'm not spilling what my bestie Bianca calls "tea" about Meredith if that's what you're looking for."

"Good, because I'm not thirsty."

I smile a bit at that and so does he.

His eyes warm as he inches a bit closer and puts his full attention on me, those brilliant green eyes lingering on mine.

"You're right about needing a spine in business, Ginger. What about you? What about yours? Don't you want to protect how special you are? What you bring to the table?"

"I'm just a small fish in a huge freaking pond, Everest. I need this job. I'll climb my way up eventually. It just takes time."

He hesitates. "I think you're not giving yourself enough credit."

"Meredith asked me to create something. I mean, I'm already doing bigger things than I ever thought I would at my age."

"Don't you think that's a little odd?"

"What?"

He sighs a little, scrubbing his hand across his chin. "Listen, you said it yourself, Meredith is a goddess in the beauty industry, so why would she ask you—a self proclaimed small fish—to create something for her, if she's so damn brilliant?"

I sit up straighter. Who does he think he is?

"I'm sorry, are you suggesting Meredith is only using me?"

"No, *Jennifer*. I bet she really believes in you."

"You have some serious nerve, Everest." I hop up from the couch and the whole world goes wibbly-wobbly.

Everest's hands steady me as he rises from the couch, holding me steadfast in his arms. For a moment, I don't want to despise him, but damn it, he grins and it's all fire and brimstone again.

"I think it's time for you to leave, Snow."

"I'm really only trying to look out for you. I wish you'd believe me, Ginger. I wish you would trust me."

"Trust you? You? I don't even know you."

"You know how I feel though, right?"

And right now, I feel a whole freaking lot of him pressed up against me as we stare in a deadlock stare-off of all stare-offs. Is that even a word? Phrase? Who cares.

I'm gazing deeply into his green eyes as he stands towering over me with his tall frame and broad shoulders. My fingers itch to hook around his muscles and climb up on the mountain of man that is Everest Snow. I run my hands across his shirt, his jacket now flung artfully across the back of the couch, forgotten. I can feel so much more of him, finally. He's hard as a rock all over. I mean *all* over, people. His hips thrust a little as he grips my hips tightly, staring down into my eyes. I brace for his kiss, how hot it's going to feel on my lips. I can feel his breath on my face. I close my eyes.

"Ginger," he whispers as I feel his fingers strum soft as a feather across my cheek.

"Everest…"

He cups the back of my head.

The front door unlocks. Crap.

Instantly, we pull ourselves away. Bianca comes bounding in, smiles galore as she runs over to me. "Guess who I saw shopping in Times Square?" She shakes my shoulders and I try to smile at her. I don't think she's even noticed Everest. She doesn't give me a chance to guess. "It was Trinity," she squees.

"Awesome." I fake a smile. "Um…"

She finally turns to see Everest. "Oh, crap."

He laughs. "Nice to meet you, too."

"Bianca, this is Everest Snow." I smile in a way that begs her to play along like she's never heard his name before.

Her eyes grow double in size. "Oh. Crap."

She's horrible at bluffing. I shake my head but laugh a little.

"I was just making sure our girl got home ok," he says and my insides rattle.

His girl.

Butterflies invade my stomach in a frenzy. Our eyes meet and he's all fire. I try to swallow and not act like a total fangirl of this man. But there's just something about him that sings to me. Ever meet someone and just feel like you've known them forever? It's so easy and familiar with that person? I feel like that but with a serious undertone of attraction that leaves me all squirmy and longing for him.

"Yeah." That's all I can muster when he looks at me like

this. A wave of heat rolls over me, as if winter was just obliterated by his stare, and summertime is back in full force.

"I should go," he says. "You're in good hands now."

"You can't leave," Bianca says. "It's snowing like crazy right now. Haven't you been paying attention to the news today? There's a big storm about to blow through." She grins a little. "I'm sure you guys have been really busy working, though. It's totally understandable."

Holy sugar plum lip balm. I'm going to be stuck here with Everest. Maybe he won't stay.

He turns to face the window and his green eyes sparkle against the cast of bleak greyish light that filters through the window. It's a mess out there. I can *not* ask him to leave.

We stare at each other.

Bianca squeals, not at all keeping her feelings about him being here lowkey.

I roll my eyes but can't help but smile.

"I guess you're stuck with me," he says.

He says it like it's a bad thing, but damn, why does it feel so good?

"YOU HAVE TO HOLD STILL."

Listen, if Everest is going to stick around he's going to help me work. Snow, Hailstorms, lightening, floods, earthquakes...you name it...it has nothing on what Meredith will do if I don't come through with an amazing collection.

So, I use his forearm for my swatches. I have a first run of colors that have already come back from the lab. It's quite impressive, even for Meredith. I turned in my choices at lunch and they had already been formulated in just a few hours and shipped right to my office before I even left for the day. Talk about power and influence.

"I need a picture."

Everest shakes his head. "No, I think I'd rather not."

"Are you scared to be a man with makeup on his arm?"

"I'm just not into having my picture strewn across social media."

"You'd be the first." I chuckle at him but he's being serious. In fact, he looks pretty stressed about it. My curiosity is piqued. "We could do a full makeover and glam you up big time. What do you think about that?"

"Hard no."

I laugh. "No one would even recognize you, after I'm done."

"Still a hard no."

"Everest," I protest a little. "This is your chance to hit the big leagues. Being Mr. Muah. Oh, that has a nice ring to it."

"Keep swiping my arm, Ginger."

"Swatching, babe. It's called swatching."

He smiles and it's warm. Or maybe that's just me. I'm tingling too. We're shoved close together in my mock studio where I film my tutorials. It's actually just a small corner in my bedroom that I converted into something that on camera seems kind of plush and rich looking, but is actually much smaller than a linen closet.

Everest and I are just inches from the wall, under the heat of the lights, our legs intertwined as we sit on stools in front of the camera.

"Where did you learn all of this stuff?" he asks, shifting in his chair a little. "What made you want to get into the beauty world?"

I shrug. "It's just always been a passion of mine ever since I was a little kid. I used to steal my mom's heels and walk around in her bright red lipstick and my church tights. I thought I was so damn cute."

"Wow." He laughs. "That's quite a look."

"Yeah, it wasn't."

He laughs harder. "Well, you've grown into your own, at least. Trial by error."

"That's a good way to look at it." I sigh, swiping a bright neon orange across his arm. "My mom thinks I'm wasting my time. She doesn't understand any of this. I thought it would change after Meredith hired me, but my mom just wants me to be something normal. Whatever that means. I guess, in her world, it's a doctor or lawyer or something."

"That must be hard." He swallows, and I try hard not to look at him but it's difficult when he's this close to me. His skin is so warm and inviting as I hold his arm in my hand.

"Yeah, um..."

"Sorry. I'm not trying to upset you, Ginger."

"No, it's cool. It's just that not many people know about it. Because I have like this dual life. In the beauty world, I'm someone cool. Like Bianca thinks my job is awesome, even though, most times, I have to cancel our plans. But still, she understands why I love it so much and gets behind me, supports me. And then all of these people online who follow me and watch my videos, they believe in what I do. Hell, they take my advice and send me pictures of my looks that they have implemented on their faces. That's epic, you know? But then there's this whole other side that just feels like...well, like this set. I'm exactly like my film set."

"Hot and tight?" Everest grins, playfully.

"You bad boy." I smack him, jokingly. "I was thinking it looks great from the frame but inside, babe, I'm a mess. I'm just faking it, you know?"

"But you're not." He turns his head a little, looking honestly like he's listening to what I'm saying and understanding me. His deep green eyes gaze into a part of my soul as he disputes my insecurities, sending my heart into a tailspin. "This is real Ginger." He waves his hand over everything around us. The desk filled with all my make-up I have sweat hours away at Guru Girl to get my hands on and brushes that are a colorful array of powers. The lights. The background in cobalt blue. Me. He holds on to me, putting his hand under my chin in such a gentle, yet possessive, way. "Think of it this way...you're a girl in New York, a city full of dreamers, fucking millions of people who live here all looking for their big break, and you're doing it. This is not faking it. This set, this gig you have, this is what it takes to fucking make it. It takes someone who believes so much in what they do that they're willing to take whatever they have, whatever they can do, and make something more out of it. The people who win, baby, look at me, don't cry, the people who win, Ginger Darling, are the people that treat it like oxygen. That's how badly you have to want it. And that's why Meredith hired you. Because she was once that type of girl that needed to catch her breath when she was drowning." Everest wipes the tears from my eyes, but keeps ahold of my chin.

"But listen here, there's also the part where you make it,

and then you lose it. So believe me, this is the best part right here. The moment right before the magic happens."

I sniffle a little, keeping my eyes locked with his. "What do you mean?"

"Tell me, what's the best part of Christmas? The night before and the morning after, right? What's the worst? The whole year of waiting in between, right?"

"Yes." I nod.

"A dream is like that, too. Right now, is the night before. You have all this built up excitement, not knowing what's under the wrapping paper, and tomorrow after it's revealed... well, what comes next?"

"The clean up." I laugh.

He nods, his mouth smiles at me and his face lights up so warm it leaves me feeling toasty all over.

"And more work to make it happen all over again next year, only on a bigger scale, because there will be more people to please. Well, what if not everyone is so good at that part? What if Santa relies on his elves because he sucks at making toys and has no ideas of his own?"

My eyes widen as my fingers tremble at his words. "Are you suggesting..." I can't even finish my thought.

Everest shakes his head as if to silently tell me to be quiet. "I'm only asking questions. I'd never make an accusation about a person without proof. Good, solid proof."

"Everest..." I'm left speechless.

He caresses my chin. "You need to know your worth, Ginger Darling. Don't be someone's hard working little elf taking cookie crumbs when you can be Santa and get to eat the entire cookie."

I nod. "He also gets to sleep the whole year. Lucky bastard."

Everest smiles and nods his handsome head. "Just be careful who you trust. Not everyone is your friend. Remember, salt looks exactly like sugar until you taste it."

"And you?" I boldly ask. "What about you, Everest Snow? Are you salt or are you sugar?"

He leans in closer, drawing my chin toward his. "Well, you've tasted me. What do you think? Sweet or savory?"

"Hm," I hum, "I might need another sample. You know, just to be sure."

He smiles right before he kisses me, and I don't even remember our kiss in the elevator. This kiss replaces every kiss that has ever been kissed in the history of kisses. This kiss is searing and binding. It's a kiss that Romeo would kill himself all over again just to feel a second of, if it were Juliet on the receiving end. I've never felt anything so powerful in all my life. Forget the storm outside, it has nothing on the magic and fury that is happening in my fifty square-foot studio.

Everest frames my face in his hands, deepening our kiss and the air sizzles with heat.

"Ginger." He attacks my mouth with the tongue of a painter who knows exactly how to artfully run his brush along a blank canvas.

"More," I cry out, not even coming close to getting as much of him as I desire. I'm soaked through. It's more than just wanting him inside me for good sex. I want to feel him take me. I want to feel what it's like to have that kind of unbridled connection with someone, that shit that makes my soul's inner compass point right fucking at him.

He brings it to life as he swoops me up in his arms and we totally crash the set around us. Lights falls. Makeup breaks. Brushes scatter. Everest rests me on my beauty counter and we tear at each others' clothes in a cyclone of lust, need, and urgency. I rip his belt from his pants as we stay locked in a kissing frenzy.

"I want you so fucking bad," he whispers against my lips. "You're all I ever think about. Fuck, Ginger."

"Everest..." I cling to him, pulling his mouth harder against mine as he grinds between my legs.

SEVEN

Everest
> One Month Earlier

IT STARTED as a night of simple things. A new client on the books. A steak dinner. And my cock staring back at me from my laptop screen. Ok, hold up, that doesn't sound right...but follow along, anyhow, please.

I realize the last item on that list wasn't simple, or so I've been told. You see, I usually like the fact that women are plentiful. Living a playboy lifestyle, where I can dabble in the beauty world and get a little sample of this and that, has always been exciting. But, after the reigns were handed to me five years ago, after my father passed down his empire to me, I changed how I thought about things. I no longer had shit handed to me, and I actually had to understand and deal with the responsibilities that accompany being a king. Well, a king that hides from the limelight.

Now...sometimes when you're a king, your throne is going to be tested, and even an attempt to overthrow it is possible. Hence, my dick staring back at me. Yes, I'm talking about a dick pic, people. Please try to keep up.

Somewhere between sliding bites of succulent prime rib into my mouth and going over a new client's product line, I was staring at my dick in my direct messages.

After I hit the thumbs up button, I debate whether or not I should reply. And the longer I stare at it, the more I want to die. Impressive or not, and of course it's a fucking rockstar, I'm responsible for stopping scandals, not starting them, let alone being the star of one.

Fuck it. I start typing.

:*How much do you want?*

No response.

:*Are you familiar with our Lord and Savior Jesus Christ?*

No response.

:*This isn't exactly the worst thing you could post about me. It actually might up revenue. Imagine that on a poster in Times Square. "Beauty Babe. We've got your best interest in the palm of our hand." Genius, right?*

No response.

There's only one thing that could drive a person to do something like this if they don't want humiliation or money. Revenge. Ugh. That's a long line. Who *wouldn't* want to hurt me? Other companies. Ex clients I've dumped for multiple offenses and not following the golden rules aka my expert advice. Ex-lovers. *Huge line.* But one that definitely makes sense.

You have to understand one thing about me though—the truth trumps everything in my world. I'm threatened on a daily basis with all kinds of shit. It's part of what I do, and I have to accept this duty and everything that comes along with it. I don't handle being backed into a corner very well. I'm a bit like a pissed off wet cat when it happens. My claws come out and I'm not negotiating with your ass. I'm just looking to draw blood. But first, I have to find out who you are.

So, I put on my hat. I fix my fucking tie. I push my food to the side and I bait my hook. And in order to do that, I also take a deep breath, and then I type out my most honest response.

:*How badly did I hurt you?*

EIGHT

Everest
>Present Day

LINES HAVE BEEN CROSSED. For a lot of fucking reasons, this is not good. Number one, I'm now part of the lines being intertwined. Number two, I now care about someone getting hurt. The only way to save the day, unfortunately, is to also ruin it. I have to take one for the team, so to speak. That is basically the only thing these days that separates me from the rest of the herd that is looking to use the people around them as rungs of a ladder and step on their faces to climb to the top.

It's going to hurt. But at least it's not going to hurt *her*.

NINE

Ginger

I HAVE a new pep in my step. My colors are picked and perfect. I have my Christmas shopping done. I feel like I'm just floating on air as I wait for the elevator. I'm not even scared of it today. I couldn't care less about riding eight floors up to my office today.

Everest Snow rocked my world. I can't even think of him without giggling like a schoolgirl. Holy Kris Kringle. How did this happen? I swear I am not this girl, but man, I love it.

Even though the elevator is once again taking forever to make an appearance, it's ok. I'm going to set my worth today. It's almost the end of the year, and I'm going to go out with a bang at the top of my own world. And my worth says I bring a hell of a lot to the table, and if I'm a few minutes late with Meredith's breakfast croissant and matcha tea, that's ok, because my worth extends beyond these silly little errands. And today she needs to know it.

Santa wants good toys? Then Santa better take his own advice and be a little bit nicer and a lot less naughty. I refuse to be the nice girl who finishes last. And that goes for Everest too. I'm not going to serve him up on a silver platter to someone who probably couldn't care less about having him in her life. I'm done being the supplier of goods and getting shit on in return. Yes, Ma'am. This is a brand new Ginger Darling and I'm *not* going to take anyone's crap any longer.

I jab the button again on the elevator to show it who's boss. Me, baby. That's who.

"I already pressed it," a deep voice says from behind me.

I spin around this time, unlike last time when I was too angry to meet my not-so-helpful hero, because this time I want to see this beautiful man. "I know."

I'm met by an incredible set of emerald green eyes. I almost can't turn away from them. They match his green sweater hiding a perfectly sculpted body underneath, the one that was all over me, inside of me last night. My body feels electric as I gaze at him, so tall and handsome, and charming.

I play along.

"So why did you press it again?" He smiles and it nearly knocks me off my feet with his straight white teeth shining from behind his full bottom lip. "Are you a model or something? They're not known for having much in the smarts department, no offense."

He laughs. "No, I'm not." He pulls his black trench-style coat a bit closer, shuffling on his feet for a moment.

"I didn't mean to imply anything. I'm sure you get that all the time from girls, don't you?"

"Hm...girls? No. But I do appreciate a beautiful *woman* thinking I'm something special. So, thank you. Um, your name again?"

"Wouldn't you like to know." I grin and spin back around, feeling pretty damn proud of myself.

I turn back to face the elevator doors, waiting for the lift to arrive. I jab the button for good measure one more time.

"The button is lit. Pressing it won't make it go any faster."

I huff a little, fixing the strap of my purse on my shoulder. "I know." I do a little eye roll, but it's ok, though. I'm not facing him, so he can't see me.

"Did you just roll your eyes at me?"

This man is hot...and possibly a wizard. "No," I lie.

"Yes, you did. I saw it in the reflection of the glass up there."

I glance up, seeing our reflections in the glass above the door. I roll my eyes again.

"You just did it again," he says with a soft chuckle. I love the sound of it. I want to laugh too, but I have to keep my poker face on.

I spin around to face him, rolling my eyes again. They seriously have a mind of their own. They can't seem to stop rolling around in my head. "I didn't mean to, but I really don't like being told what to do." I stand a little taller to match his height.

He steps closer, getting extremely close to my face and reaches out a hand to touch the button again. "There. Maybe that'll help."

I press it once more. "It was fine when I did it all by myself."

The elevator arrives, the doors whoosh open and Everest rushes me inside as if our pants are on fire.

He steps even closer, leaning in until his lips are teasing me to take a step and claim them. "I think the button likes it better when I do it." He ups the ante and double clicks the button for floor eight.

I go weak in the knees.

It's hot. *So hot.* White Christmas outside and red hot Christmas all up inside this elevator. Let me tell you. I cannot get my clothes off fast enough, but I try to keep playing along.

His eyes glance up. "Well would you look at that. Some really naughty person hung a mistletoe inside of the elevator."

My eyes follow his to see what he's staring at, and that's when I see it. My eyes immediately fall to his lips. It's almost like I'm trapped in some sort of spell, and he inches closer.

He inches closer.

Oh my God. This is so going down. Possibly literally.

Whoever thought of the idea of kissing under a mistletoe, is a genius. I could kiss that person. And this hot as hell man trapped in here with me, of course.

My mind is no longer on Meredith and her breakfast sandwich and demands. Nope. They are gone. Because this is Ginger's moment to have everything in life she deserves. Hot man. Hot job. Hot boobs. What? Oh shit. Like, literally hot boobs. Everest smooshes Meredith's dumbass matcha tea between us as he goes for my mouth, and I pour the blazing hot brew down my top.

"I'm sorry. Oh, fuck." He tries not to laugh but fails miserably at the absurdity of this.

"It's ok. I'm sure I can make blistered nipples a hot fashion trend."

"Oh, baby," he says softly, and I melt at how he looks adoringly at me. "I'll stall Meredith so you can change before the meeting. I'm so sorry."

"I'm fine really."

He removes the cup and everything in my hands, setting it all on the floor and then presses the emergency stop button on the keypad. We come to an abrupt halt and he steadies me in his hands. His skin already feels hotter on my skin than the matcha tea.

When his lips meet mine, all the brain cells in my head have shrunk or exploded, either one, making all rational thoughts leave my body. Because I'm about to keep kissing this guy, and I won't let anything stop me from doing so. Not even burnt boobs or wrathful bosses.

He cups my cheek with his featherlight touch, and I sigh. And then the next thing I know, his lips are on mine. I'm floating away. His mouth is pure magic and his hold on me tightens just a tad, and I grip onto his shoulders not wanting to let go. How did I get here?

When I woke up this morning, late I might add, I never could have imagined the events of today transpiring to this moment. To this heady moment where I'm trapped in an elevator with this non-model, but looks like a model, kissing him underneath a mistletoe. Thank heavens for Christmas. It's my new favorite holiday.

My mind stops wandering and focuses on the way his mouth moves over mine, his tongue begging my lips to open. I do. I do it for him. Everest deepens the kiss, and I let him. I let him all the way into my heart.

He moves me up against the wall, the kiss turns more urgent as his hands explore my body.

Before we can move this along any further, the elevator springs back to life and we break the kiss.

"What the hell?" Everest says, dropping his hands to his sides as he takes a step back. "I didn't mean.." his words fall away but I smile.

The elevator finally reaches the eighth floor, and the doors open with a high-pitched ding.

"Are you guys ok?" a man in a grey button-down shirt asks.

"We're fine." Everest steps over the threshold. "It all worked out in the end. Just a little accident with some tea." He nods and pats the guy hard on the back.

I want to die, but crack a smile instead. My face must be so smug and painted even pinker than my cheeks, right now. And I don't even care.

"Um..." Everest turns to me for a moment. "I'll see you inside."

"Ok." I'm a little confused. But he turns and walks straight inside the office where Guru Girl operates. The door closes. And then I remember my shirt.

I rush to the closet where sometimes there's lost and found items, or leftover things from photoshoots, and find a simple white t-shirt still wrapped in plastic looking brand spanking new and haul ass to the bathroom to toss it on. It's not nearly warm or upscale enough for Guru Girl, but it's better than tea spilled over my shirt. Ha.

I make sure to take a selfie of my stained shirt and text it to Bianca, joking about how she finally got her wish and I "spilled some piping hot tea." She replies back in an instant with a fire flame and laughing-tears emoji. I laugh too, before I shove my phone in my bag, and then brace for the storm that is Meredith, especially now that I'm both late *and* drinkless. But, I do still have breakfast. Oh, shit. No. I left it in the elevator.

Breathe.

I suck in a big gulp of expensive beauty guru air, then straighten my spine, and prance my little confident self into the office, unlike any time before. And to my surprise, Everest and Meredith stand close to my desk, laughing away like they're the best of friends. Or lovers. But what's the real "tea" is that she has her hands on his chest and they look almost as if they were having a moment. He touches her arm in a soft caress as he sees me, keeping that sexy smile on his face that I have grown to adore.

I have to be honest, I feel stung. Like someone just told me Santa isn't real. But I don't let it show. I just smile back and walk straight toward them.

"Good morning," I say, brightly.

"Glad you could join us," she says, her voice dripping with sarcasm. "Where's my matcha?"

And I expect Everest to speak up with a good cover story, since he was the one who spilled it on my shirt, but he just waits for an answer right along with her. So much for being sugar.

"I had a run in with a really big jerk in the elevator."

"Hm," she replies. "Seems to be a running theme with you lately. Perhaps you should take the stairs. It could do you a great service in more ways than one."

"What the hell does that mean?"

She doesn't expect my boldness, and quite frankly, I've even surprised myself with my outburst.

"It means," she leers at me, "you get paid to perform tasks

for me in a swift and perfect manner, and when you don't, it throws off my whole damn day, Jennifer."

"My name is Ginger."

"Yeah?" Meredith scoffs. "Well, congratulations. You still fucked up, no matter what I call you."

I hoist my beauty box onto my desk. "You know what I didn't fuck up, Meredith? My new line that is perfect for your brand. You know, the one you can't come up with yourself. Would you like to talk about that, or maybe we should talk about Trinity Sykes and how her collection is a million times better than yours, and I think you know exactly why."

She laughs me off. And it doesn't escape me that Everest is still as a statue, silent as the dead, as this goes down. But, it's like I'm a volcano erupting and there isn't any stopping the lava from overflowing out of my stupid mouth as I spill it at her designer-studded feet.

"How dare you imply such things. You know the penalty for smearing my name like that? You will never, ever, work in this city, or anywhere in the country, as long as I'm alive."

I smirk a little. "Yet, you're not denying it."

"It's because she can't." Everest finally speaks and when he does it's to defend Hell-on-Heels?

I see blood red.

"You have to be joking, Snow."

"Ginger," he says softly, but sternly, "you need to leave. Now."

"That's right. I've found your replacement. This is Everest Snow. He's one of the most talented new artists I have come across in a very long time." She clings to his arm like it's made of gold, and I want to puke. But, I won't let them see me wounded. I grab my things and blow past them, not stopping until I reach the empty stairwell where there is only the sound of my

tears as I call Bianca.

"Hey, what's up, G? Did you blow her away with your collection? Are you now the CEO because Meredith is deceased after swatching your palette?" And I know she means well, but it only hurts worse that she was expecting me to kill it and I failed.

"No, Bianca," I sniffle, "but now I know why some Christmas stories have been told as miracles and others as nightmares."

SO, here we are again. I'm back on my couch with my bestie, sipping wine and "spilling the tea" as she calls it. Except, my tea is as cold and bland as the snow falling outside, because I should have seen this coming from a mile away. We have a fire going and Bianca even made Christmas cookies shaped like trees and elves. I take one look at the green and red sprinkles on the elf's little pale face and I feel an unatural amount of rage as I bite his sweet little head clean off, thinking about Everest's stupid advice to me about not being an elf, but trying to become Santa.

"Is there a problem with my cookies?" Bianca asks, trying not to laugh, because I'm sobbing like a crazy person.

Mouth still full of cookie I shake my head. "He's fiiiine."

"This isn't about my cookies. Are you ready to talk about it yet, G?"

"No." I sniffle again and toss the headless elf to the coffee table where his poor little body smashes into a million bits. "I'm going to just cry my eyes out in my room for awhile."

"Whatever helps," she smiles. "I'll bake some more snacks. Something tells me we're going to need a lot later."

"Thanks, Bianca."

Inside my room, I take a shower that washes away most of my tears. After I toss on a tank and sweatpants, I roll down the top of the pants and walk over to my little makeshift studio and scoff as I stare at myself in the mirror all red and puffy from crying. And normally, I'd be horrified and mad at myself for letting it go this far. But not today. Today, I use my anger for the greater good.

I flip the lights on and turn on the camera. I sit there for a moment until I find the words. In the monitor, I look terrible. The tip of my nose is bright red, and I'm blotchy as hell all over my face.

I take a deep breath.

This is normally when I would upload something about how great Guru Girl's new holiday collection is and how everyone should run right out and buy it. And while the product is just fine, the ringmaster behind the circus is not.

"I don't really have an intro for this," I say to the camera. "But you know, not everyone gets what they want for Christmas. The thing about all of this is everything we celebrate in the beauty world, well, it's all kinds of bullshit. This face you see right here is the truth. This is what I look like today. So," I laugh a little and reach for Guru Girl's Frostbitten collection, "let's see if seventy-five dollars can make you believe less than an hour ago I didn't have my heart ripped from my chest, shall we?"

I start going through my normal routine, blotting on foundation and concealer.

"Well, that looks a bit better, doesn't it?" I show the camera my face and it looks like a filtered pic you'd find on Instagram, so smooth and luminous.

"Maybe, Meredith Taylor, you should have called this the Betrayal Palette. Look how it smooths out a scandal. Flawless, right guys?" I show them my face again. And then I toss the fucking palette. "Let's get real here. It's the holidays. The merriest time of year. I want to talk to you, yes you, the people out there who actually help to support a girl like me, a small little dreamer who just wants to create something full of passion and integrity. I want you to know that beauty is not found on a shelf in a store. And I know that sounds super cliche, but it's true. Beauty is how you feel, no matter whose name is on your face or the tag of your clothes. If you're a beautiful person, it'll shine through. Stick with the people that make you feel glamorous year-round and never falter. Those people are the real gifts in your life. I love you guys. Stay pretty." I blow them my signature kiss and cut the tape.

It posts without editing because it's not meant to be anything special. I just upload it as is. My soul feels a little lighter.

TEN

Everest Winters

YES. You read that correctly. My real name is Everest Winters, not Everest *Snow*. It was a quick choice to throw off the people trying to take me down. You see, I'm a snake in the grass. No one sees me coming until I strike. My bite can kill a brand instantly. But if I like you, if I believe in you, then I can also be an angel of mercy and bring you to life in the click of a button. And if you fuck with someone I love, you were dead the moment you decided to give it a go.

ELEVEN

Ginger
Christmas Day

A WEEK away from the drama of working for Meredith has done me good. A week away from Everest, though, has me still feeling like I've lost a part of myself. It's unnerving how quickly he got under my skin and bones. I feel a bit shattered. Just at a loss. I think closure is part of it. I need to know why he did what he did. Why would he trick me like that? Why use me to get closer to her? Why would anyone be so cruel? Over money? A job? A status? Nothing in life could ever make me betray a person or use someone like that. Ever.

But there's more than that. I looked in his eyes. I felt him. I don't feel like he was just trying to fool me into believing a lie. He was too raw for that. I could feel his truth.

I busy myself by doing the only thing that could possibly torment me worse than thinking about my ex-lover, I go

Christmas shopping the night before Christmas. In New York. Yeah. I'm *that* girl.

As I sniff around a candle store, I run into a face I least expect. Trinity freaking Sykes.

She's glammed out from head to toe, looking like a walking talking magazine editorial. Hot pink big designer sunglasses. Black Gucci tracksuit that rich people wear to feel average, even though the look costs two months of my rent—and you know how big city living costs are. She has a group around her that is like incognito security slash assistants. It's all very posh and upscale and over the top. Because it's the beauty industry in a nutshell, folks. Ri-freaking-*dick*-u-lusssssss. But still, it's amazing to see her in person. Like witnessing a unicorn or mermaid in the wild.

"Holy Frostbite, Batman."

She laughs, tilting down her frames. "Do I know you?"

"Not even close." I shimmy my shopping bags down my arm to free up my hand and offer her a shake. "But I'm a huge fan."

"Thanks. What's your name?"

"Ginger. I really look up to you. I've always wanted to have a makeup line."

She looks me over. "Sweet. Who are you wearing, girl?"

I feel flushed. I rushed my routine this morning and didn't do a full beat. Just brushed on some colors I blended from her palette and a smear of shimmery pink gloss. I don't even think I brushed my hair. And I'm still in the same raggy sweatshirt and hot pink Guru Girl logo sweatpants from three days ago. It's been rough and these are comfy, ok? Judge me not.

"It's mostly yours, actually. Your winter collection."

"Oh, well it looks pretty amazing. I never thought to put

the colors together like that. Not many people can pull off more than a couple shades."

Normally, I'd feel super insecure and wonder if that was a drag, but she looks honest about it.

"Thanks. It's a great palette. A lot better than um...you know."

She giggles. "Oh darling, don't believe all the hype. People love to cause drama. I love Meredith."

"You do?"

"Sure. World's big enough for everyone to have a dream." She tosses her long jet-black hair over a dainty shoulder. "We should take a picture."

With me?

"We should?" I ask.

"Of course. Any woman that can blend to filth my palette has some serious talent. And darling, you're more blended than a Ninja."

"I have no idea what half of that means, but thank you. It really means a lot if you think I'm even semi put together in a decent fashion."

"You're funny." She laughs, holding up her phone for a selfie. "Ok, guru tip number one, just smile and make a duck face with me. We'll add filters. Don't even sweat what the real thing looks like."

We kiss at her iPhone and she takes a pic and then uploads it to Instagram.

"So you really don't care that someone stole your idea?"

Trinity raises her oversized hot-pink sunglasses to the top of her head and comes closer to me. Her face turns serious and she speaks in a hushed whisper, "Ever hear the expression 'ideas are cheap, execution is everything'?"

I nod. "Yes, I have heard that before."

She smirks. "I'm not bothered by some woman trying to steal my hustle. This is a billion-dollar industry. You have to be a warrior with hot-pink war-paint smeared under your eyes to survive it. The customers know at the end of the day who has it and who doesn't. Trust your execution. Perfect that, and you won't spend a day bothered by an imposter, baby." Trinity goes back to her phone. "You have an Insta or blog or something? People are asking who I'm with...they like your look, too." She shows me the post. Already over a hundred-thousand hearts. Holy shit. Is that for real?

"Um, yes. Yes. I have a tutorials channel."

"Well, baby, you better put that address in there. Give them the map that leads to all things...damn, what's your name again?"

I quickly tap out my info on her phone and hand it back. "Ginger. I'm Ginger Darling."

As soon as the words leave my mouth, my phone vibrates and beeps out of control. I snag it out of my purse, dropping most of my shopping bags as I do so, looking like a complete idiot.

She laughs a little.

"I'm so sorry." I look at my screen. I have over a thousand new subscribers. "Is this real?"

Trinity grins and slides her phone back into her designer purse. With her two perfectly manicured hands she holds out what looks like a frame using her long fingers around my face.

"I told you, baby...execution is everything."

I SIT with Bianca for the next two hours on my couch going through every single comment, like, and new subscriber, thanking them and crying tears of joy at what has happened. It's amazing. A Christmas freaking miracle. We're both shoveling sugar cookies into our face-holes, enjoying our little moment in the sun, when suddenly everything turns gray.

New notification. Everest Winters has subscribed to your channel. I'm shocked, but not because I think it's...*him*. But because Everest Winters is an amazing fashion and beauty icon. One of the most respected editorial reviewers in the industry. And he's also been dead for the last five years.

Bianca and I stare at each other. My phone alerts and we both jump.

"Holy Ghost of Christmas Past," she presses her hand over her chest, "I am not drunk enough for this."

"Me either." I tap on my phone and it's Everest.

I chuck the damn thing clear across the room, shrieking in horror. This escalated quickly. A ghost is freaking calling me from the grave? What in the world?

It sounds again. A little beep from inside a pile of Christmas presents under the tree, buried between boxes.

"I'm not getting it," I say.

"Maybe we could just move."

"The landlord would surely understand."

It sounds again.

"He really wants to talk to you," she says. "Maybe we should answer it."

"Whose side are you on? Me or the ghost?"

"It's obviously the real Everest. Just a coincidence."

"Ok, then you go answer it. I'll stay here. Safe next to the cookies."

"It's your phone. I mean that would be rude to answer it."

I sigh. "If I don't come back alive, you can have all of my beauty room."

"Sounds fair."

I snort and lift myself from our super comfy couch. With a deep breath I take a step, and then another, until I'm by the tree. I rummage around to find my cell, locating it finally under a box of five pounds worth of gummy bears I bought for Bianca. Long story.

There are four new messages all from Everest. And now that I actually look at it closely, yes, of course it's *him,* not some ghost. I feel so silly.

"Well?" Bianca asks from the couch.

"Here..." I walk over to her and toss the phone on the couch. "I can't talk to him."

I hide in the kitchen, rummaging through our tins of cookies and cheese popcorn. Our apartment has become a sea of holiday foods and I'm taking full advantage. I'm also seriously avoiding what needs to be done. I know I'll have to talk to Everest sooner or later. There's no way I can just leave things like this. I'm walking around with a pit in my stomach and it needs to be purged. I just need to know why. And how.

I will never be able to understand how a person can take advantage of another. Using me to climb the ranks, all the while sweetening me up with nothing but lies. I hope it burns when he thinks about it. I hope he loses sleep. I hope Meredith gives him an STD.

Ok, that's too far. And the rumors of her with her previous boyfriend were never proven true. But you get it. I want him to feel hurt like I do. I want him to just...feel anything. I don't want to be some tier he used as a footing until he got where he was going. I want to be the girl that didn't ever need that fucking job in the first place.

Fuck him. Fuck Meredith. I storm back into the living room and pluck my phone from Bianca's hand.

"Ginger I think you should—"

"Nope. Don't stop me. I'm going to do this. I'm not being a doormat any longer in my life."

"But—"

"I'm good. I can handle this."

I tap out a quick message, ignoring his, and tell Everest freaking Snow *exactly* what I want. Trinity is right. Ideas are cheap. Just like people. And execution is *everything*.

TWELVE

Everest

SWEET LITTLE BABY Jesus in the manger. She actually text me back. It's only three words, but still she responded to me. This is something.

My house. Tonight.

I hurry from my desk, leaving my glass of half-sipped scotch behind, and find my suit jacket. I had spent the entire day putting together one of the best motherfucking campaigns of all time. I'm spent, but also extremely lit up at the idea of seeing Ginger. Even more happy about her wanting me to come to her house. I can't think of a more fitting place to lay it all out for her.

From my office, I grab all the materials and things I need to make good on this moment. She's going to feel as if she'd never even worked a day for Meredith Taylor after I'm done with her. She's never been a part of something this grand or amazing. There's only one company in the world that can pull it off, and I won't rest until I make sure she knows...that company's *mine*.

TEN MINUTES before the nine o'clock hour strikes, I knock on the door of Ginger's small apartment. It's a nice place with decent furnishings, but nothing like the lavish style of a home I'm accustomed to. I grew up surrounded by wealth and plentiful things. But, I was also taught the value of people. My father, Everest James Winters, Sr., came from humble beginnings, but poured himself into his business until he was the guy at the top. I never failed to see him treat taxi drivers or waitstaff like gold. He cared about people. He really cared about *hard working* people. After he died of cancer a few years ago, I fell off my game for a while. It ate at me. I didn't want to be the man who had to fill such big shoes. But it was also a wake up call. Cancer destroyed what was once such a strong and decent man. I could not let him die in vain. I had to carry on his legacy in an honorable fashion.

And then, Meredith "Hell on Heels" Taylor came into the picture. And nearly destroyed everything.

The sound of the door unlocking pulls me from my thoughts and I straighten up, tugging at my tie a little to loosen it around my neck. And then there she is. Ginger Darling.

"Hi," I say. "I'm glad—"

"Shut it. Just come in."

I bite my lip so I won't laugh. She seems fired up enough

without adding fuel to the fire. Rightfully so. There is so much to iron out.

I step inside of her cozy apartment and haul all of the things I've brought along with me. She takes note, nudging her chin toward the box in my hand.

"What is that?"

"It's a gift," I say. "For you."

"I didn't ask you here for a gift exchange."

"I know. But it's part of the message I sent you."

"I didn't read your message." She shrugs and I nearly die.

"You didn't?"

"No."

"So why did you ask me here?" I ask, my heart beating out of control.

"Because you're going to tell me what made you into such a jerk."

This time I do laugh. "Excuse me?"

"You heard me." She takes a step closer. "I want to know what makes a guy like you think he can just walk up to a place he's never worked a day in his life at and steal everything I have worked for in the blink of an eye...just because you swindled my boss into loving your...candy cane."

"Ginger—"

"No, you wait. I'm not done with you, mister." She steps closer. "Everest Snow, you're charming and handsome as sin, and you have no right to whittle your way into a girl's life, make her fall in love with you, and then just dump her like yesterday's...like yesterday's... "

"*Cold tea!*" someone hollers from the back of the apartment.

"Thank you, Bianca," she says. "Dump me like some cold ass tea."

I take a breath and sigh. "Ginger, just let me show you what's in the box."

"If it's your dick, you can just leave right now. Regift it to someone needing your dick in a box. Because I don't." She points at herself, dramatically. "This girl right here, is dick in the box free and loving it. Understand?"

I shake my head at her and settle the box (that does not have my dick in it) on the coffee table. I give a tug to the ribbon on top and motion for her to have a look.

Slowly, she glances at it, like she's afraid a snake will pop out. Or a dick? And then, she catches the magic. The thing she needs to see the most. The thing that makes her face light up like a kid on Christmas morning.

"That's my name." She points at the box. "That is my name on that box. Holy shit. Is this what..." She covers her mouth.

"That's your collection. You didn't answer my emails or text in time, so I hope you don't mind, but we're calling it Magic Maker collection. Because that's what you do, Ginger Darling, you make magic happen." I step closer to her. "In an elevator." Closer. "In a board meeting." Closer. "In a studio in your bedroom the size of a pantry closet." I reach for her hand and press it to my chest, allowing her to feel how my heart beats for her. "There isn't anything you can't do, and you deserve to have your dreams come true. You deserve to show the world the kind of magic you are truly capable of, Ginger."

"Everest, I don't know what to say."

"Then maybe you should just let me kiss you." I hold her

face in my hands. "Because I'm fucking dying to kiss you, baby."

Her eyes softly flutter close, and she tips on her toes for my mouth. I get lost in a heated, searing kiss that binds our heartstrings, lacing us together forever.

"I love you," I whisper against her warm mouth.

"I love you," she says. "But I don't understand anything. I thought you were stealing my job. How did you do all of this?"

"I'm the owner of Beauty Babe, Inc. My father was Everest Winters. He left it all to me after he died. Meredith knew I was going to blast her for stealing ideas. She's been doing it for many years and getting away with it. She didn't take too kindly to me finally trying to put a stop to her thievery. So she found some very unflattering dirt on me after my father died. I went a little off the rails, so careless about drinking and who I let into my life, and she threatened to use it against me."

"Holy shit," she says. "So…dating her?"

"Just a cover to try and get into her computer and get back whatever she had saved. I hired a few people from the inside too, like Watson, to help me. In the end, we made a deal. I'd let her keep peddling her shitty products, as long as she'd let you go."

Her eyes go wide. "You wanted her to fire me?"

"I told her to. Yes."

"Everest."

I soothe her face. "I didn't want her taking advantage of you. The way she acted, her business practices—she would have ruined you. And Ginger, you're so very special. You have no idea."

"So you did all of this?" Her eyes mist over.

"I took the sketches you gave Meredith and based it off

that, yes. And don't worry, she won't even think about copying it. Trust me."

"Oh my gosh. I can't believe this."

"Believe it, Ginger." I kiss her nose. "Because baby, I believe in *you*."

THE END

Want more Everest and Ginger?
CLICK HERE to receive your free copy of Magic Maker.

GRAHAM

Graham Steele is the owner of the Mountain Goat Resort and Zoe would love nothing more than to get her handmade soaps in every room. "It was only supposed to be one night of bliss before my big meeting. But, I never expected to run into my one-night stand the next morning as I pitched my proposal. And I never expected his counter proposal...a fake engagement."

CHAPTER 1

Zoe

HELL ON EARTH is the twelve days before Christmas. It's a hodgepodge of demonic last-minute shoppers on a quest to find the must have special something that sold out months ago, tired and cranky workers, and Satan's own special lair smack dab in the center of Pineview Mall—Santa's Winter Wonderland.

It's sad I feel this way. Christmas is my *thing*. Rudolph is my spirit animal. I'm *that* person. The one whose tree goes up at midnight on Thanksgiving. The one who has a gingerbread man counting down the days until I can give perfectly wrapped gifts with exquisite bows. Christmas music all day, check. Holiday movies, hot chocolate with homemade whipped cream, and Christmas pjs, check, check, and check in green and gold glitter. I last minute shop just to be a part of the excitement. It's a holidaygasm. Or was, rather, until I got fired from my marketing job a month ago. You'd think they'd have the decency to downsize after the holidays, but apparently, decency doesn't fit into the new business model. And neither did I.

Instead of moping, I took that big lump of coal I'd been given, and applied for a position with the most powerful man on the planet—Santa.

Not until I started working as head elf and picture taker for the bearded man himself, did I realize that Satan and Santa are synonymous, just change the letters around.

Ornery people have sucked away my Christmas spirit, but I've got one last chance to hold onto it. In a few minutes, I'll escape this sea of snarled faces and drive to the mountains where my future awaits. Marketing is all about hashtags, so I'll hashtag this moment #seeya.

"Zoe, you tell them," Jenna, one of my fellow elves, urges.

Impatient parental eyes in the mile-long line filtering past the twinkling ten-foot Christmas tree throw daggers at me. There will be no crying and screaming in Santa's lap today, because, thanks to an unexpected bout of stomach flu, Santa has left the building.

A jingle wafts from the bells on my green felt shoes as I walk to the red velvet rope holding the rambunctious crowd at bay and latch the lock into place.

"Santa had a sleigh malfunction," I tell the mob of people. "Unfortunately, he won't be here today."

A groan rumbles like a wave down the crowd, before they disperse in a murmur of disapproval.

"Can you let Santa know I want an Xbox?" the towheaded boy, who was first in line, asks.

"I sure will," I tell him with a smile. "The elves are in short supply this year, though," I add as a disclaimer, just in case he doesn't get one. I'm not sure how I feel about this almost satanic ritual of lying to little kids. He gives me a thumb up before darting away with his mom.

"Where is Santa?" a deep voice demands. I turn and am accosted by frosty chocolate eyes set in a face so ruggedly beautiful the tips of my shoes would curl, if they weren't already. He runs a hand through his jet-black hair, leaving it in perfect disarray. Broad shoulders square off with me and my lies.

"He's not here," I answer, glancing down at the dark-haired girl, whose hand he holds.

"Yes, you mentioned his *sleigh* troubles." His eyes glide over the red hat covering my brown hair. "But I'm sure he could Uber to fulfill his obligations. So, where is he?"

Does he really think I'm going to tell the truth in front of little ears? Tall, dark, and handsome arches a brow, waiting for my answer.

"How old are you?" I ask, losing my last bit of Christmas spirit.

"He's thirty-two," the little girl answers.

"So you're old enough to know how this works." I place my hands on my hips. "There is no Uber at the North Pole. There's a giant sleigh with reindeer, that's how it works. If your daughter—"

"Niece," he corrects.

"If your niece would like to leave a letter, you can pop it in the mailbox by the candy cane."

I point to the massive postal setup a few feet away.

"Can I?" the little girl implores, full of glee. He gives

permission with a nod, and she rushes over to the table to write a letter that will never be sent. This is all just wrong.

"Where is Santa, really?" the stranger asks, sliding his hands into his jean pockets. "Do you have any idea what it's like to stand in that line and keep a six-year-old occupied? I don't like wasting time."

"Let's be real here, half these kids don't even want to do it. They're terrified. Do you have any idea what it's like to get your hopes up, and ask the one man you're told will answer all your dreams for something, and then be disappointed on Christmas day?"

His eyes drift down my red felt mini dress and green tights to my curled shoes, and back up again. "You're very jaded for an elf."

"Listen, I don't know how to break this to you. So, I'm going to rip the band aid off." I step closer to whisper, "Santa isn't real; we're all big liars."

He looks taken aback for a moment, before he chuckles. "Thanks for enlightening me," he says, amused. The carefree transformation to his chiseled face is so startling I step back, because he smells like everything I ever wanted and didn't get.

"You're welcome," I tell him before I'm called away to deal with a disgruntled mother wrestling a toddler. Five minutes later, when she's finally appeased with a free cookie coupon, the handsome stranger is gone.

"Hope they have a backup for tomorrow," Jenna says, as we collect our handbags from the secret door behind the faux fireplace. "Don't want to have to deal with that again."

Luckily, I won't have to, since today is my last day. And where does my future take me? Into the mountains. It's a career opportunity, one I set up long before the pink slip was handed to me. If I can convince the owner of Mountain Goat Cabins to put my soaps in his resort and spa, my life just might be salvaged. Along with my Christmas spirit.

"Have a merry Christmas," I tell her.

I make a quick pit stop in the bathroom to switch my elf attire for a pink sweater, black leggings, and boots before leaving the cacophony of the mall for a quiet drive to the resort. I need to hurry if I'm going to beat the snow. It's expected to be a heavy snowfall tonight, and I want to make sure I have a stiff drink in my hand while I prepare my notes.

After nearly an hour, I arrive. *Your destination is on the right,* my GPS tells me, as if I could miss it.

"Holy balls," I murmur to myself, as I pull into the large parking lot. Pictures on the internet really don't do this place justice. It's like a Christmas village for millionaires snuggled in the picturesque Colorado mountains. I grab my bag and hustle into the lobby of the monstrous snow topped log building that's strung with enough lights to make Clark Griswold look like an amateur.

A cheery worker with a blonde bob, wearing a black button down, greets me at the front desk.

After a few types on her keyboard, she hands me a key card, along with details about free breakfast and directions to my cabin. 'Cabin' is a bit of an understatement; it's bigger than my apartment. I waltz through the living area filled with wood accented leather furniture, back to the master suite, complete with a fireplace.

Before I trek back to the lounge for a drink, I peek in the oversized bathroom to check out the competition. Average at best toiletries sit in a wicker basket on the countertop. This place needs something more luxurious.

Feeling a little more confident, visions of dollar signs dance in my head when I step into the lounge of the Mountain Goat. A large, roaring fire blazes in the stone fireplace in the front of the lounge. An oak bar sits behind a Christmas tree that almost touches the top of the cathedral ceilings. It's decked out in gold and red, and it warms me up on this dreary evening.

My hopes don't falter though, if I can land this account, my entrepreneurial dreams will come true. I've done my research, and there are one hundred cabins rented out year-round, and I figure, at least half of the vacationers will steal the bars of soap and tubes of lotions I make, so Serendipity Soaps will potentially be nationwide.

I beeline for the bar stretching along the back wall. The television behind the liquor plays the LGC shopping channel, and I spot cute red knee-high boots I'd love to buy if I had the money to splurge this holiday. Soon boots soon.

"What can I get you?" the tall, blonde bartender asks as I turn away from the TV and settle onto a wooden stool.

"Vodka and cranberry," I order my forever drink of choice, with no need to even think about it.

"Just what I pegged you for," he says with a wink.

He's cute, and he's totally flirting with me, but I'm not sure what that means. If I were to be a drink, I'd much rather be something exciting like sex on the beach. His blue eyes flit back to me as he pours my alcohol. Well now I want to change my drink to something less mainstream, but before I can, he brings it over.

"What's your cabin number?"

I'm used to forward men, but I didn't even get to taste the drink before he's trying to get in my panties.

"Oh, well, um," I stammer, glancing at his name tag,

"Brian, I appreciate the offer, but I'm not looking for anything besides the drink."

"I think he wants to charge your cabin for the drink," a deep voice interjects.

"You can pay cash if you don't want me charging the room," Brian clarifies.

"No, it's fine." My cheeks redden. "Cabin twelve." I turn away to hide my embarrassment, and my eyes collide with the mall stranger from a few hours earlier.

Recognition crosses his features, and he half-smiles. "The jaded elf?" he asks with a raised brow.

"Just an off day," I tell him. "Normally, I love Christmas."

"I don't." He takes a seat beside me.

"Didn't get that official Red Ryder, carbine action, two-hundred shot range model air rifle?"

"Impressive, but no."

"Then why do you hate it?"

He signals Brian for a drink, then looks over at me with a grin. "Because I just recently found out Santa isn't real."

I smile. "Sorry to spoil it for you."

"Take this song for instance." I listen as "Jingle Bells" lightly plays from the speakers. "Have you ever ridden in a one-horse open sleigh?"

"No," I answer, distracted by the way his jean clad knee brushes my leg when he turns to face me.

"I have. It wasn't fun."

"Maybe you were with the wrong person," I say, sounding a lot like I'm flirting.

His tongue peeks out to caress the corner of his mouth before he says, "I'm sure I was."

"What about giving gifts? And getting gifts? And spending time with family?"

"No, no, and hell no. I try to avoid my family as much as possible."

I frown a little. "Not even Christmas movies? *It's a Wonderful Life? Christmas Story?*"

"No." A cute dimple appears when he smiles. "Especially, not Christmas movies."

"*Elf?*"

He cringes. "Sounds horrible. *Die Hard* is a good one."

Don't get me wrong, I'm all for Bruce Willis, but... "*Die Hard* is *not* a Christmas movie."

"Is too."

"Is not," I challenge with a hard stare. His warm chocolate eyes hold mine. The way they study me over the rim of his drink causes a zing in places that hasn't felt a zing in a very long time. "I guess you hate eggnog as well?"

He holds up his drink. "I'd rather have this instead. Bourbon is better than whatever they put in eggnog."

"Well, you can put bourbon in it," I mumble under my breath.

Another Christmas song, "Blue Christmas" by Elvis, serenades the bar, and I chuckle a little.

"What?" he asks.

"This song is kind of perfect for you."

"I never said I was sad, just not a fan of Christmas."

I take another sip of my drink. "Is there anything you like about it?"

"Mistletoe." His eyes drop once more to my mouth. "Let me ask you this, why do you like it so much?"

"Hm." My mind overloads with all things holiday bliss. "It's maybe just the spirit of it all."

As if I'm an anomaly, he silently stares at me. Clearly my flirtdar is off tonight, because I'd swear his brown eyes are more than admiring my sweater—they're removing it.

"Let me buy you another drink." He motions Brian over to us. "Put her tab on me."

I wave off his gesture. "No, really, you don't have to do that."

"I can't let you drink alone. Just doesn't seem right."

"Well, I sure hate drinking alone." My voice just dropped like fifty octaves.

"Yeah, me too." His voice is just as low.

I've never done this before. I don't even know his name. I'm about to introduce myself, but change my mind, because, honestly, I kind of like we're anonymous. It's exciting. Don't tell Santa, but the naughty list might be *the* place to be this year.

As soon as I finish my drink, Brian makes me another. And another. And suddenly, I'm feeling great, and this stranger is not only the sexiest man in the world, he's the funniest. I've become obsessed with the way he talks, the perfect things he says. I find myself hanging on every word. I'm also becoming touchy-feely, because he's just too magnetic, and that's my signal to leave. If I stay any longer, I'll be straddling him.

"Thanks for the drinks." I stand and shrug my coat on.

"Let me walk you to your cabin," he says, rising from his seat.

Before I can object, he's lifting my hand, and settling it in the crook of his arm, so I use the opportunity to slide it up a little and fondle his bicep. And oh, what a bicep it is.

"See." He points above our heads to a hanging shrub of greenery on the door leading outside. "Mistletoe, my favorite."

"You planned that."

"Ah, you figured me out." And then he leans in and the lips I've stared at all night, meet mine. They're firm, yet soft, and irresistible. His tongue begs for entrance, and I open my mouth for him. And this is no mistletoe type kiss either. No this is the kind made for dark corners and naughty places.

He steps me outside, our lips never breaking apart.

The air between us shifts like tectonic plates and I hold onto him for fear of falling.

"Twelve, cabin twelve," I say against his lips.

"Mine's closer," he husks back.

We get there in the blink of an eye. In a rush, he opens the door, and then pulls me close, kissing me once again.

This is all very surreal. Normally, I wouldn't do this with a stranger, I'm a get to know you first kind of girl, but I want him. I've never been with a man who makes me feel so weak in the knees. As if he knows what he's doing to my body, he lifts me over the threshold and kicks the door shut.

We're a mad rush of lust driven hands, kissing and groping down the hallway, leaving a trail of clothes along the hardwoods.

His cabin is an exact replica of mine, so I know we're headed straight to the master suite.

We fall to the bed, tumbling between the covers. "I'm not going to be very gentle with you tonight," he says, between kisses.

"Do whatever you want."

He leans over, producing a condom out of thin air. I rip the foil with my teeth and watch as he rolls it down his hard length.

He spreads my legs, licking his lips as his eyes trail down my body. I need him inside me right now. And it's like he can read my mind, because he holds the thick head of his steel cock at my entrance and pushes deep with one thrust, stretching and filling me. "Fuck," he groans out.

He pumps his hips, and I move against him, with him, and together we push and pull, tugging and holding onto each other.

"Don't stop," I whisper over and over.

My body thrums with a want—a need—it's never had before. He kisses along my neck, then across my collarbone, and ends at my nipple.

"You have perfect tits," he murmurs against my skin, biting the stiff peak, as he hits that special spot inside me.

No one has ever hit that spot. My body rises and falls, closer and closer to my orgasm, closer to tumbling over the cliff with him. His hair is magical, thick and soft—tuggable. My fingers pull and clinch the strands to bring him closer. Like a vice, my legs tighten around his waist.

"That's right, take my cock." He pumps harder, hammering into me with determination. "Tell me you like the way I fuck your pussy."

I don't even have time to blush at the dirty talk he wants me to do, I just blurt it out, wanting to please him. Because he sure knows how to please me. It's insane the way he's working my body like he owns it.

"God, you're so tight. Your sweet, little pussy feels so good."

Oh damn, I can't handle his mouth. It makes me wetter, more turned on, if that's even possible. I trail my nails down his back, digging them in as my body gets so close to shattering in a sexplosion.

"You going to come for me?" he asks.

"Yes," I pant.

"I want to feel your little pussy get off on my dick." He keeps pumping, fucking me as the headboard thrashes into the wall. "Come on me."

His words send me over the edge. I come and come, breathing out of control.

He moans, pumping faster, until his orgasm crashes through him shortly after mine.

"Fuck," he says, dropping down beside me.

His skills have left me speechless, so I stare at the endless loop of the wooden ceiling fan blades until I catch my breath, until awkwardness settles over my naked body. Now what? Do I say thanks and leave?

My sex high crashes, and I scoot off the bed and rush to the adjoining bathroom. Toiletries litter the marble countertop. Instead of snooping to see what products make him so perfect, I splash cool water over my heated face, and take a deep breath. I fix my fresh fucked hair, clean up, and wrap one of the resort's towels around my body before heading back into his room to say goodbye. I've never had a one-night stand before, but this is pretty much how they go in movies and books. One and done.

He lies face down when I return. The white sheet clings low on his hips, leaving his spectacular back on display. Corded muscles ripple beneath skin my fingers already itch to touch again, so I do.

"Hey," I poke his back with a finger to see if he's asleep, "are you awake?"

He flips over with a lazy smile. "Come back to bed with me." His voice is deep, sexy, and sends a shot of adrenaline racing through me.

The clock reads midnight, chastising me and reminding me I have an important day tomorrow. As tempting as it is, I can't risk my future for another ride on the One-Night Stand Express. If I get back to my cabin now, I can possibly go over my notes before I shower and get to sleep. God, the man is sexy, though.

He stretches a muscled arm above his head, waiting.

"I have to go." The words are like razors coming out of my mouth, but this is what I have to do. I have a reason for being here and getting off is not one of them.

He doesn't say anymore, just rises from the bed in all his naked glory. For a moment, I gawk at the beauty of the chiseled abs and perfect vee leading down to the manscaped part of him that is still semi-hard, memorizing every part of him.

I turn away and find my clothes, quickly dress, and go on a quest for my shoes. Talk about the awkwardness being back tenfold. I don't even know what to say to him. 'Hey, thanks for the stress reliever?' I can't say that. I can't even think that.

Because this was so much more than *that*. This was better than any sex I've ever had in my twenty-eight years, but again, I can't let some stranger know he just upended my world.

Oh my God. I just had sex with a stranger. I don't know anything about him. I know he hates Christmas and really likes nails scratching down his back and makes the best orgasm face known to man, but I'm not sure that counts.

"I think they're by the front door."

I spin around to face the stranger, now semi-clothed in just a pair of well-worn jeans. All men should take instructions on how to wear jeans from him. The undone button makes me debate for a moment if I should take him up on his offer of getting back in the bed.

Instead, I slip into my heels, and smile. "I had a really nice time."

He stalks closer. "Are you sure I can't convince you to stay?"

"No," I say, shaking my head. "I really have to get going."

He gives a little nod, and I want to ask for his number, or email, or something, but I don't. Because, that's not how a one-night stand works.

I walk out of the cabin and leave my sexy stranger behind.

CHAPTER 2

Zoe

"HURT YOUR LEG, MISS WALTERS?" the front desk clerk inquires as I hobble across the lobby to refill my coffee while I wait to meet with the owner, Mr. Steele.

"Just a little kink," I tell her.

It's more than a kink, though—it's a full-on sex strain. Karma is not on my side today. Not only did I oversleep this morning, that spectacular sexcapade last night left me with sore muscles in places I never knew I had muscles. Hence the slight limp.

"You can go on back," she informs me, a few minutes later. "Just down the hall, last door on the left, is the conference room."

"Thank you." I set my mug down, after taking another sip to energize me, and grab my notes.

I can do this. I have a degree in marketing; if anyone can

sell this soap, I can. There's no way they can turn down my presentation. My red silk shirt is my power tie as I walk down the wide hallway, giving myself every type of pep talk known to man.

Before I enter the room, I take a deep breath and open the door with a forced smile on my face.

"Good morning," I address the two people seated at the long rectangular table.

"Hello, Miss Walters," Liv, the woman with whom I set up the meeting, greets me. "Mr. Steele stepped out for a moment. He'll be right back."

In the interim, she introduces me to Mark Feinstein, a burly man with a distracting mustache and a buyer for the resort.

I smile and shake his paw-like hand.

The door opens, and my entire sales pitch leaves my brain faster than I spread my sore legs for the man standing before me in an orgasmic black suit that clings to his broad shoulders like my hands did last night. This can't be happening; my stranger is Graham Steele.

"Good morning," I say, hiding my shock behind a tight-lipped smile.

"Morning. Let's get started."

He takes a seat as if last night didn't happen. Yes, right. Be professional. There's a reason I'm here—an important one—and it's not to admire how his skillful hands thumb through the packet of papers in front of him. I reach in my leather bag and assemble my materials on the table. My go to trick of imagining everyone naked, to ease my nervousness, is definitely not going to work in this scenario, and I silently will my hands not to shake.

Mr. Steele's eyes follow me as I pass out a sample of lavender soap with an evergreen sprig embedded. Everyone takes a sniff, except Mr. Steele. Instead, he sets his soap aside, and twines his fingers together, placing them on the table in front of him.

"Miss Walters," he starts, "why don't you tell us a bit about your soaps."

"Um, absolutely." His eyes track the movement of my hand as I push up the purely fashionable glasses slipping down my nose.

I begin my presentation with my backstory, how my grandmother owned her own candle company, and how I experimented with candle making and then became fascinated with soaps. None did everything I wanted. Some smelled sweet, but left my skin feeling dry all over. Others felt great, but had no scents. So, I wanted one that could clean, soothe, moisturize, and smelled like any place I could imagine: the beach, the mountains, clean sheets and a rainy afternoon. The possibilities are endless.

While I hand out a pamphlet on my small business, website, and sales projections, I tell them how I branched off into lotions, lip balms, and bath gels, each handcrafted in my home.

This nugget of information impresses Liv, and she smiles wide. I smile back, knowing I've got her on my side. Mr. Steele is another story. His eyes burn into me with the same fire they incinerated me with last night. When I'm done, I finally sit, and squeeze my thighs together to quench the ache inside me.

"This soap smells divine." Liv takes a long whiff of an oval bar. "What is that?"

"It's sandalwood. I have so many different scents." I grab

my bag, opening the front pocket to pull out a variety of scent cards and hand them over to her.

Each bar of soap has an original 'calling card' scent—a smidge of finely ground coffee beans—which I won't ever disclose. Kind of like a secret ingredient.

Liv passes the cards to Mr. Steele, and I watch as he brings a card close to his perfect nose. His eyes bore into mine as a small smile graces his lips.

I try so hard not to smile back.

"Can you imprint the company goat logo onto the bar?" Mark inquires after the scent cards are handed to him.

"Absolutely. I can make a stamp, which I can place into each bar upon production."

Before I can get into numbers, the door opens, and a woman with red hair twirled into a bun on top of her head, enters.

"Mr. Steele, sorry to interrupt, but there's been some damage from the storm last night."

"Damage?" He rises from his seat, and I can see my meeting is now finished.

"The roads at the base of the mountain are blocked, and they're not sure when they'll be able to get them cleared," she explains.

"What do you mean blocked?" Liv asks with concern, standing.

I grab my bag, and follow everyone out the door.

"The storm created an avalanche on Briar's Pass, and there's some downed trees blocking the road," the woman says.

"Ok, Maggie, do a wellness check on everyone," Mr. Steele instructs. "Make sure we don't have any emergencies that need off the mountain immediately. We're ok on supplies to be holed up here for a few days. Let the guests due to checkout know they won't be leaving today."

I trail behind listening as he doles out instructions to call the sheriff and ask for a timeframe on when the roads will be operational. I'm supposed to be at my mom's at five, so this isn't going to work for me.

"I won't be able to stay," I say, realizing I don't really have the money to book a cabin for another night.

"Non-negotiable," he tells me. "Maggie, re-book Miss Walters in her cabin, on us, until the roads are open."

"Thank you." I'd love to fight his generosity, but I can't afford it right now. Plus, I can see this is a battle I'm not going to win. I excuse myself and head back into the conference room to grab my things.

When I turn to leave, Graham leans against the door frame. "I'm sorry we can't finish your presentation."

I wave him off, thankful he didn't bring up our fuckfest. "It's ok, Mr. Steele."

"Graham."

Should it feel weird calling the man I had sex with last night by his first name? "Thank you, Gra- Mr. Steele."

He leans closer. "I think after last night you can call me by my first name now."

Avoiding his mention of our tryst, I reach in my bag for a sample of my soap. "Just do me a favor." I step closer, holding it out. "Try this tonight when you take a shower."

The left corner of his lips lift into a sexy smirk, as his fingers curl around mine, silently tempting me to join him in the shower for a two-night stand. Even though I'd really love to lather him up and lick his skin dry, I step away.

Fate sucks. Last night it was fine when I didn't know he's

the man who holds one of the largest accounts I could possibly ever acquire. Now I do. This would be huge for my company—my soapany—so I tamp down my overwhelming desire to lather up his muscular body and think about my future instead of my vagina.

"Thank you for your time."

"Right." His eyes darken, growing narrow as he stares right through me. "I'll let you know what we decide."

"Have a good day, Graham." I brush past him and curse fate for screwing me. Literally.

CHAPTER 3

Graham

IF SANTA WERE REAL, I know exactly what I'd ask for—Zoe's sweet pussy. Unfortunately, there's no Santa, and it looks like I won't be getting to enjoy her anytime soon. The cardinal rule is no mixing business with pleasure. I had no idea the beautiful jaded elf was a potential supplier. Fucking figures. I can't really confirm that would've stopped me had I known, but judging by the look on her face when I walked in, she had no idea either and it certainly would've stopped her. I should be making sure everyone in this resort is safe, not replaying sex with Zoe over and over in my head.

I came up here to get away, not meet someone new. Try telling that to my dick, though.

After changing into a black sweater and jeans, I shrug into my coat and step from the warmth of my cabin, back into the frigid, ice-cold air. Mounds of freshly plowed snow line the walkways connecting the cabins to the main building as I wander around the property.

A pink knit hat in the parking lot, covering long dark tresses, catches my eye. Zoe, her previous sexy as sin black business skirt and heels now replaced with jeans and calf-high boots, stands by a black Camry, loading her suitcase into the trunk.

"What are you doing?" I call out, making my way over to her car.

"Leaving." She smiles and brushes past me, throwing her purse into the front seat.

I grab the door. "You can't leave. I thought I made that clear?"

"Well I thought about it," she grabs the door, and stares into my eyes with something akin to panic, "and, I have to get off this mountain."

I smile at her dramatics. "Well, that's impossible."

"Nothing's impossible if you try hard enough." She jerks the car door from my hold.

"You sound like a motivational poster." She doesn't think that's funny. "I prefer the demotivational ones, they're more accurate."

She scrunches her face at me. "Demotivational?"

"Yeah, like overconfidence. The cat walking toward the eagle," I explain, "and a little tagline saying 'This is going to end in disaster. And you have no one to blame but yourself.'"

She jerks the door. "Like I said, nothing's impossible."

"Try stapling Jello to a tree."

She parks a hand on her hip. "I really have to go."

"No one's getting off the mountain," I say again.

"We'll see about that."

"No, we won't." I lean down, pop her trunk, and make my way to the back of her car.

"What are you doing?"

"You're staying." I remove her luggage and set the bag onto the ground.

"I'll ski if I have to." She lifts it back into the trunk. "I have somewhere to be."

I step back. "I'm sure you can call your family, or boyfriend..." I don't finish the thought cause the glare in her eyes directed at me is enough to silence me altogether.

She stalks closer, her red-tipped nail poking into my chest. "Do you think I'd..." she does a quick check over her shoulder to make sure no one is around, "sleep with you if I had a boyfriend?"

Honestly, I don't know the answer to that. I sure as fuck hope not. I shrug.

Her plump lips open into an o. She jabs me again with her finger, this time in the ribs. "You have a girlfriend, don't you?"

"I don't have a girlfriend." An idea sparks, though, and I step closer. "Technically."

"Technically?" She shakes her head at me, then rolls her blue eyes in indignation. "What does that mean?"

"I don't have anyone. Ok?" Everything I'm saying is coming out all wrong, so I grab her suitcase and head toward her cabin. This is probably the craziest idea I've ever had in my life on this Earth. But I didn't get to where I am by being mundane.

"I can't believe this," she grouses, following me up the steps. "I can't believe I'm stuck here."

I open her door and let her step inside, before I follow and set her suitcase in the entryway.

She removes her hat and tosses it onto the mini sofa.

"Sorry," not really, "but I'd never forgive myself if something happened to you on your way down the mountain."

"For the record, I don't normally have one-night stands," she says. "I hope that doesn't affect... things."

"Well, there wasn't a lot of standing going on," I walk closer, "so, technically, you didn't."

She crosses her arms, not appreciating my effort to ease her worries. "Since you're stuck here, why don't we take advantage of some of the things we offer. We can discuss business."

"Outdoor stuff?" I nod, because if I don't get her outside, I'll have her legs over my shoulders. "Well, I didn't bring anything, but I can put some extra layers on."

I like her resourcefulness but that's not going to work. "I'll have Jean hook you up with everything you need from our store. Do you ski?"

"Like a pro." She does this little motion with her hands and hips, mimicking the motions, but to me it just looks sexual.

"I'll see you in an hour." I give her a smile and flee. In a manly way, of course. I phone Jean and make arrangements for her to connect with Zoe. She may think the business to discuss is soap, but I've got an even bigger proposal for her.

CHAPTER 4

Zoe

I'VE NEVER SKIED in my life. The closest I've gotten is a patch of ice in my driveway. That didn't end well, so I'm not sure why I didn't just tell him no. Well, I know why I didn't. This is my chance to get him to agree to my soaps and show I'm a professional. It's a little unconventional, and I may break my legs, but at least I'll look fashionable doing it. He wasn't kidding about Jean hooking me up—black pants and turtleneck, teal jacket, scarf, hat, gloves—I'm a walking endorsement for his fashionable Mountain Goat clothing.

The snow crunches under my black boots as I hurry to the dark-haired god waiting by the ski rental shop. I was hoping for a puffy marshmallow man, but much to my chagrin, he looks just as sexy in his all black outfit. He probably caused the avalanche with his hotness. It probably slid right off the mountaintop from being near his heat, just like my panties.

"Hey," he greets me, lifting his aviators onto his knit hat to give me a thorough eye fuck. "My brand looks great on you."

I'm thankful my cheeks are already flushed from the cold, so he can't decipher the blush now spreading across them. I flip off the hooha switch and hold out my hand to shake his, because that's appropriate behavior between potential partners. They shake hands, not run them along a whisper of stubble and into the dark hair peeking out from his hat, like mine want to do. "Hello, Mr. Steele. I appreciate the opportunity to discuss business with you. And the clothes to do it in."

His brows rise a fraction, and he extends his hand to clasp mine. "It's like that, huh?"

"Well, yes." Unfortunately, it can't be any other way. This is business. I release his hand and divert my eyes away from his encompassing stare to the white landscape dotted with skiers. Looks pretty easy. "So, do I just shout out things as we ski?"

He chuckles. "If you'd like, sure."

He leads me into the shop where I'm fitted for the gear I'll need and twenty minutes later, I'm clinging to the poles in my hands I have no idea what to do with, looking down an endless sugary slope. There are no obstacles in my way, so that's a plus.

"So, as I said earlier, I can brand all my soaps with your logo." He looks over at me. "You may think soap isn't that important, but your guests will appreciate the moisture. No one wants alligator skin. I only use my soap and my skin is extremely soft..." I trail off, realizing he knows exactly what my skin feels like—he licked it. Just like he's now licking his lips.

"That it is," he muses. "Great point."

"As I was saying, take away all the clothes and skin is all you have left..." This is not going well. Now, all I see is his nude body covering mine. "Ready?"

"How about a wager, Zoe?"

"What kind of wager?"

"You beat me to the end of that slope and I'll put your soaps in the cabins—"

"Seriously?" I cut him off in my excitement.

"Well," he says, looking very dark and devilish against the pristine terrain, "if you don't, then you agree to my proposal."

"What proposal?"

"Well, if you win, you won't have to find out."

Maybe this is some kind of eccentric businessman test to see how bad I want this deal. My former boss had a bad habit of giving impromptu assignments that later turned out to be his way of 'separating the sharks from the guppies.' I'm not really one to venture into the unknown without cautiously dipping a toe in first, but I've had sex with Graham, so, yeah, this isn't exactly following my guidelines. Time to be a shark. "Let's do it." Once again, his eyes flare at my word choice and it's suddenly blistering hot on this mountain. "Count to three," I tell him, getting into position and hunkering down a little.

I look over and a small grin plays at his lips. I really wish he'd take off that hat that's making him look so ruggedly handsome.

"Ok, one," he starts, but I'm already gone. I figure it's only fair I get a head start. Besides, he should admire my tenacious desire to win. Since I don't really know how to get started, I give an awkward attempt to run. It may not be the most graceful thing, but it works, and the next thing I know, the wind is hugging my face. I ski like a champion. For about a second. I wouldn't exactly call what I'm doing skiing, more like trying to keep my legs together, which is what I should have done in the first place. Pricks of snow pelt my face, and my heart races faster than I'm flying as a tall black-clothed body whizzes past me like a gold medal skier.

"My soaps are hypoallergenic," I yell out in a futile attempt to distract him. It doesn't work, and my survival instincts kick in as he swooshes to a winning stop. Something I don't know how to do. "Oh fuck," I mutter as I drag my useless poles and then slam them down, sending myself face first into a bed of snow.

"Are you ok?" Graham asks, kneeling beside me.

"I seem to be." I roll over, cautiously, making sure all my body parts work. "Am I bleeding? Don't tell me if I am. If I have any major trauma, I don't really want to know."

With a gentle swipe that sends warmth all the way to my toes, he removes the snow from my cheeks, then releases the skis from my feet to help me up. "No, you're not bleeding."

"Best out of three?" I try, knowing there's no way I could beat him in a rematch.

He smirks. "So you can cheat again?"

"Guess cheaters never win is a real thing." Resigned to losing, I dust myself off. "Ok, congratulations. What's your proposal?"

And then, he nearly knocks me off my feet with a snowball of words. "We're getting married."

CHAPTER 5

Graham

MAYBE I SHOULD'VE SOFTENED the proposal blow. I've been told I'm too blunt, maybe it's true. I have no experience in the fiancée department, but It can't be good that Zoe is now the same color as the snow beneath our feet. Silent and owl eyed, she stares at me as if I've just grown another head. Which, I guess she would. On the romantic side, however, a light snow falls all around her, and if this were a real proposal, it'd be perfect.

"We're not really getting married," I explain. "I need someone..." I trail off, rubbing my thumb along my jaw. "I need someone to come home with me for the holidays."

After what seems like an eternity, she finally squeaks out a "Why?"

For some reason, it reminds me of the helmet wearing little

mouse approaching a trap on a demotivational poster in one of my employee's office.

"It's my mother. It's complicated." I smile, hoping my charm will help land my proposal. "Come on, you in? You did lose, after all."

My charm must be rusty, because she gives me a little eye roll. "What would I have to do…exactly?"

"Just pretend to be my fiancée. My mother thinks I'm engaged."

"Why does she think you are?"

"Maybe because I told her I was?" It sounds ridiculous coming out of my mouth, but my mother is relentless. "You'll understand when you meet her."

As a little Jedi mind trick I learned along the path to success, I speak in certainties so she's already envisioning it as a done deal.

"You mean *if* I meet your mother?"

Of course, it wouldn't work on someone like Zoe. "I know this is crazy. Really, I do. It would be a simple meet my family, and after, we can break up." And then I throw in the clincher, because she doesn't look sold just yet, "And your soaps will be in every cabin on this mountain." Her eyes shine at that, and I tuck away the unfamiliar feel of disappointment that she clearly doesn't like me enough to just go along with this insane idea. "We'll just need to get you a ring."

She glances at her glove-covered left hand. "A ring?"

"Yes, you know, an engagement ring."

"Why?"

"No mother would believe her son is getting married without a ring on her finger."

"Can't we just say we wanted to wait?"

I step closer. "Look, we want to sell this engagement, right? Make it look real? So, you need a big fat rock."

She laughs a little. "Ok, but I'm returning it to you after this is over."

The non-business part of me is kind of fucking pleased that Zoe isn't the type to milk this for all its worth. I like that. It says a lot about her character. The women I've dealt with in the past have all been about the money. "I'll have Jean select something. What's your ring size?" I grab my cell, ready to make the call.

"Oh, hm. If we're really going all in, we should pick it out. For authenticity."

I blow out a breath. I swear the way this girl stares at me makes this all harder. And not just the situation, my dick swells at the thought of spending a long weekend with her. But I throw the sexual thoughts in the trash bin of my mind and try to focus on this ring situation. The thought of actually stepping into a ring store leaves a fine sheen of sweat on my forehead. "I have a jeweler friend, Charles, whose shop is on the way. And after that I'll buy you some clothes to save time. So, that's a yes?"

"I'm not loving the idea of pretending to marry someone who hates Christmas." She pauses, worrying her lip. "This is only business, though. So, we shouldn't have sex again."

"Of course," I agree.

She taps a red-tipped nail against her plump bottom lip. "Ok, yes. I'll marry you."

Thank God. Before she can change her mind, I whisk her away from the ski slope and head inside the warm cafe nestled under snow laden pine trees. While Zoe waltzes to the counter to grab a hot chocolate, I put a call in to my mother and tell her

Zoe will be joining us this holiday. Needless to say, she's shocked, but it's not like I haven't shocked her before. After we hang up, I dial the highway patrol to check on the conditions of the roads. The patrolmen lets me know it'll be any time now. Thank God. As soon as we're given the all-clear, I want to be headed to Charles's and then to my mother's to get this holiday over with. When I hang up, I walk with Zoe back to her cabin. "I'll pick you up tomorrow," I almost ask it like a question, because more than anything I want to ask her to dinner. I want a repeat of last night. But, I keep my wits about me, remembering not to mix business with pleasure, and I say goodnight.

She smiles a soft smile, and whispers her goodnight, almost as if she's thinking the same thing as me. Like she wants the repeat too.

Once she's inside, I head back to my cabin, alone. I check my emails, and do some push-ups, but nothing calms the lust swimming around in my veins. Zoe isn't too far away. I could go knock on her door and just get a kiss. Instead, I pretend I'm not going out of my mind insane with desire for this girl.

When my mother invited me for Christmas, I wanted to decline just like I did for the Fourth of July. During the summer, I holed up away at this mountain resort, and pretended the world didn't exist. It's not that I hate my family. I don't hate them at all. It's my mother's incessant pushing of the neighbor's daughter, Trudy.

So, to appease my sanity and deal with the holidays in semi-peace, I'm bringing Zoe.

I head to bed, and after tossing and turning half the night, finally pass out.

The next morning, I get the ok from the highway patrol that the roads are open.

"You ready to get this show on the road?" I ask Zoe after she opens the door.

"Sure." She's dressed in a baggy off-white sweater with dark, skinny jeans and the same calf-high boots she wore yesterday. Never knew boots could be so sexy, but these are.

Once the Range Rover is loaded, and my fake fiancée is buckled in, I head off down the road.

I wish I could say I hated everything about this, but I'm actually kind of enjoying it. Which is probably not a good thing. But, I've always been a little bad. I'll just have to keep my hands to myself. Easiest deal I've ever made.

CHAPTER 6

Zoe

MY GRANDMOTHER, Lila, used to tell me something every year when I'd visit her for the summers. We'd sit on her porch, molding candles, and she'd look over at me and say, 'Zoe, you can't wait for things to happen. You have to *make* them happen.'

I remind myself of that as I scan the jewelry shop—I'm just making things happen.

I'm sure she didn't mean try to land a soap contract this way, but it's too late to take it back now.

What's the big deal, though? I spend a few days at home with his family and he puts my soaps in his resort? Like this is easy. Too easy. Mothers usually love me. And I already like having sex with her son, so this should be a breeze. And oddly enough, I feel comfortable around him. I mean, we've seen each other naked, there's nothing that strips away the pretenses more than that. I'm sure Granny is haunting this shop right now, shaking her head at my justifications.

The glass cases lining the rectangular shop are filled with stunning rings of every shape and size. Graham guides me closer, and I swear every diamond in here is judging me.

I'm sure his mother expects status and a diamond that eclipses the moon, but I feel guilty taking a ring from him for a fake relationship.

Maybe his friend will just let him borrow it?

"Graham," a distinguished gentleman, wearing a black suit and bow tie, calls out in a regal voice. I almost feel like curtseying. He steps from behind the counter, and his blue eyes give me a once over before he reaches out and embraces Graham into a hug.

"Charles, I'd like you to meet my fiancée, Zoe," Graham introduces us.

"Fiancée?" Charles' eyebrows shoot up to his receding hairline. "So, you're the one who finally got him to put a ring on it," he says to me.

"Well, not yet." I hold up my empty ring finger in an awkward attempt to be funny.

Graham's hand slides onto my lower back, searing me through my sweater. "Let's find you a ring, Dear."

"Let me get my special reserve from the vault," Charles offers. "I'll be right back."

When he is out of sight, I whisper to Graham, "Don't take this the wrong way, but could you pick a different pet name?"

His brow furrows. "What do you mean?"

"My father used to call my mother 'dear' and it always sounded so patronizing. If we're going to pretend, I want something sexy, like baby."

He gives me a sultry grin and then sends a jolt of electricity to every fragment of my DNA when he says, "We can do that, baby."

"Yes," I whisper, taken aback by how much I like it, "perfect."

His eyes drop to my mouth, and I fight the urge to grab him and make him kiss me while he murmurs baby against my lips. I like it that much.

"Let me show you these," Charles says, bringing out three rings, which I'm sure all cost more than my apartment.

I lean closer to Graham, breathing in his scent as I say, "Maybe this isn't such a good idea."

"Pick one."

This isn't real, so I point to a platinum band with an oval diamond. It's the smallest of the three, but still heavy and cumbersome when I try it on. I'll need to cart my hand around in a wheelbarrow.

"We'll take it," Graham says, appreciating the ring on my finger.

I smile, trying my best to gush like the bride to be, but then another ring catches my eye. One not from the exclusive vault collection. It's different, with a rose gold band and vintage vibe, and judging by its positioning in the case, probably much less expensive.

"May I see this one?" I just want to see it closer. It's like the ring is calling my name. It's probably my grandmother's ghost, and when I slip it on, her face will appear and ask me what the hell I'm doing.

Charles frowns, but obliges anyway. "This is a James Allen natural diamond ring."

Thankfully, grandma Lila does not appear as I study the

facets and fall in love with its character. When I get engaged for real, this is the one. I remove the gaudy spectacle on my left finger, and slide this one home. And that's exactly how it feels, like home on my finger.

Graham takes my hand, sending little goosebumps flaring across my skin. "This ring was made for your finger."

"It's...wow." I can't find the words to finish my thought.

"We'll take the vintage style one instead," Graham informs Charles.

"Really? But the other is premium."

"What my baby wants, my baby gets."

His words send a ripple of lust through my veins. It's silly, I know, and this is all pretend, but this desire is also what I want when I'm for real engaged. I look up at Graham. "It's really ok," I say. I don't want to ruin the facade before it even begins.

He leans down and whispers against my ear for only me to hear. "Every ring in this shop is an acceptable ring my mother would believe."

I nod, and my heart kind of has its own hesitations, but I throw caution to the wind, and take the offer. Twenty minutes later, it's official: we're fake engaged.

After we finish with the ring, and buy me some new clothes for my stay as his fiancée, we hop into the SUV and head off toward his mother's. I flip the radio to a station playing "Silent Night."

He switches the station to another.

"Not even Silent Night?" I balk.

"No."

"Graham the Grump. No wait, Graham the Grinch. That's what I'm going to call you from now on."

"If you know what's good for you, you won't."

The authority he says it with, and the hooded gaze he gives me, causes me to shift in my seat, envisioning a spanking from him. I think I'd like that. Nothing too much, I'm not into whips and chains, just a hard spank, while he calls me baby. God, I have to stop this. No sex. This is business. "Why do you hate Christmas so much?" I ask to swipe the smut from my mind.

"Because, listen...," he turns the radio off, "it's just not enjoyable."

"I think you're just not doing it right."

He glances over to me with a wicked glint in his eye. "There's a wrong way to do it?"

His words drip with sexual innuendo. "I didn't mean that." Judging by my epic orgasm, we both know he knows exactly what he's doing in that department.

"I should probably warn you, my mother is kind of old school."

"What do you mean?"

"She's going to assume we haven't had sex."

"Ah, I see." I can play angel around his mother. Heck, I can be an angel and wear wings around his mother.

I don't really understand all of this, though. He's a grown man, a very sexy grown man. He's successful and fucks like a stallion. So, I don't see why he needs to pretend that he's engaged. He could probably have a real fiancée in the blink of an eye.

Old money, I guess. Elite eccentricities I've never been privy to in my life. Like helicopters and helipads. Because that's where Graham pulls in and parks—a helipad.

"My parent's vacation house is a bit hard to reach after a heavy snowfall," he says as if we just pulled into a gas station.

I point to the white helicopter, its blades already spinning. "We're going in that?"

"Yeah, we are." He turns to face me before we head over. "You're not afraid to fly, are you?"

I shake my head, hoping the fear of flying falls away as I keep shaking. "No, no. I'm pretty sure the pilot knows what he's doing."

Graham laughs, softly. "He sure does."

And the joke's on me, because as soon as we get to the chopper, the man in the front gets out. "It's all ready for you," he screams over the roar of the blades. "And you'll have a vehicle waiting for you at your parent's house when you land."

Graham nods before helping me inside the chopper. He takes the headset from the man and climbs into the pilot's seat.

Remember how I said it was all easy before? Like taking cake from a baby, or whatever idiotic thing I said, well, I'm terrified now. This is real. What kind of house do you travel to by helicopter? Who are these people? Is there going to be a red room when I get there?

I try to smile as Graham hands me a headset, but my nerves get the best of me. "Are you sure you know how to fly?"

His sensual lips curve slowly into a smile. "I've seen a lot of movies." He grabs the control stick. "I think I just wiggle this thing around."

His humor isn't funny at a moment like this, and he must sense I'm about to jump out, because he reaches his hand across, and gently squeezes my knee. "Relax," he soothes, "I wouldn't let anything hurt you."

I believe the sincerity on his face and take a deep breath, or at least I try to, and the nausea settles a bit.

And then the helicopter leaves the Earth. The ground

below gets further and further away, and I keep my eyes glued on it, watching the helipad get smaller and smaller.

"You doing ok?" Graham's voice fills my headset.

I glance over and force a smile. "Define ok."

He laughs. The intoxicating sound relaxes me. I mean, if he can laugh we're obviously not crashing to our deaths. I finally look out the front window, watching the trees in the distance get closer as he flies us over snow-covered pine trees.

It's really kind of beautiful up here.

He navigates between a gap in the mountain, racing through the skies, and I relax a little more. It's actually kind of freeing up here. I could get used to this. I could get really used to experiencing new things with him.

But, I remember why I'm here, and let those thoughts go. After a few more minutes, Graham points to a speck of a cabin in a clearing.

And as we get closer, I realize the word cabin is too tiny for what we're approaching. The place is massive, sprawling across the land like a wooden castle. Glass windows cover three-quarters of the house, and it's stunning.

"You grew up here?" I ask.

"No, my parents bought this after we moved out."

"We?"

He laughs. "My sister, Lindsey and me."

"Ah, will she be here as well?"

"I'm not sure. She has two kids, and a great husband, but sometimes they spend it with his family."

"The little girl from the mall?"

He nods. It's hard to imagine Graham attached to people. That came out wrong. It's hard to picture him as anything...normal. Or human. Because all of this has been a whirlwind, with no time to process.

"Won't she recognize me?"

"Probably. You're kind of hard to forget."

My face blushes, and a warmth spreads through my body. And as he smiles, landing on the helipad, I'm not sure it's a good thing if I see the real man behind the business deal, because, once this is over, he's definitely going to be hard to forget.

CHAPTER 7

Graham

IT'S GO TIME. I hope Zoe is up for this.

As we approach the house, I reach down and twine her fingers in mine, for appearance sake, because I know curious eyes are watching. And, well, because my fake fiancée looks like she needs it. "I would like to apologize now," I tell her.

She looks up at me, stricken. "That bad?"

"Sort of," I answer, honestly.

She stops. "You're not bringing me here to make me some kind of sex slave are you? I probably should've asked that before now." Panic widens her eyes. "Is that why you flew me here, all Christian Grey-like, so I couldn't escape? I just wanted you to use my soaps, not punish me."

"Zoe, god no..." I try to interrupt, but she continues to ramble.

"I'm not calling you Sir, and if I have to chew my way through those wood walls, I will."

And then I do the only thing I can to stop her freak out, I cup her flushed cheeks with my palms and kiss the fuck out of her. Like a second skin, her curves meld to my body. I didn't mean to kiss her, well actually that's a lie, but maybe I don't mean for it to go on this long. Zoe's words are long gone from her lips as I kiss away the ache burning inside me.

With one hand in her hair, I finally pull away. "Everyone's going to love you." I try to calm her worries, because it's true, everyone will love her. It's me that's in for the earful. "I'll give you every key to every car and door, if that makes you feel better."

"I'm sorry," she says a little breathless, and still clinging to me. "I didn't mean to freak out."

I kiss her again, soft and slow, slipping my tongue in her mouth for a taste of sweetness, just because I want to, not because I know people are watching. She breaks the kiss, darting her eyes to the house, and I reluctantly step away.

Now it's show time. We stroll to the front doors of my parent's vacation lodge, and I don't even need to knock before it opens.

"I was about to send out the search party," my cousin, York, says. His dark eyes scan over Zoe. "But then I saw you trying to be all alpha and shit."

"Shouldn't you be chasing a puck or something?"

He grins. "You're just jealous you're not a hockey god." His eyes shift to Zoe. "Aren't you going to introduce us, Graham?"

"This is Zoe. My fiancée."

"I know you," Zoe chimes in, looking a lot star struck. "York Steele. You're the center for the Colorado Blizzard."

"Hockey fan?" he asks, looking way more interested than he should in my fiancée. I narrow my eyes, listening to Zoe gush stats at him like she's a sports announcer. What is this madness?

"I can hook you up with tickets to a game," he tells her, and she looks like he just offered her the moon.

"I can get her tickets." Hell, I could buy her the team. And maybe I will. I don't know where this territorial feeling is coming from, York and I are like brothers. I mean, technically, if she were interested in him, she's free to do so, but there's no way she'd prefer him over me. If I'm being objective, he's alright, his dark hair is a bit too long. Women seem to love him, but they love me too.

They continue their chit chat as we step inside.

My mother, dressed like she's going to a boardroom in designer slacks and pink silk blouse, stands beside a life size nutcracker in the entryway. Her hazel eyes hone in on Zoe.

"Zoe, it's nice to meet you," she finally says, walking over to pull me in for a quick hug.

"Nice to meet you too, Mrs. Steele."

"Please, call me Eleanor." She beckons her staff to fetch our bags and take them to our rooms. "York, why don't you take Zoe into the kitchen for some refreshments."

Zoe gives me a wary look, and I smile and let her know I'll be there soon. When they're out of earshot, the interrogation begins.

"Why did you bring her here?" my mother asks.

"We're in love. We're getting married." Being with Zoe the past few days, I almost kind of like the lie I'm telling.

"What's her favorite color?"

I blow out a breath, fuck. "What do you mean?"

"If you're in love, you'd know her favorite color."

"Red," I guess, based on the amount of the colors she's worn in the whole two days I've known her. "I should check on her," I say, abruptly walking out of the foyer and heading into the kitchen.

I spot Zoe standing at the island with York, and that's when a laugh echoes that makes my skin crawl when I hear the small unmistakeable snort that goes along with it. Trudy Vesterlane.

Let me lay it all out on the line here—my mother is dead set on getting me hitched to Trudy Vesterlane. My mother thinks it will be a marriage made in Heaven since she's best friends with Trudy's mom. Her family vacations next to mine every year, and every year, despite my objections, it's the same thing: Trudy and I paired up. Not this year. This year, I'm engaged.

Trudy enters the kitchen and stops short when she sees Zoe and I.

"Who's this?" Trudy asks, her blue eyes glaring right at Zoe.

"My fiancée."

"That's unexpected," Trudy says, assessing Zoe like a pony at a pony show. The contrast between them is stark. Where Zoe is warm and inviting, dark hair and carefree smile, Trudy is an ice queen, cold and snooty, blonde and a pinched smile that looks like someone shoved an icicle up her ass.

I grab Zoe's hand. "Let me show you where you'll be staying." We leave the frostiness in the kitchen behind and head toward the garland-wrapped grand staircase. She follows me up, quietly.

I peer over my shoulder. "Sorry about all of that."

She smiles, but it's strained. "It's ok. It's part of the deal, ya know?"

"Well, it shouldn't be."

"Were you and Trudy..." she trails off.

"Fuck no. Not for her lack of trying, though."

"Ah," she says as we enter the first room on the right. I shut the door behind us.

Zoe moves further into the large space, taking in the view of the mountains from the floor-to-ceiling window on the far wall.

"This room is huge," she says, admiring the dark wood furnishings. Her eyes stop on the faux reindeer head jutting from the wall between two butter-colored overstuffed armchairs, and she laughs. "I love it."

"My mother themes the room every year, looks like you got Vixen."

"Which do you get?"

"Prancer."

She studies me, contemplating. "Well, I can see that. I read an article once where they ranked the reindeer, and Prancer came in second. He's sweet and kind. A sensitive soul."

Is that how she sees me? I make a mental note to be more badass. "I don't like to be second," I admit, resting my shoulder against the door frame. "I'm guessing red nose won."

She shakes her head. "Nope. The only female on the team, obviously." She thumbs over her shoulder, with a wink that sets my heart racing. "Vixen."

How fucking appropriate. Cause that's what she is. My

dick hardens just from being alone with this girl. What is wrong with me? I can usually handle being in the same room as a pretty woman; I'm not a teenager for fuck's sake. Right now I don't care about the situation, or all the people downstairs most likely talking about this relationship. I cross the room with purpose, that purpose being the need to touch Zoe.

For the second time in less than an hour, our lips meet in a hungry kiss that makes me wonder what voodoo she possesses. Her tongue tangles with mine, and I tighten my grip on her. She tastes like peppermint and holiday wishes.

"Graham," she whispers, breaking the kiss to run her lips along my jaw, "we shouldn't be doing this here."

She's right. We shouldn't. We should be on the bed.

I don't know what's come over me. It's like a demon has possessed my body and put it into this constant state of horniness when I'm around her.

"I can't help myself."

She smells so good. Maybe it's her soap. Maybe she's put some pheromone into it that turns me into this wild beast. I make another mental note to get an ingredient list.

I tug her closer, tearing at the button on the top of her jeans. Our lips meet again, and I slip my fingers into her panties. "You're so wet." I groan against her mouth, dipping into her heat.

"Graham," she pleads, moving her hips against my hand.

So, I keep going.

I slide a finger inside her tight heat, and rock myself against her to ease the pressure in my cock. "Tell me you want me, right here, right now."

"I do," she says as pump my finger inside her, hooking it at just the right angle. Her moans increase, and I slip another finger into her pussy and circle her clit with the pad of my thumb.

"Zoe, come for me, baby." I'm so hard. I can't take much more of this, and I want to come right alongside her.

"Oh god," she murmurs, bucking faster. "Call me baby again." Her fingers grip tighter at the base of my scalp, her nails digging into my heated flesh.

"You like it when I call you baby?"

"Yes."

She moans long and hard, her pussy vibrating around my fingers.

I kiss her as she rides out her orgasm. When her body calms, I release my grip. "You're so fucking hot when you come," I tell her. My dick is painful when I pull my hand from her jeans and lick my fingers, savoring the sweet taste of her.

She blushes and then zips her jeans. Just as the door flies open.

CHAPTER 8

Zoe

HELLS BELLS, it's hard to pull yourself together after an epic orgasm when two children are prancing around the room, yelling for their 'Uncle Graham' to pick them up and see their pretty pink dresses.

"This is Gia," Graham holds the youngest dark-haired girl, "and this is June." He wraps his arm around the older of the two little girls, the girl from the mall. He gives a kiss to Gia before putting her down. "Ok, go downstairs, girls, and I'll be right there."

They bound from the room, and Graham gives me a half-smile. "My nieces." He scrubs a hand at the back of his neck. "I wasn't expecting that."

I'm mortified. "Ok, no more of that. Can you imagine if they had..."

Graham cuts in, "I'll make sure the door is locked, next time."

There can't be a next time. There shouldn't have been a this time. I blame my lack of control on the fact he's one of those guys who's too good-looking. You know the type—the ones you can't stop staring at because your brain can't handle all the deliciousness at once. It's like standing in a bakery shop. You can't process all the things that look so great all at once, so you just keep staring in disbelief. Gawking, really. And then you tell yourself you'll start your diet tomorrow, because you just can't resist.

After a quick freshen up, we head back downstairs to rejoin his family. When we enter the gargantuan living room, a dark-haired woman, with eyes the color of Graham's, pulls a plethora of coloring books and crayons from a large ottoman next to the couch.

"You must be the fiancée," she says, extending her hand for me to shake.

"Hi, I'm Zoe." I shake her hand and she does something unexpected, she pulls me in for a hug.

"I never thought he'd settle down," she says for only me to hear. I can hear the happiness in her voice, and even though this is as fake as fiction, I still feel a warmth spread through my chest at the thought of being the one he's picked to bring home.

Absurd, I know.

"This is my little sister, Lindsey," Graham introduces us. "And you already met the girls, Gia and Junebug." He holds each by the hand, and they lead him over to the couch to color with them.

"He's so good with them," Lindsey says. "So, what do you

do?" she asks, plopping down onto one of the two leather sofas.

"I make soap." I peek over at Graham coloring with the two young girls and try to ignore the explosion in my ovaries.

"That's a cool job. I'm always looking for good soap. Gia has such sensitive skin."

"Well, I have all kinds of soaps you could try." We talk about mundane things, but it's oddly easy. I like Lindsey.

She's nice. Things are going well until I catch June staring at me.

"Are you the elf from the mall?"

Graham's head pops up. Well I can't lie to a child, can I? Well, actually, I do by even pretending to be an elf, so yeah, I can. "No."

My eyes collide with Graham's and I wonder how in the world I'm going to survive Christmas in this house. The rest of the day passes in a blur of pretending to be in love, and after everyone is tucked in their beds, including me, I toss and turn replaying every touch and glance from Graham until I finally pass out and dream I'm in a runaway sleigh, careening through soap bubbles toward a cliff, unable to stop my demise.

"YOU HAVE to take it slowly, and just let yourself glide," Graham instructs, with his hands cradling my hips.

We left his mother's house early this morning, and thanks to York, we're at an indoor rink.

"Well, I'm trying," I say, as York skates up to us, like the pro he is. He sends a fine mist of ice flying when he twists to a stop.

"Want to play a game?" he asks Graham.

"Yeah, right." Graham laughs. "I think the odds are not in my favor. Besides, I'm busy."

York smiles at me, and I still can't believe I'm actually in his presence. Not only is he the best player in the league—he's the hottest. I know that sounds bad to downplay his skills on the ice, but obviously I don't watch hockey because I love the game. Of course, he's not Graham gorgeous. And it would be nice if Graham wasn't either. Instead of clinging to his masculinity wrapped up in jeans and a black sweater, I cling to the wall. "I guess my secret is out," I say.

"What, you're really a professional skater?" Graham teases.

I laugh, almost losing control of my skates, but his large hands steady me. "My secret is I didn't grow up in the snow like you all did. I'm a Florida girl."

"I couldn't tell." He kisses my nose. It's an intimate gesture that's hard not to twist into something other than what it is—a ruse. It's part of the act, since his family, and Trudy, are here to enjoy the show.

Lindsey and her kids fly along the ice like they were born on it. Is there anything this family is bad at? I really need some space to keep my head straight, especially after that crazy dream.

"Go scrimmage with York," I tell him.

"You'll be ok?"

"Yes, go spend time with him."

Graham lands a soft kiss on my forehead and then skates away. I manage to get myself off the rink and out of my skates without incident, and find a seat where I can be a voyeur. I watch as Graham and his cousin pass a hockey puck back and forth between their hockey sticks. It's just me and my mom—no cousins, no siblings, no dad—and we don't do this whole family thing. This is all new to me. It's all so busy, and loud. Yet, I'm finding myself loving every minute of it.

After the ice skating, we head back to Graham's to relax before dinner.

"I have some business things to take care of before we leave," Graham informs me when we arrive at his parent's house. "Will you be ok on your own?"

"Of course," I assure him. It's actually nice he seems concerned, but again, as much distance as possible from him is probably best, lest I forget the purpose of this arrangement. "I'm just going to grab something to drink."

Wine, preferably. He leaves me with a promise to be back soon, and I watch him ascend the staircase before unrooting myself from the foyer. When I enter the kitchen, Eleanor stands at the granite counter filling a glass of Chardonnay to the rim. I suppress the urge to bolt. Maybe, just maybe, I can get her to like me. I don't know why this is so important to me, but for some reason, I feel if she likes me, maybe it will take some of the pressure off Graham. I mean, it's obvious why he asked me here. His mother has probably been arranging his marriage to Trudy since his birth.

Such different worlds we grew up in. Hell, my mother would be happy if I just brought a guy home...ever. It's not for lack of looking that I've not found anyone. Believe me, I've tried to find true love. After a while, it's time to stop the dreams of fairytales and start getting a plan in place for your life. And that's exactly what I'm doing. I don't need a man to make my dreams come true by asking me to marry him and live happily ever after. Sure, it would be nice to have that special someone to share things with, but I'm not going to settle just to say I have someone. I've never felt that undeniable spark—until Graham. On that scary thought, maybe I need the whole bottle of wine.

"Mind if I join you?" I ask, moving across the room.

She looks taken aback for just a second, before masking it behind a smile. "Not at all." She slides another glass from a fancy contraption beneath the cabinet. "How was the rink?"

I tell her about how skating just isn't for me—I'm more of a coffee and fire kind of girl—while she pours. She stops three quarters from the top. "Oh, don't be shy, fill her up."

She laughs. "I can see why Graham likes you so much."

"Why's that?"

"Because you're different from anyone he's ever dated in the past. Most women like what he likes."

I don't know if I like this answer, but I smile as she slides the now full glass to me.

To seem cultured, I breathe it in, before taking a sip. "Well, if I didn't have my own thoughts and opinions, I wouldn't be me." I take another sip. I'd like to think differences can be appreciated. "Christmas, for example, he's not a fan. I can't pretend to not like Christmas to please him."

She leans back against the counter, looking very philosophical. "Sometimes in life, you do have to pretend though. For the greater good." Don't I know it. "Do you love him?"

Her direct question makes me wonder if she can see right through this transparent sham and knows I don't. I like him, a lot, but I don't love him. I mean, I could easily fall for a man like Graham. So far, he pretty much has it all: personality, brains, and great bedroom skills. Like otherworldly on the last one. And now that I think about it, why am I not rushing to love a man like Graham?

"Yes, I do." I'm in love with the idea of being in love with a man like Graham, so, even though I feel guilty as hell, I'm not technically lying.

Her hazel eyes watch me over the rim of her glass as she drinks. "Since you're going to be a part of the family, why don't you take Thursday as your entertainment day."

I'm not sure what that is, but I'm probably supposed to know. As terrified as I am at this prospect, I feel like this is some type of honor being bestowed upon me. One I can't refuse.

"I'd love to," I agree, feeling like this is becoming way more than I thought it would be when Graham and I made our deal. I'm just going to stay as far away from him as possible.

"Great." She drains her glass. "We're going out for dinner in an hour, so you should probably get ready."

"Well, that's what I'm doing," I mumble to myself before taking a large gulp, as she exits.

How am I supposed to entertain these people? Instead of finishing off the entire bottle, I head to my room for a quick shower and dress in a mid-thigh cranberry sweater paired with black tights and boots. Because I don't want to make a faux pas and be late, I slap on mascara and gloss in a hurry and quickly descend the staircase to find Graham standing in the entryway, looking like a GQ model in dark jeans and a slate grey sweater.

"Let's go before anyone wants to ride with us," he says, taking my hand and leading me quickly out of the house to a black SUV.

"Listen, we need to talk," I tell him as he backs out of the driveway.

"Uh oh," he says, looking over at me.

"I've been assigned an entertainment day. What does that even mean?"

"Really?" He looks over a bit incredulous. "My mother has a tradition of assigning everyone a special day to come up with things to do. She either likes you or is testing you. "

"Well I'm not sure I'll pass."

"Something tells me you will." His hand lands on my thigh, giving me reassurance with a gentle squeeze. "Whatever you need let me know."

What I need is to be able to resist the lure of his hand caressing my thigh. "We don't have traditions like these. Can't you just make cookies like regular people?"

"You're turning me on," he says in a husky voice, trailing his hand higher.

"What? How?"

"Talking about cookies." His fingers inch into the zone, running along my seam.

"Talking about cookies turns you on?" That's a strange fetish, but the thought of him being turned on, turns me on.

"Cookies," the pressure he touches me with intensifies, "make me think how I only got a small taste of your pussy. I need more."

My face is on fire at the casual and unapologetic way he says such naughty things. And then I can't help myself, I test my dirty talk skills in a breathy voice as his thumb presses against my clit. "You like the cookie warm?"

"Fuck, you're turning me on more. I'm hard over here." He pulls over in a wooded area, and cuts the engine. "I'm starting to crave you, Zoe."

"I already do crave you." And I do. So bad. I grab his face with my hands and devour his lips.

"I need to feel your tight little pussy, right now."

"What about dinner?" I say as he unlatches my seatbelt.

"Fuck it," he answers.

I'm so turned on, I can't think straight, and after a wrangle of removing my tights, I climb into his lap. He moans as he slides in deep, filling me completely. We're loud and feral. Like wild beasts, unable to get close enough to one another.

He pumps his dick inside me, and it feels too good. I love having sex with this man. This can't be normal. His hands fondle my breasts, and I lean my head back, eyes closed, and bite my bottom lip.

"Yes, don't stop," I say, riding him faster.

He keeps thrusting, and we rock against each other as our moans escalate. "Zoe, do you feel what you do to me?"

I keep grinding, seeking release from his torture. And then his fingers massage my clit, his thumb tracing circles against it, and I can't hold back.

"I feel you," he pants out. "Come on me."

All my built-up angst explodes, and I tug at Graham's dark hair as he slams into me, hitting that treasure spot that only he's ever reached. Before my orgasm is done, he sends me into another with his ragged breaths and soft pleas of *how good it feels* and how he's *so close.*

His head falls back against the seat, and I bring my lips to his. "I'm coming," he groans.

As I hold his gaze, my hands cupping his beautiful face, I want to tell him things. I want to tell him how good he makes me feel. How it's never been this good before. And how I don't care about the soap deal. But instead, I kiss him through his orgasm. And when it's all over, he kisses my fingers. "I like doing that with you."

"I like the way you do it." I smile.

He laughs, then is serious once again. "No, I mean I really like it."

"I really like it too."

I like it way too much. It's something I could easily become addicted to and not have the willpower to quit. But, I can't ignore the fact, he didn't say he liked *me*. So, I can't let multiple orgasms cloud my judgement and twist this into something more. Because that's all this is—sex. If I tell myself that enough times, maybe it will stay true.

CHAPTER 9

Graham

"I SHOULD JUST TREK off into the damn forest, and keep going," my father grumbles. "We have enough money to buy a tree so why am I chopping one down every year?"

"Because it's tradition," I mimic my mother's words. Every year, we do this, and every year dad complains and then complies.

"Yeah, well, so is turkey, doesn't mean I'm going out to shoot it." And then he gets to the real reason he woke me at the crack of dawn when he arrived to hike into the woods for a Christmas tree search. "You're going to need a prenup if you really plan on marrying this girl."

Even though our engagement is fake, I'm offended for Zoe. Having her sign a piece of paper essentially expecting it to fail wouldn't be in the cards, if this were real. I don't do failure.

"We're good," I say, stalking away to scope out trees while

he continues to advise me of the dangers of not having an agreement in writing while he surveys our choices of pines.

"Listen," he says, "I don't care who you marry. Your mom has her heart set on Trudy because of what she brings to the table."

"Yeah, well, she can sit at the table with her then. I've got what I want." I don't want to be at the table, I want to be coming hard in the car because I'm with someone who makes me forget about the table. Zoe has my head all fucked up. Two nights ago, after I took her back here, and kissed her goodnight, I couldn't sleep. At All. She's avoided me since that night, and I'm sure she's compartmentalized all of this into not mixing business with pleasure. And she's right; I shouldn't mix business with pleasure. But, it's too fucking late. Now I'm trying to not mix pleasure with *feelings*. I'm not supposed to have feelings. And getting feelings for Zoe is not what I need right now. It's not what should be happening. But guess what? It kind of is happening. Maybe after we break off this engagement we can go on an actual date.

"Up here, Graham," my father calls to me. "Found one."

I trod through snow, over to where he stands, eyeing a gorgeous Douglas Fir with full branches.

"Ah yeah, it's perfect."

We get to work chopping it down and then tie it with rope atop the red sled my father brought along. No one is stirring when we arrive back at the house, and my father and I set the tree up in the living room.

"A real tree," Zoe exclaims as she comes into the living room. She takes a deep, calming breath, and lets it out slowly. "I've always wanted one, but my mother always does a fake tree."

"Oh, there's nothing fake when it comes to me." Except our relationship, and that thought stings when my mind goes there.

"It's really beautiful," she says, stepping closer to examine it.

But what's really beautiful this early morning is *her* in something as simple as jeans and a cowl necked black sweater. Her dark hair is pulled back in a low ponytail, emphasizing the beauty of her face. Is it bad that all I want for Christmas is Zoe? I want her wrapped in a big red bow, that I can undo and use to tie her to my bed. She's smart, and sexy. And she's ...cute. Have you ever met a girl who's just plain cute? Every smile, every little glint in her eyes, is just cute.

"I'm Douglas, Graham's dad," my father introduces himself. "Nothing better than a real tree. Chop one down every year."

I give him a little side eye as she shakes his hand and compliments his tree finding skills.

"It's great to meet you. I better go find Eleanor so she can inspect it."

When we're alone, I curl my arms around her from behind as she continues to marvel at the tree. There's no one to pretend around, but I still can't let go of her. Truth of the matter is, I don't want to let her go. I like holding her close.

The smell of warm vanilla takes over my senses, and I nuzzle my nose into the crook of her neck, smiling as I kiss along her smooth skin.

A cough behind us breaks us apart before I can get any further. We both spin around and come face-to-face with my mother.

"Hey, Mom, didn't see you there. Like the tree?"

"It's perfect," she says. "Trudy brought breakfast."

I pinch the bridge of my nose. "I'm not hungry."

My mother moves closer, whispering, "Graham, it's bad manners to not acknowledge her effort."

"It's actually kind of bad manners to have her here with my fiancée."

My mother stops short, because she knows I'm right.

"It's ok," Zoe says, placing her hand on my arm, attempting to defuse the situation. "Let's eat. I'm starved."

Her eyes plead with me to agree, so I do. Ten minutes later, I wish I hadn't. Trudy brought the cavalry of breakfast. Catered eggs, French toast, bacon, sausage, and anything else you could want fill the chafing dishes in the dining room. Blueberry and chocolate chip pancakes are on display complete with flavored syrups. I'm expecting a damn omelet station, but to my surprise there isn't one, Trudy explains this is supposed to be an 'intimate' breakfast.

Intimate, yeah, sure.

The crystal chandelier in the dining room twinkles over the linen draped table as the clatter and clang of the cutlery surrounds us. I'm not even sitting near Zoe, which kind of pisses me off. I'm wedged between York and Trudy. It's as if everyone is working against us in their rush to the buffet style set up along the wall.

"How's resort living?" York asks, shoveling eggs into his mouth.

"I'm sure he loves being away from everyone, hiding up there in the mountains," Trudy says, holding her glass of breakfast sangria close to her lips. "You've always been a bit antisocial."

"Actually, *York*," I stress, "it's going great. I'm just about to add Zoe's soaps in each cabin." I give a little wink to Zoe from across the table.

"Soap?" Trudy says as if I said shit.

"Zoe makes soaps," Lindsey offers, when I don't make any effort to answer.

"That can't be cost effective." Trudy lowers her glass, her eyes narrowing on me. "How much are you probably paying for soaps now? Probably like three cents a bar." Trudy won't let up.

"Something like that."

Trudy's blue eyes glance over at Zoe, and we have the attention of the whole table now. "I'm sure Zoe can't beat that cost, and even if she did she'd lose out."

And listen, Trudy is one hundred fucking percent correct —I'm taking a loss by bringing on Zoe's soaps.

"It's fine," I say, my voice low and deep, demanding not to be questioned.

Because that resort is *my* resort. And if I want to pay extra for soaps, then I fucking will. It's not going to make or break me. And there's not a damn thing anyone can say about it.

Zoe's face falls flat, and I try to telepathically tell her everything is ok.

"Zoe," Trudy turns her attention onto her, "you understand that's not cost effective, right? You understand business?"

I don't give a fuck if Trudy questions me all night about my business practices, but don't fuck with Zoe. Leave her alone.

"Trudy, drop it already. I didn't come all the way here to talk business over the holiday. I'm here to spend time with *my* family, which by the way, you aren't a part of."

"It's ok," Zoe says, focusing her gaze on Trudy. "I'm sure

you understand you could've gotten this breakfast at a much cheaper price at the grocery store, but you wanted something premium as a luxury for the people enjoying it. Even though it's not cost effective."

York smirks beside me at Zoe's damn good response. I push back my chair and head over to the spot where Lindsey sits next to Zoe. "Can I sit by my fiancée?"

Lindsey gets up without saying a word. I slide into the seat, and take Zoe's tiny hand into mine and bring it to my lips and give it a kiss.

"I agree with Graham," my mother says, "we're not here to talk about work." She turns her attention onto Lindsey and asks her a question about the girls, effectively ending the discussion.

And then the whole table comes alive with easy conversation, and I know one thing is for sure, Trudy does not look happy. And that makes me very happy.

THE NEXT DAY, I'm not so happy. After Trudy's little breakfast debacle, Zoe seemed to be avoiding me the rest of the day. And night. I knocked on her door, only to get a crack with her eye peeking out telling me she was fine, just needed to rest up for her entertainment extravaganza today.

"I never thought I'd see the day," York says, patting me on the shoulder.

"What day is that?"

"The day you'd become pussy-whipped over some chick."

"Ok, let's get one thing straight. I'm not pussy-anything. She's my fiancée."

"So, you've told us. I don't care how much I love someone, I wouldn't wear an ugly Christmas sweater for anyone," he says as we watch my mother, sister, nieces, and fake fiancée all drive away to shop for Zoe's entertainment day—an ugly sweater party.

"Well you will be," I inform him. "It's her day, and you'll be participating."

We step back inside and move to the family room.

"Ugly sweater party." York takes a seat on the sofa, raises his hands behind his head and leans back, propping his feet on the coffee table. "I repeat, she's going to get you an ugly sweater."

"It'll be fine."

"Don't mind him," my father says, dropping down into the recliner, "he'll be single for the rest of his life. I think I like Zoe for you."

I meet his eyes, a little shocked by his statement. "Oh really? Why's that?"

"She's lively."

Ain't that the truth. I've never met anyone like Zoe before. And I find myself loving that about her, loving the fact she's unique, like the engagement ring around her finger. "Yeah, I kind of like her," I let slip out, forgetting the moment. "I *really* kind of like her."

My father chuckles, loud and deep. "Well, I sure hope so, son."

Before I mess up any more, I excuse myself to take care of business. When they arrive back a few hours later, giddy and laden with bags, I pull Zoe to the side. "What's my sweater look like?"

She dabs my nose with her index finger and then digs into

a white bag. She pulls out a red and green sweater, unravels it and holds it against her chest.

Horrified, I stare into the button eyes of Santa, and well, she's got to be kidding. "Umm, what is that?"

"It's an ugly Christmas sweater."

"Ugly is right. I'm not wearing that."

"Why?" Her face twists into an adorable pout of disappointment, complete with big eyes and plump bottom lip. My dick hardens instantly, and all I want to do is kiss this girl.

My hands land on her hips. "I just can't wear tinsel."

"I think you can." She inches closer.

I stare at the sweater again, then at her lips. And I lean in. "Fuck it, for you I'll do it." Our lips meet in an instant.

I've never been one for PDA's—yeah, I'm *that* guy—but, with Zoe, I can't keep my hands off her. At this point, I don't really care who's around, so I keep kissing her. Until a familiar cough interrupts us.

"Guests will be arriving soon," my mother says.

Guests? How big of a party did they plan? An hour or so later, I find out a pretty damn big one. The house is alive with friends of my parents from the club, and community. My mother doesn't do small intimate affairs. Go big or go home is her motto.

Everyone is having a great time in an ugly sweater, and I glance around looking for the one person responsible for it all. Zoe. Her sweater takes place in outer space with kittens wearing Santa hats and eating pizza. It's god awful. How she can look so beautiful in such an ugly sweater is beyond me.

"Graham, haven't seen you around in a long time," Mr. Vesterlane, Trudy's father, says.

His sweater is atrocious. A fuzzy reindeer protruding from

his belly bumps me as I shake his hand. "I've been busy with the resort, sir."

His brow rises. "Quite a spunky little fiancée you have."

"Yes, she sure is." It comes out like I'm talking about her spunk in the bedroom, but I don't care. She is spunky, both in and out of it.

He walks away after patting me on the shoulder, and I can't say that I miss him. I know the Vesterlanes aren't happy I came home with a fiancée on my arm. Mr. Vesterlane has been trying to get his hands on my resort for a long time. And if I marry his daughter, that's one step closer to his hands in my business.

My mother saunters over in a gaudy green cardigan dripping with garland and tiny ornaments, still managing to somehow look couture. "You must really love this girl if you're willing to wear that in public." She points to the Santa sweater I'm wearing, like she has any room to talk.

I laugh. "I guess I do."

My mother lifts her champagne to her lips and takes a sip. "The Vesterlanes won't be happy about this."

I face my mother. "Who would you rather see happy? The Vesterlanes or me?" I walk away and head straight for the bar. I grab a bourbon, and then I spot Zoe heading right for me.

"You look upset," she says, concerned.

I throw an arm around her shoulders, putting on a show, but not really. "I'm great now that you're here." I lean in to kiss her. "Want to get out of here?"

She nods.

I know this is her event, but my mother always plays the gracious hostess, and I doubt anyone will even miss us.

After grabbing our coats, we slip out the back door, and I

fire up the SUV and speed away before anyone even notices we're missing.

"Where are we going?" she asks.

"Not far." I turn onto the gravel road that leads down to the lake. "I want to show you something." My headlights illuminate the frozen lake as I park along the riverbank. I cut the engine and step out into the cold stillness.

She exits the car as well, and I grab two lanterns and a blanket from the back of the SUV, meeting her on the other side. "This way," I say, taking her hand.

Her warm tiny hand fits so perfectly in mine.

"Where are we going?" she asks as I lead her into a wooded area.

"You'll see." I squeeze her hand as we walk just a bit further until what I want to share with her comes into view.

"What is that?" Zoe asks, peering with wonder at the old wooden bridge and small deserted bridge house next to it that time passed by and left untouched.

"Isn't it cool?"

I open the door, following in after Zoe.

"Wow." She spins around, slowly, taking in all the wood detailing and carvings.

"I used to come here a lot over the years." I point to some of the woodwork. "Whoever built this place took their time with all the details. They hand carved all the designs into the walls."

She traces her fingers over some of the intricate wood carvings. "These designs are so amazing. Look at this flower." Her fingers flow along the petals of a hydrangea carved into the wall. "What is this place?"

"A long time ago this little house would be a place for

passing boats to stop and take a break as they traveled through the lake. I think they would sell ice fishing gear here as well."

"Ah." She faces me. "And you use to come here?"

"Yeah, growing up whenever I wanted to get away from life, or my family."

"I love it here." Then she turns to face me, her eyes growing serious. "Thank you for bringing me here."

"I'm happy I brought you." I step closer until we're toe-to-toe. Her eyes flutter closed as I graze a finger along her cheek. I like touching her. She's so soft and feels like silk and happiness. "This place is really special to me."

Her eyes open, their vibrant blue color shining up at me. "You're special to me," she whispers.

And damn if that doesn't do things to me. I pull her in, capturing her lips with mine. Fire blazes through my veins when she moans.

I can't think about anything but taking this girl, making her know just how special she is to me. Is it possible I could be falling for her?

No, it's too soon, too risky. Here's the thing, though—I want her. And not just sex. I like being around her. Holding her today on the couch while my family decorated the tree, felt all too domesticated. But, I liked it.

I deepen the kiss, running my hands all over her body as she clings to me.

"We shouldn't..." she doesn't finish her thought, because I kiss her again. Oh yes, we should. Fuck the negativity. I lay the blanket at our feet and kneel down, bringing Zoe with me.

There's way too many clothes in the winter time. She removes her coat, sweater, bra, and then pulls me in until I'm up close and personal with her tits. I trail my tongue along the stiff peak, sucking her nipple into my mouth, and then doing the same with the other.

Her intense gaze, trembling body, and little moans tell me she likes the way I touch her. And that thought makes me greedy for more, so I rid her of her jeans and panties to run my tongue over her silky thighs. Chills erupt along her skin. I spread her legs and stare at her, and not at her eyes. She's ready and wet. Her cheeks blush and she tries to close her legs, but I *tsk* her. "Don't be embarrassed."

And then I drop my body, settling on my elbows between her legs, and plant a few kisses over her thighs, making my way to her sweet spot. I swipe my tongue over her wetness and her legs try to close again. "Relax, Zoe, let me enjoy all of you."

She closes her eyes, and leans her head back.

I bring my hands under her ass, cupping each cheek in my palms, and feast, sucking and nibbling against her heated skin. It's heaven, and she moans, grinding her body against me. Fuck, she's so hot.

She rocks forward, her hands in my hair, leading me exactly where she wants me, and I don't disappoint. I take her in all the ways I can. I lick at her skin, playing with her clit between my lips and teeth. She gets louder and louder, and I keep fucking her with my tongue, my face, and then my fingers. And my fuck, she's so turned on, and so am I. My body is iron, my cock made of steel, as I hum my lips along her skin. The moment she loses control is a beautiful sight. I wrap an arm beneath her, squeezing tighter, as if I can hold onto her forever by not letting go.

"Graham, oh fuck," she whispers as her body calms after her orgasm.

I don't want the moment to end, I want to drag it out for

fear of never having the chance again. So, I bring my lips to meet hers, kissing her until I can't stand it anymore. A ragged groan tears from deep within my throat as I push my way inside her. Goddamn I can't get over how tight she is. And how good she feels.

Her legs grip around my back, and I keep pushing, keep trying to go in as deep as I can. Until I can stop the incessant want and need of this girl. But, it'll never end. I have a feeling I'll keep wanting her more and more after each time.

I lean my forehead against hers, our lips a millimeter apart, and whisper her name again and again.

Her eyes crash into mine, owning me. Completely fucking owning me. My orgasm rips through me as she tells me how *she's never had it so good*. My heart beat ramps up, and I know in this exact moment, I am completely fucked over this girl.

CHAPTER 10

Zoe

THE NEXT MORNING, I sleep in. And it's heaven in this big comfy bed with thoughts of Graham swimming in my head. Sounds like a Christmas rhyme. What happens next, is exactly what's in the poem. *When out on the lawn there arose such a clatter, I sprang from the bed to see what was the matter.*

I look out the window and this can't be happening. I mean this really can't be happening. Eleanor has a thingy, an actual wedding thingy, assembled in their backyard. An arch, with white flowers snaking around the frame of the trellis. The only thing missing is the wedding officiant underneath.

I get dressed in a hurry and fly down the stairs.

"What do you think?" she asks as I step outside.

"What is it?" I rub my hands along my arms to warm up.

"Well..." she draws out, "I was thinking why not have the wedding here and now while the family is all together?"

She can't be serious. I grasp at straws. "I'd want my mother here, so I don't think that'll work."

At that precise moment, Graham steps outside, and like a saint has my winter coat in his hands. He helps slide it over my arms, and then smiles at his mother. "What is this?"

"A wedding. It's already decided," his mother exclaims, nodding at me.

My mind can't comprehend all of this. I glance over at the deer-in-the-headlights look Graham has on his face, waiting for him to step in and explain everything. Or to come up with an excuse as to why we can't get married this weekend.

He doesn't. Instead, he strides over confidently to his mother, places a kiss on the top of her head, says, 'perfect,' then walks back inside the house.

What the...? Men.

I turn back around to face Eleanor and try to lift my lips. "I love it."

Ugh, I guess I'll play along until Graham tells everyone the truth, preferably before my mother shows up.

"You have a lot of explaining to do, Zoe."

Oh my god. My mother. She's here. I blink to make sure the petite woman with a dark bob stepping onto the patio isn't a hallucination. It's not.

I can tell by the tone of her voice she's not happy. And why should she be? Her only daughter didn't even tell her she was getting married.

"I'll leave you two alone," Eleanor says with a smile, moving around us to go inside.

"Zoe, you're marrying Graham Steele?" my mom asks, once we're alone. "I searched him on the internet. How did you end up engaged to a man like that?"

"Mom, it's a long story. It all just sort of happened."

I know this is so wrong, and I'm probably going to Hell, but I'm actually beginning to like the lie. I'm kind of believing it too. Just like the kid says in that movie, 'Oh fudge.' I decide to sit on my throne of lies a little longer. "I'll explain everything later. Let's go inside; it's cold."

We step inside to find Eleanor and Lindsey sitting on the couch with a million bridal magazines. Graham is nowhere in sight. And I'm not in the mood to plan a wedding I'll never get to enjoy. A wedding to a man who doesn't truly want me. I think it's this thought that depresses me further.

But then, I remember our deal and plaster on a fake smile, because, let's be honest...the only way to put on a fake smile is to plaster it on. Right?

I move closer, feigning interest. "Are you looking at dresses?"

"Yes, and this one would look so perfect on you," Lindsey says, pointing to a form fitting gown with a low back. "Mother knows the owner of Fantasy Dresses, Pierre Von Ludwig. Yes, *the* Pierre Von Ludwig. And he's coming...here...today." Her voice rises on each word.

Eleanor taps away on her phone. "Yes, what's your dress size? I'm texting him now."

I tell her my dress size, and then sit on the red wingback chair before my legs give out. Pierre is a legend in the wedding arena. Well, in the famous socialite wedding arena. He designs all the top dresses of all the top brides. Ugh, put it this way, I'm so out of my freaking league here.

There's no way Graham will let this happen. I just need to pretend until he reappears to fix this.

A few hours later, it's not fixed, and I stand in the middle of my room, wrapped all in white, looking like a bridal nightmare. That's basically what I'm in right now. A nightmare.

This just doesn't feel right anymore.

Flutes of champagne are passed around as everyone waits to see me in the dress Pierre has brought over. Pierre has basically brought the whole store with him. He says it's because this will be *the* event of the century because I'm marrying one of the country's most eligible bachelors. And I haven't even been able to find that most eligible bachelor anywhere, let alone talk to him.

Hopefully he's planning our escape.

I close my eyes and count to ten, taking a deep breath for good measure.

It's like a fairy tale gone rogue. How do I say I love the dresses and not actually have them purchase one?

Lindsey and Eleanor sit like jurors in the high back chairs waiting to judge me in the next greatest creation of Pierre's. And somehow, Trudy has managed to weasel her way in to this fashion show. She looks disgustingly pleased with the way each dress isn't the right one.

"You look like a giant snowball," my mom says in regard to the silk organza mess of madness that I can't even figure out how to sit in.

Lindsey laughs a little, and Eleanor gives a dismissive shake of her head. "That's not the one," she says.

Pierre prances over to his portable rack. "I have another."

Of course, he does. This is more than a 'few' dresses. I'm on my fifth fiasco. Each one more extravagant than the one before. If this were my real wedding, I'd want something simple and elegant, not full and frilly. But, no one listens to me.

I step inside the bathroom with my mom as he hands me another dress.

After mom zips me up, I study myself in the mirror of this makeshift dressing room. I twist and turn, admiring the dress from all angles. This dress is kind of perfect. It's classy, with art deco beadwork on the bodice. Sometimes less is more, and the drop back ends in a tasteful v.

"It's stunning," my mother says to me in the mirror. I can't believe it's me in the reflection. I really can't.

"Oh my," Lindsey says, when I step out, her eyes shining with excitement.

Eleanor rises from her chair with a smile on her face. "I think it's perfect." And then she does something I'm completely not expecting. She turns to Pierre, and says, "We'll take this one."

"Wait," I squeak out, but no one is listening to me. They're all occupied with a little mini-chaotic party that just erupted the moment Mrs. Steele spoke her approval.

Oh my God, she just bought this dress.

I'm sure this dress is a small fortune, and it's not a real wedding. I want to say something. I open my mouth to actually do it, until a knock at the door stops me.

"Zoe, are you in there?" It's Graham. Just the man I need to see.

Lindsey hops up from her chair. "Don't come in here. It's bad luck."

Pierre and Eleanor hurry me back into the bathroom to change, and I do, as fast as possible. I need to talk to Graham. Now. Before I can get to him, the door to the bathroom opens and Trudy steps inside.

"Listen," she says in a low voice, "we need to talk."

"I can't right now," I say, trying to move around her.

She blocks the door, leaning back against it. "If you marry him, my dad takes his resort."

"What do you mean?"

"There are things that have been in the works long before you came around." She eyes me, coldly. "Do you want to be the reason he loses everything? It's me or the resort. And if you tell him any of this, my father will move hard and swift to take control of it. So you need to stay as far away from him as possible." Her words slide in my ears and go straight to my heart. "Let's be real, you're not one of us anyway."

"I can definitely see why he doesn't like you," I tell her, before nudging her out of the way. This is all fake, and it's time to get out of the fantasy. No matter how much I want it, Graham and I will never be anything. And it's time to end the charade.

CHAPTER 11

Graham

"YOU CAN'T GO in there. It's bad luck to see the bride in her dress before the wedding," Lindsey chastises me as she slips out the door of Zoe's room.

Fuck, a dress?

I need to put a stop to all of this, but I don't even know where to begin. I can't believe how on board with this wedding my mother is.

"Ok. Ok," I grab her arm to pull her away from the door, "Lindsey, I have to tell you something."

I'm pretty sure it's shock that freezes her face as I blurt out all my lies, everything Zoe and I have been keeping secret. She looks like she's watching a train wreck happen right before her eyes. And that's how I feel about my life right now—it's one giant train wreck.

"Well, shit," she says, after I finish telling her everything.

"That's your best sisterly advice? How do I tell Mom?"

She shakes her head. "I can't believe you're so blind."

I run a hand through my thick hair. "What?"

"She loves you."

"Who?" Is she talking about Mom?

"Zoe." She places her hands on her hips, her eyes shooting bullets at me. "And you need to stop being an idiot."

"No, she's not. Trust me." No, Zoe is doing this for a soap deal. And I don't blame her.

"I know love, and she's got it. And so, do you."

"I do not," I scoff.

Her brow rises, and her hands stay firmly rooted to her hips.

"I'm not in love." I raise a brow back. "I'm not." Right? I mean, Zoe is great—really fucking great—and I'd love to date her and all, *but*...

I don't long-term date. Ever. My life is simple, easy, it's the making of my own design. And I like things the way I like them. I wouldn't call me stubborn, but I'm definitely not one to go and fall in love.

Yet, Zoe just fucking does something to me, like makes my heart beat this whole new rhythm. If there was anyone who could get me to hang up my bachelor suit and tie, it would be her. She'd be the one I'd settle down with, *but again...*

I'm *not* in love.

Lindsey nudges me. "Are you still sure you're not in love?"

I scowl at her. "It doesn't matter." Because Zoe doesn't love me.

"You need to just come out and be honest with mom." She grabs my arm. "But, you need to be honest with yourself first."

I kiss her cheek. "Thanks." For whatever that advice meant. Be honest with myself? Sure.

The door opens, and Zoe stands before me looking like a vision in her ivory sweater and jeans.

"Zoe, I'm sorry." I step inside and Trudy brushes past, leaving the room. Good. "Everyone—"

"Graham," Zoe cuts me off, "we have to end this."

"I know," I whisper.

She looks around at the curious faces assembled. "We're not really engaged," she blurts out, and my mouth is drier than. And then she confesses to everything, including being the mall elf. "I'm really sorry about that," she says to Lindsey.

My mother stands statue still in the center of the room. "I don't understand. So, you're not getting married?"

"Mom, I'm sorry," I say, feeling a pit of sadness forming in the middle of my chest. "I can explain." I step closer to my mother, trying my best to get control of the situation.

"So, no dress?" the skinny man in a fedora, holding a white gown in his hands, asks.

"Pierre, not now," my mother snaps. "Explain, Graham."

Before I can say anything, Zoe rushes past me with her mother in tow.

"Wait, Zoe," I say, following her out the door. I touch her arm. "I want to see you again."

She shakes her head. "No, I don't think that's such a good idea."

"Why?"

"It's just too complicated."

"What's complicated?" I drop my hand from her arm as she steps further away. My mind can't process what exactly is going on. I know I just want to see this girl again. A lot.

"Just let me go, please?"

I hate this idea. I hate every word flying out of her mouth. "Is that really what you want?"

"Yes."

"But..." I slide my hands in my pockets to keep them from holding on to her. "You're sure?"

"Yes." She tilts her head up, shoulders back and smiles. "I am." She quietly removes her ring and slips it in my pocket. And then her and her mother take off.

I want to chase after her, my feet beg me too, but I do the right thing and let her go.

CHAPTER 12

Zoe

DON'T CRY. Don't cry. Do not shed one single tear. The stars come into view out the window as I gaze up, trying my best to stop the tears. We've been driving for what feels like hours now, and I can't wait to get home. The scenery passes by in a blur and I wish I could just erase the last few days.

This is all my fault. Waltzing around that room, dolled up in white, pretending to be the doting fiancée of Graham Steele, I enjoyed it. I wanted it. I should have said no to his offer. I shouldn't have let my dreams of becoming the soap queen of Colorado overcome my sense of right and wrong. More importantly, I shouldn't have developed feelings for him.

I mean, so what if I would have lost the Mountain Goat Resort account? It's not like I had any accounts to measure it with.

"They just live different lives than us," my mother rambles

on in an attempt to make me feel better. "They just use people for their own silly games." She drives us down the mountain, away from my fake family. Away from Graham.

It's late, I'm tired. And I can't stop thinking about the way he asked if I was sure. Like I had any other choice. I force the tears away as my mother continues to lecture while I watch the trees pass us by. It's like watching my life pass me by.

The one time I decide to pave my own way—to make things happen and head my life into a new direction—something like this happens. The only person I can really blame is myself, though.

By the time we get home, I'm too emotionally exhausted to do anything but fall into bed and hide under my covers.

I spend the next day, Christmas Eve, at my mom's moping and listening to "Blue Christmas." Part of me, I realize, thought when this ended, maybe Graham and I might actually be something. It felt like we had one of those connections you read about and hope you find. Trudy effectively erased that idea, though. I would never jeopardize his resort for my own selfish happiness. That night, I send a little Christmas wish out that I won't miss him more than I already do, because that might break me, and then I go to bed the same way I woke up—moping.

Thankfully, there's something magical about waking up Christmas morning. And when I wake, I try to pretend the whole mess never happened. I traipse downstairs with the spirit of Christmas propelling me forward. I'll be jolly today, if it kills me.

My mother is already doing our own Christmas tradition of blueberry pancakes and coffee. Lots and lots of coffee.

"Morning," I grumble as I pour myself a mug of Christmas bliss. Think I can say Christmas anymore times?

I wonder if I say Christmas more, if it will make the pain of losing Graham go away? It can't hurt to try.

So, I grab my mug of Christmas coffee, and sit my Christmas ass on the Christmas stool at the Christmas bar.

It's not working.

Is it even worse I checked my phone this morning in the hopes he may have called? I know, sad and Christmas pathetic.

"I figured I'd make a big breakfast and then maybe we can cuddle on the couch and watch Christmas movies?"

See. This is why I don't need a big family. All I need is my mother. "Sounds perfect."

And that's just what we do. We spend the afternoon watching movies and drinking hot coffee, until I get a call I never expected.

I KNOW IT'S CONTROVERSIAL, but I love pumpkin spice. Like hook it to an IV and pop it into my veins. Yum. Today, however, sitting in Baked Beans, the corner coffee shop, listening to a Bon Iver song playing through the speakers while nervously tapping my foot to the beat, I can't taste my pumpkin spice latte at all. My taste buds have shut down from pure nervousness, and I'm just going through the motions. I'm so nervous, I'm sweating. I tug my coat off as I wait, hoping I don't look as nervous as I feel. It's been a few days since Christmas, and I'm sorry to report, I still miss Graham. It's like a gentle tug at my mind, he's always there, following me around throughout my days. I can't seem to get over it. And I don't know if I even want to.

"Thanks for meeting me," Lindsey says, sliding into the booth.

"Sure, of course. I was surprised to hear from you." I take a sip, to busy my hands, letting the burn from my tasteless coffee calm my nerves. When she called and said she needed to meet with me, I was shocked to say the least. I'm assuming it's about Graham.

"I didn't bring you here to rehash what happened with my brother." Well, that's what I get for assuming. Lindsey's expression is unreadable as she remains quiet, peering at me from over her coffee cup.

"I appreciate that," I lie, a little disappointed it wasn't about how he's pining over me too.

"I don't know if Graham ever told you, but I'm one of the VPs over at LGC."

"The shopping channel?" I ask her.

"Yes." She leans forward, like she has a very important secret for me to hear. "Those soaps you gave me for the kids cleared them right up." She snaps her finger. "They're amazing, and I'd like to offer you a contract with us over at LGC."

My whole world gets turned upside down with just those words. I'm at a complete loss of what to say, but nod, knowing my soap dreams are coming true.

"Yes," I finally agree after about a minute of awkward nodding and smiling. She must think I'm crazy. Maybe I am.

I can't wait to tell Graham. And that thought right there knocks me straight out of my happy-fest. There will be no sharing excitement with him.

Lindsey goes over important details while I try desperately

to listen and not ask any questions about Graham. It's nearly impossible, but somehow, I manage.

"I'll be calling you after the New Year to plan a meeting," Lindsey says, once everything is squared away. "I have to run and get the girls."

I hug her, thanking her profusely before saying goodbye. As she leaves, I resist the urge to stop her and ask for one little something about Graham, because as great as this is, I'd be lying if I said it didn't feel a little hollow.

CHAPTER 13

Zoe
One month later

"HAVE YOU MET LOGAN CHANCE?" Hope, the host of "Holidays with Hope," asks me as the stylist for LGC flatirons her wavy blonde hair into silk. Tonight, I'm her guest for thirty minutes, showcasing all of my soaps. To say I'm nervous is an understatement.

"The owner of this channel? No, not yet. What's he like?"

"He's a great guy. It's funny, he became addicted to a shopping channel and decided one day to buy it. And that's how LGC was created."

"Ah. Where does the 'G' come from?" I ask, adjusting the red bow tying my shirt together.

"Graham Steele, you must know him. He's the other owner."

Just the mention of his name, sets my heart racing. To say

I'm not sad about the fact I haven't seen or heard from Graham would be a lie.

His purchaser, Mark, held up Graham's end of our bargain, even though I never would have expected that, and I'm currently in production to have my soaps in every cabin of Mountain Goat Resort. I debated whether to accept, but in the end, Mark convinced me by saying Graham really wanted the deal. It feels flat somehow.

"Oh, I didn't know that," I finally respond. "I know his sister is a VP. That's who offered me the deal."

The producer of the show calls us on set, and everything is pushed out of mind except for the fact I'm about to be on television.

"We're going to sell the fuck out of your soap," she assures me, rising from the makeup chair.

"Let's hope." I laugh. "No pun intended."

She cringes, slightly. "Honey, you just leave the funny stuff to me."

I follow her on set, unable to believe I'm really here. Ever have your life happen in a whir of commotion? That's how the past month has been. Busy on top of busy, getting ready for LGC to run a Valentine's Day promotional preorder for my soaps. We have a seat on the white, comfy couch, and I smooth down my black skirt, and take a deep breath.

The cameraman counts down and then the red-light flicks on, showing us we're live. My heart jumps into my throat, but I keep a smile glued on as Hope does her little intro.

"So, next up, we have Zoe Walters here with her Serendipity Soap collection. I just love these soaps." She turns to face me.

"Thank you, Hope," I say, not really sure where the words

are coming from, but somehow, I launch into a little memorized promo spiel about my soaps.

"Let's go show everyone what you've made."

We stand and move over to a display table with a variety of my products. Hope picks up the peppermint bar shaped like a heart. "This is great for a Valentine's Day gift. It not only moisturizes, but it also leaves the skin feeling supple and smooth."

"That's right. These soaps are designed with that sensitive winter skin in mind."

"Be sure to grab these soaps," she speaks to the viewers at home with a toothy grin, "they're currently flying out the door."

"We should shut that darn door, Hope," I say, giving her a wink.

She smiles back. "We have a caller on the line. Let's see what they have to say."

"Hi, this is for Zoe," the caller says. The familiar timbre of the voice on the line sends chills all over my skin. "I've used the soap and I have to say," he chuckles softly, "it kind of turns me on."

Unable to believe Graham would call, I stand statue still, blinking wildly like everything is ok. Hope intervenes as quickly as possible. "Well, thank you for calling."

"Wait," Graham's voice calls through the speaker, "Zoe, I want to talk to you."

Hope glances nervously at me, and the cameraman talks rapidly into his headset. I still have my smile plastered on my face, trying my best to remain calm, but my heart is galloping a million miles a minute. Say that three times fast.

"Graham," my smile slides off my face as I stare into the

camera, hoping Trudy doesn't see any of this, "it's probably not a good idea for you to call in?" I need to end this call, stat.

The Christmas music lightly playing in the background comes to an abrupt halt. I'm not even sure if the camera is even still filming at this point, and I no longer care. All I care about is the man on the other end of the phone line.

"Zoe, I've missed you. And not the 'hey, I haven't seen you in a while' type of miss you. But, more of the 'I need you here right now' type of miss you."

My heart aches, my eyes misting over with unshed tears, and I can't do anything but tell him the truth, "I've missed you too."

"I have something for you."

I stare into the camera, because I'm not sure where to look at this point. All I want more than anything is to see Graham. Just this one time. "Ok."

"Come outside."

I look over at Hope. "Well go, honey," she urges.

"Oh ok, right." In a rush, I remove the microphone pack from around my waist, set it on the table with my soaps, and exit the set. I grab my coat and then rush out the back door. When I step outside, the wind blows the last of the snowfall around from last night. And then I see him. Graham, in all his glory, standing next to a one-horse open sleigh.

"Graham, what are you thinking? What if Trudy sees that or someone tells her?"

"What are you talking about? Why would I care if Trudy sees that? She can fuck off." He moves closer. "I wanted to call you so many times," he whispers.

"I wanted you to. But, I don't want you to lose the resort."

"What? How would I lose the resort?"

I tell him everything Trudy told me about the marriage, and her father taking over if their wedding didn't happen. I tell him how I just wouldn't be able to live with myself if he lost his resort.

He laughs. "Yeah, well that shit is just not true."

"No part of it is?" I ask unable to believe she'd be so manipulative.

"None of it." He kisses my cheek. "He isn't even on the board." Then he kisses my other cheek.

"I could've never seen you again..." my words fail me.

"You should have asked me." He kisses the tip of my nose. "It's ok. I forgive you." He gives me a sexy smirk. "But, this means you more than care about me."

"Was it you who got me the deal here?" I ask, stepping closer to him, trying my best to read his eyes.

The cold wind can't put out the heat between the two of us. He steps closer, his arms wrapping around my waist. "You got that on your own. I was telling the truth, your soaps turn me on."

Even though I know it's selfish, I can't help myself. "Are you turned on right now?"

He leans in. "Very turned on."

Wanting to feel him again, I wrap my arms around his neck. "We should take care of that."

He smiles against my lips. "We really should."

He helps me into the sleigh and nestles me under a faux fur blanket with him. The horse trots off through a small park filled with snow as we sit cuddled in the back. The driver steers the sled around, and I smile up at Graham.

I pull back, gazing into his chocolate eyes.

I kiss his lips, his nose, his cheeks, his lips again, and then lean back. "I do more than care about you."

A light snow falls all around us and Graham gathers me in his arms, holding me close.

"See isn't this fun?"

"Yeah, it kind of is." I rest my head on his chest and can hear his heart beating faster. "You were right, baby. I just wasn't with the right person."

He's so perfect. I'm going to love dating this man.

And I'm going to make sure he loves dating me too.

THE END

GRAHAM BONUS
CHAPTER ONE

Zoe

WHAT DO you get the man who has everything for Christmas? Graham, billionaire mogul and sex god, literally has anything he could ever want. The man owns a shopping network for Christmas' sake. The twelve day countdown is on, and I'm still presentless. This is unheard of for a Christmas savant like myself. The trees were decorated and the stockings hung with care on the enormous mantle in Graham's home before Thanksgiving was even finished. Why wait?

I'm not one to crumble under the pressure of a challenge, though, and I've finally found something he definitely doesn't have.

"York, I need a favor," I whisper as soon as Graham's cousin answers the phone.

"Why are you whispering, Zoe?"

I glance over my shoulder to check I'm still alone. "Congratulations on the hockey title," I say before I dive into what I need.

"Thanks, but again, why are you whispering? Is something wrong?"

"I need help with Graham's present."

"Ah, and what is that?"

To ensure this remains top secret, I move further into the bedroom at Graham's mother's home, where we're spending a few days of the holidays, and step into the closet. "A baby goat."

His laugh fills my ear. "Wait. A living breathing goat?"

"Yes." I don't tell him how Graham thinks baby goats are adorable, nor how he watches YouTube videos of fainting goats, because I feel like that would be breaching the unspoken boyfriend/girlfriend confidentiality agreement. "I need your help getting it."

I've already been in contact with The Mountain Goat Resort and a heated barn with ample enclosure is already in the works. And who knows, maybe friends will be added.

"I'm all in," York says, with a smile in his voice. "I'll be there tonight."

"Perfect. Don't forget your ugly sweater for the party."

"Never," he says.

"You should see the little sweater I bought for the baby goat. I'll show you tonight."

"Zoe," Graham calls out.

"Gotta go," I whisper. "Don't tell a soul about this."

"Oh, don't worry. I won't. Can't wait to see his reaction."

I disconnect the call and step from the closet. "Hey, babe. How was your meeting?"

It's been a year and I still get that dip in my belly, like I'm skiing down a snow-covered mountain at lightning speed, when I see him. His dark hair, full of fuckable Christmas magic, gleams under the lights as his tall body closes the distance between us.

"Hey. It was good. Sorry I'm having to deal with business."

"It's ok." I hone in on what he's wearing. "Are those real?"

"Yeah." Graham's crooked grin is hot enough to toast the marshmallows dangling on his ugly sweater. "Check this..." He pushes a button and flames ignite in the fireplace on his chest.

I'm thoroughly impressed with his hideous creation of a Santa roasting marshmallows by a fire. *Real* marshmallows. Like everything he does in life, Graham went the extra mile. It's hot. He's hot. "Your creativity is such a turn on."

He leans in for a sultry kiss that curls my toes. "I have something for you," Graham tells me.

He produces a small black pouch from his jeans pocket.

"What is this?" I take the velvet bag from his fingers and peek inside. "It's not Christmas yet," I say as I pull a delicate silver chain out.

"Well, it's the first day of Christmas."

I study the charm. "Oh my god." I look up at him. "Is this a partridge in a pear tree?"

"Yep," is his smug answer. "Are you singing the song in that beautiful head of yours now?"

"Maybe." I want to cry that this man loves me. He's the ultimate gift—he got me a freaking partridge in a pear tree. And I have nothing for him. Well, actually, I do have something...

His family won't be back for a few hours, and everything is

ready for the ugly sweater party tonight, so I'm about to go all ho ho ho on my man.

I place my hand on his hard chest and push him back toward the bed. His dark eyes incinerate me as he sits.

"I was going to save this until tonight, but now is the right time." I knee his legs apart and step between his muscular thighs. "Unwrap me, Graham."

"Fuck, Zoe." As if I'm encased in expensive paper he doesn't want to ruin, his hands slowly dispose of my t-shirt and then slide my leggings down and off. My panties are next to go. "Beautiful," he murmurs at my freshly waxed and vajazzled vagina. He traces a finger along the sparkling candy cane, followed quickly by his tongue.

My knees nearly buckle. "Bre told me at the salon it's the best way to spread Christmas cheer."

As soon as I speak the words, I'm flipped around and on the soft comforter with Graham hovering over me.

He sucks each nipple in his warm mouth before moving down my body in a flurry of kisses. "Oh, baby, I'm definitely going to spread you." He opens my legs. "And lick you." His tongue takes a swipe through my wetness. "Mm. And suck you." He toys with my clit and does that nipping thing with his teeth I love so much. My back arches off the bed, and I moan as he works my pussy with expertise. To give him better access to his present, I plant my feet on his broad shoulders.

Really, it's hard to decipher who is getting the gift here. With Graham feasting on me like I'm plum pudding and his tongue is the spoon, I think it's me. I need to give back. Before I can, he inserts two fingers and white hot heat ignites low in my stomach and spreads until I'm coming all over his gorgeous face.

"God, I love to hear you come," he rasps out.

He licks the candy cane again. It really is the most wonderful time of year.

CHAPTER 2

Graham

I STILL DON'T CARE for Christmas. But I do care about Zoe. This past year with her is worth the array of atrocious sweaters surrounding me. None of them can hold a candle to mine, though.

"Having fun?" Zoe asks. Even in her fuzzy green sweater, decorated with god awful soap ornaments, she looks stunning.

"Loads," I tell her.

Her blue eyes narrow on me over the rim of her eggnog glass. "Admit it, Mr. Grinch. You love it."

"I'll give it to you, this ugly sweater party is pretty damn funny." I steal a kiss from her ruby lips as we wait in line to have our picture taken before the tapestry draped on the wall that reads "The Uglier The Better."

If the ghost of Ebenezer Scrooge himself would have told me a year ago that I'd be holding a giant candy cane while wearing a sweater with fucking marshmallows on it, I would have laughed in his pasty face. But here I am. It's ok, though. Not many can rock this ensemble like I can.

Zoe blushes when I look at the candy cane and then down to the sweet spot between her thighs. And just like that, my dick hardens. It's a hazard of being within twenty feet of her.

After picture taking, Zoe is swept away to deal with hostess duties so I check in with the Mountain Goat Resort to make sure everything is ready for our stay. Then I check email. Vacation is never really vacation. There's always work to do. Thankfully, Zoe is very understanding.

"Can you grab some sparkling water from the kitchen?" my mother, draped head to toe in gold tinsel, asks.

I slide my phone in my jeans. "What have you become?" I ask with unbridled amusement.

"Says the guy wearing marshmallows," she retorts, with a smile. "Love looks good on you."

I laugh. She knows she's said the words to send me off like a rocket to retrieve her request. "I'll be right back."

I pivot on my heel and walk away before she can say anything else. It's not that I mind discussing my feelings for Zoe, I just don't want to field all the questions I know are coming. Marriage. Babies. Forever.

I'm not opposed to any of that, but I'm still enjoying the dating phase with Zoe. I want to savor each part of the journey —things like candy canes on a bare pussy—and my mother wants to express mail us to the end. It already seems like time is moving at warp speed with Zoe. I'm forever wanting to slow it down, so the seconds tick by at an excruciatingly slow pace. So this sublime feeling of freefalling never ends. Besides, Zoe is busy becoming a soap mogul and who says *she* wants to get married? Hm. Would she marry me? We haven't had that discussion. She loves me, but does she love me like *that*?

Speaking of...my little vixen has disappeared from her party.

As I weave through the chattering guests in the living room, there's no sign of Zoe's dark tresses under the twinkling lights. I want to steal her away for an impromptu fondling, put my dick in her box, but she's nowhere to be found. Probably because she's tucked in a corner...next to the refrigerator...amidst a bustle of workers...whispering with York.

She's oblivious to my entrance, and I'm a little offended she's so wrapped up in her conversation with York that she didn't feel me enter the room. Isn't that cheesy shit supposed to happen? I'll admit, there is an ugly insecure part to love that rears it's demonic horns at times like these. York's dark head is bowed down toward hers and the carrot protruding out of his ugly ass sweater pokes her breast. Twice. Instead of yanking it off and slapping him over the head with it, she continues talking to him in an animated frenzy, the golden star atop her head bobbing.

I amble closer, still undetected, and stop cold when she pulls what looks like a baby sweater from one of the wrapped presents dangling from the bottom of her cardigan. He shakes his head and grins.

And I may faint.

Zoe is pregnant?

CHAPTER 3

Zoe

"HOW ARE YOU FEELING?" Graham asks for the millionth time as we leave the French restaurant where we dined on an extravagant dinner of roasted hen. Yes, he ordered three. I'm flabbergasted at the thought he's put into this. Yesterday, he gifted me a bracelet with two diamond turtle doves. For someone opposed to Christmas, he deserves an award. Maybe I do too, because my return gift to him was my ass. TMI?

"I'm fine," I assure him. "Why do you keep asking that?"

He takes my elbow and leads me to his Range Rover across the parking lot. Although the pavement has been plowed from the recent snowfall, small slushy spots remain. He navigates me around them as if I'm made of porcelain.

"Careful," he warns as I sidestep an icy patch. "Want me to carry you?"

I laugh. "Um, that's very chivalrous of you, but I think I can manage to walk."

His brow creases and his dark eyes bore into mine. "You'd tell me if you were feeling sick?"

"Sick? I mean, I'm stuffed, but I don't feel sick."

I didn't eat *that* much. I'm not shy about eating, and I certainly wouldn't let a good meal go to waste, so yes, I had two hens. But honestly, the portions were tiny, so it's really like I only ate one. He nods, and opens my door.

As we pull away from The Chateau, I reach over and palm his cock through his black slacks. "So," I coo to his stubbled profile, "that was very romantic. I'd like to show my appreciation with a little surprise when we get back."

"Oh, damn." His head whips to me. "You feel ok to do that?"

"Mhm. Better than ok."

His cock stiffens beneath my caresses. When I lick my lips, he lets out a nipple-hardening hiss. Even his sounds are sexy.

The passing car lights illuminate his chiseled face as he glances over at me. "You're irresistible. Do you know that?"

"You're amazing. Do you know that?"

"Maybe," he jokes. Traffic is minimal on the ride back and it seems like only a few minutes before we are pulling in the drive of his parents' home. We hustle past the snow laden shrubbery and indoors. His family is still out at a showing of *The Nutcracker*, so we fly up the staircase to our room where I'm about to give true meaning to it's namesake, Vixen.

"I need you to shower or something so I can get ready."

"Fuck. This is something you have to prepare for?" He locks the door and kicks off his shoes, followed by his clothes, until he's completely nude, already erect.

I nod, tempted to just skip the surprise and impale myself on his thick cock.

"Don't peek," I tell him as he strides across the spacious room into the bathroom.

Once he's inside and closed the door, I spring into action. Graham told me once, he found my elf uniform incredibly sexy. Obviously, I catalogue all these things in the Graham Rolodex in my mind, so I brought it with me. And now I'm about to become a very naughty elf on a shelf.

Graham takes exactly fifteen minutes to shower, so I grab paper from my bag and scribble off some notes to help him locate me.

Follow the clues to find your naughty elf on a shelf...Here's a hint, you light a fire in me.

If you found this, woohoo! The next clue can be found beneath a tiny version of the giant tree where we first met. You better get this one! Kiss. Kiss.

Your naughty elf is behind a door where clothes you won't be needing are located.

The first goes on his pillow, because he'll go to the bed immediately, the second on the mantle of the fireplace, and the final in the Nativity scene on the bookshelf. Ok, that's just wrong. Forgive me, Jesus. I snatch up the clue and place it beneath the miniature tree on the dresser and then snag the strand of lights off of it.

Five minutes later, I'm dressed in a red felt dress, elf hat, and thigh high candy cane striped socks. Since I won't fit on an actual shelf, I'm perched on the square cabinetry/island thingy in the walk-in closet. I cross my legs and wait for Graham. Hopefully, he doesn't find this creepy. I've never liked the idea of the Elf On A Shelf. It's his grin. He looks like a serial killer who will come alive and smother you to death while you sleep. But, sacrifices.

Which, how can this even be considered a sacrifice, when Graham enters wearing nothing but a Santa hat on top of his still wet hair? It's another gift.

"I've been a very naughty elf, Santa," I drawl out. "You may need to tie me up." I hold up the string of lights.

"Damn, you are such a bad girl but no, I want you free to touch my cock." He strokes his dick and walks closer, a confection of abs and rippling muscles. He's so delicious, I want to devour him whole, but also not, because then I wouldn't have anymore.

"I love these." He trails a finger up my socks. Explores the exposed skin of my thigh. Then discovers I'm not wearing panties. He groans.

When all is said and done, Graham is a simple man. Six dollar Target socks turn him on just as much as expensive lingerie, and I love that I can still be me.

He leans in and nips my bottom lip with his teeth before he hoists me up from my seat on the cabinet. Forehead to forehead, he walks us to the oversized leather chair in the corner of the room. I wish I could capture his scent for a soap. I'd call it...well, I don't know what I'd call it. Man-a-licious seems too ordinary. Maybe I'd just give it a symbol like an exclamation point. That's how he makes me feel.

He sits, and I straddle his lap. "Tell me what you want," he rasps.

"Well..." I reach between us and fondle his balls. His hooded eyes mesmerize me. "I want a dark eyed man who doesn't like Christmas, but loves to give." I ease down on his dick and moan as his thickness stretches me. His fingers grip my hips. "I want a man who fucks like a god, but is so mortal he feels everything." I rock against him. "You. I want you."

"Fuck, Zoe." His hips buck and heat spreads throughout my limbs. Sometimes I worry this insane sexual chemistry we have will destroy us both. He cups my face in his warm hands and seizes my lips. Our tongues mate with each other as he thrusts into me. I wonder if this longing for him will ever fade. This need to make him as happy as he makes me. I hope it doesn't.

He pulls back. "Do you love me, Zoe?"

His earnest question stabs my heart and confuses me all at once. We've said the words so many times. "More than Christmas," I whisper.

He pumps his hips in a frenzy and then I shatter, like a million snowflakes drifting and swirling.

"Yeah, baby, keep coming." He pumps faster, sliding me up and down, until he groans and his own release sends me spiraling again.

My heart drums against my chest and our pants fill the room. "Wow. You really jingled my bell." I remove my hat and toss it.

He chuckles just as a knock sounds at the door. I spring from his lap and bolt into the bathroom. Don't really want anyone wondering why I'm dressed as an elf. After a few minutes, Graham peeks his head in to let me know his family is back and his dad needs help bringing in firewood.

While he's gone, I shower, and once I'm tucked in bed, my phone buzzes. I retrieve it from the nightstand and read the text message from Nick, my future baby goat's owner.

"I've got some other people interested in Jack." I gasp. "Just want to give you the first opportunity. Can you come by tomorrow morning?"

"Yes," I reply instantly. "I'll be there by ten am."

Well, this is throwing a wrench in my plans. Tomorrow, I've been invited for tree cutting with Graham and his dad. To say I was excited is an understatement. I slump in the bed. I've never been on a tree finding expedition. But, baby goat trumps everything. It's a small sacrifice. Now, I just have to figure out a way to sneak off with York without Graham knowing.

I'VE NEVER SEEN anything as cute as Jack in my life. He's white, and soft as a marshmallow, with a chocolate smudge between his doe eyes. But now I have to take the mom too. Cause I can't take a baby from its mother. Even if Nick assures me it's ok. Baby momma studies me like she knows what I'm up to, and I just can't.

"I want Star too," I tell Nick. "They'll have a great home at the Mountain Goat Resort. Thanks to York," and his connections, "a barn and fence have already been installed."

York slides his hands in his coat pockets and grins. If it wasn't for his hockey star status, I wouldn't have been able to pull this off. I'm very grateful for all of his help. But if I can't have Star too, it's a deal breaker.

Nick drapes his arms on the wooden fence. "I can come up and help them get acclimated."

I clap my hands, full of glee. "Yes. I'd appreciate that."

"Tomorrow I'm free. Sorry, that's the only day I can do it."

"That's fine." We return to the lodge tonight and there's no way I can hide the barn until Christmas, anyway. "Thank you so much. They're going to be so happy."

We work out the details, and I sign the papers. Graham is going to be a father.

CHAPTER 4

Graham

MY BABY WILL BE cuter than baby Yoda. My feet trudge forward through the snow, but my mind is back at the house where Zoe is sleeping. This morning, after I gave her the custom made pajamas with four birds talking on the phone, and she cried over how 'adorable' they were, she said she felt a little nauseous and needed to skip the tree cutting. I offered to stay, hold her hair back, but she shooed me away.

While I have a mini panic attack over a baby shooting out of Zoe's tight as fuck vagina, my father scopes out the abundant evergreens and inspects their branches, like his life depends on it. "What do you think about this one?"

I walk next to him and touch the stiff needles. "I think Zoe is pregnant."

His head turns in slow motion to me. "And how do you feel about that?"

"Like I'm going to fail as a father."

For the first time in my life, I realize this is something I might not succeed at. Sure, I've got more money than I can ever spend, but that doesn't mean I'll be good at parenting. There's psychological shit that goes into it. I sit on a fallen log and look up at the clear blue sky. It's the color of Zoe's eyes.

"Well," Dad says, "you probably will at times."

"That's reassuring."

Dad laughs. "It's all trial and error." He rubs a hand against his red cheek. "I'm happy for you."

I stand and give him a wan smile. "Let's get this tree. Zoe and I have to head to the resort early."

Thirty minutes later, we're on our way back with a fat evergreen loaded on the sled. When we enter the foyer, Zoe stands by the stairs, radiant and beautiful.

"Oh, it smells so good," she says.

"How are you feeling?" I ask.

"Much better."

She stands on her tiptoes to give me a kiss and then heads toward the living room. Dad and I drag the tree in while mom gives directions as if we don't do this every year. We set the tree in the stand and Zoe helps my mother string the lights.

"Looks good," York says.

I turn and meet his brown eyes. "Can I talk to you for a second?"

"Sure."

He follows me into the kitchen.

I lean against the counter and cross my arms. "You'd tell me if you knew something?"

He tilts his head. "About what?"

For some reason, Zoe has decided to confide in York.

Unless it was an immaculate conception, that's my child in her, so shouldn't I be the first to know?

"Zoe."

He rubs a finger against his lower lip, then clasps his hand on my shoulder. "I can tell you this, your peaceful existence is about to be no more. Double trouble is coming your way."

Fucking hell. I've got super sperm. Twins. I can't parent one, much less two.

"Hey," Zoe says from the entrance, "we need your help."

In a daze, I follow her to the tree and with numb hands hang ornaments until the tree is barely visible beneath the array of glass baubles. The rest of the day is a blur as we pack our things, say our goodbyes, and drive to the resort.

"Are you ok?" Zoe asks as we settle in our cabin.

"Yeah, I'm just beat. I have an early call in the morning."

Worry floods her blue eyes and she places a cool hand on my forehead. "You don't have a fever, so that's good."

She mother hens me and once we're in bed, I pull her close. She falls asleep immediately, but I lie awake, running through all the ways I'm going to fail at being a father, until my lids become heavy.

And then I dream.

A dark figure enters the room garbed in a long black gown. For a moment, I think it's Darth Vader. He's breathing that heavy.

Because I'm cool, and don't dream like an ordinary man, we don't walk down the hallway—we fly. Right through the damn walls, over a canopy of trees, to a two-story log house adorned with Christmas lights and smoke puffing from its chimney.

"Why are we here?" I ask faceless dude.

"You'll see."

I stand next to him in the snow. Two children, in coats so puffy their arms barely bend, waddle across the snow. Giggles float through the air and claim my heart. Zoe chases after them.

"Wait. This is my future?"

"Obviously," he drawls.

"Well, you skipped over past and present," I point out.

"Well, sometimes you need to just fly to the end."

Ok, this isn't so bad. I'm not freaking out. Palms aren't sweating. No reindeer hooves battering my chest. Until York zips across the snow and lifts up a squealing tike. Zoe rips a snowball at him. He laughs and they proceed to have a jolly good time. Twin One in his arms giggles as he runs from Zoe and Twin Two.

"Am I in the house?" What the fuck?

"No. Europe."

I stalk across the snow to take my child but my arms go right through her. Her. The hazel eyed, chubby cheeked cherub is a her. Dark curls peek from beneath her knit hat. She lays her adorably adorable head on York's shoulder. That should be my shoulder.

Twin Two waddles past me and dumps a pile of snow on York's boots. Good boy. A boy. Twin Two is a boy. Because he's bundled like an Eskimo, he tips over. York squats to help my little man up but they topple to the ground. Squeals abound. Squeals sweeter than a chorus of angels. And I'm in fucking Europe. Zoe whips out her phone and takes a picture.

I move closer and watch as she texts it to me. "No, don't text it," I say to her. "Call me and tell me I'm missing out."

Her fingers pause. She glances over at me and I think for a moment she heard me, but her blue eyes look through me until frost covers my soul. She shakes her head and hits send. I watch *in horror as she tells the kids it's s'mores time and York is going to build a real fire. And then—as if s'mores wasn't bad enough—they're going to watch Rudolph.*

"Ok, first," I tell cloaked figure, "York can't toast a marshmallow without burning it to a crisp. Second, this is my family, I should be watching movies with them."

He shrugs his ghostly shoulders. "Well, you're in Europe."

"Well, you're annoying," I mutter.

"I wanna watch da Gwinch," Twin Two *announces with mittened hands on his hips.*

"We can watch that too, little man," York *appeases him.*

Twin Two's precious pout transforms into a grin as he lurches against York and gives him a leg hug. My legs ache for a hug.

"Thank you for coming," Zoe *tells him.*

"Of course," *he says.* "I wouldn't miss Christmas Eve."

No way. I look over at ghostman. "Christmas fucking Eve?" *He nods.* "Let's go. I don't want to see anymore."

"Go where?" Zoe says.

I open my eyes to morning sunlight streaming into the cabin and Zoe's blues staring back at me. "Just a dream."

"You're going to be late for your call," she says, snuggling against me.

"I'm taking the day off."

Her eyes widen. "Really?" She throws the covers back and hops out of bed. "Well, this is unexpected."

"I thought we could do something fun."

You'd think I just said Christmas is cancelled. She tugs her t-shirt down over her panties and worries her plump bottom lip. "Isn't the call important?"

"No." I pick up my phone from the nightstand and postpone everything for today. "I'm free."

And I do feel free. We dress and as I pocket my wallet, Zoe types on her phone before saying, "Santa has arrived."

"Yeah?" With twins in his sleigh? I swallow back the urge to ask her to tell me already. There's a lot of shopping and preparation and freaking the fuck out to be done.

We step out into the cold air. "I have a surprise for you." Zoe grins and takes my hand. She places it against her chest. "Feel my heart beating? I'm so nervous."

Same. This is it. She's going to tell me today. But I got this shit. I'll be brave for both of us. Or hell, I'll hire someone to be brave for us.

CHAPTER 5

Zoe

"SO WHAT NAMES would you pick for kids?" Graham asks.

My steps falter for a moment. "Um, I haven't thought about it."

"I don't like fancy names. Just good solid names," he adds.

"Me too," I say. Are we having the talk? Honestly, I've fantasized about a family with Graham, but I don't want to jinx it.

My nerve endings buzz with anticipation as we walk hand-in-hand to the main lodge. Nick is already here, and I'm sweating buckets beneath my coat. What if Graham hates the idea? I sneak a peek at him as we near the building. He looks very rugged today in his flannel shirt, jeans, and black coat. He looks masculine. Like a man who needs a goat, I reassure myself.

Before he can enter the lodge, I tug his hand and redirect him with a head nod. "This way."

"Where are we going?"

"I have something to tell you. Well, show you."

I lead him around the building, down the side, toward the back.

Before we make the final turn that will reveal his surprise, he stops and moves in front of me to clasp my face in his hands. "Listen, I'm going to be there for everything." His serious eyes plead with mine to believe him. And I do, even if I don't know what he's talking about. "I'm going to have snowball fights, and light fires, and watch Rudolph. I'm going to enjoy the hell out of being in a gingerbread house. I will *not* be in Europe."

"Ok," I say as a bleating goat prevents me from asking what in the heck he means.

He drops his hands. "Was that a goat?"

I grin and take his hand again. "Merry Christmas, Daddy." Nick waves as we round the corner. "Meet Star and baby Jack."

I've never seen Graham stunned, until now. His footsteps slow. He volleys his eyes between me and the goats. "You got me a baby goat?"

"Yes," I exclaim. "He's so sweet and I got his mom too. York helped me."

"You're not pregnant?"

My head draws back. "What? No. Why would you think that?"

He scrubs a hand on his jaw. "Well...I saw you show York a baby sweater. And then you said you were sick and York said double trouble was coming my way." He blows out a breath. "A baby goat?"

I nod. "The sweater was for Jack. There are no human babies."

"Yet," he adds to my statement. "But there will be. 'Cause I want them with you," he says, causing an explosion in my ovaries. He grins. "Let's go meet Star and Jack."

Give a man a goat and he'll give you a ring. Five. With Nick, Star, and baby Jack looking on, Graham opens a red velvet box containing the engagement ring from a year ago and four slim rose gold bands twined together. "I need a real fiancée this time. I love you, baby. So damn much. And I want every Christmas for the rest of my life with you. Will you marry me, Zoe?"

"Does Santa have reindeer?" I step into him and wrap my arm around his waist. "That's a yes, in case you don't know Christmas speak."

And then he kisses me. Heady and deep. A kiss full of promises of Christmas magic to come.

THE END

NORTH

North Caspian, a very successful alpha boss and his lively employee, Holly Winterbourne, will heat up your holiday and kindles. North owns a store for the celebrity babies of Hollywood. When Holly accepts a job there, she is immediately intrigued by her Scrooge of a boss. THIS BOOK IS FUN. (No celebrities were harmed in the making of this book)

CHAPTER 1

Holly

I DON'T HATE my job. I don't hate my job. I so hate my freaking job. Don't get me wrong, I'm grateful that I have a job at this time of year. But, I really hate it.

Ok, not so much my actual duties of the job. But I do really despise my boss. He's gorgeous, talented, and a ruthless prick. That's not why I hate him though. Today is Christmas Eve and instead of being extra generous to the employees that have busted our butts off (I have legit dropped twelve pounds) over the last four weeks to get the last leg of holiday retail sales (quite literally) in the bag, he has decided tonight we are going to work. All. Night. Long.

That's right. There will be no sleep. No eating. No breaks. No going home to wake up on Christmas morning to the ones we love. Scrooge bastard. There aren't even any Christmas cookies in our shop. Speaking of our shop, did I mention I work for *the* Caspian Wondrous Emporium? Sounds fun, right? Surrounded by toys and cool gadgets all day long? Well, it's not.

This shop is basically the gateway to hell, because it's where every celebrity and big-time somebody shops for gifts for their brattylicious ankle biters. I have nothing against kids, I actually like them, but the parents...holy tricycles.

The demands are as high as the prices in our store. And what they demand of the shop, North Caspian demands of his "little elves" slaving away to bring the most exclusive, fresh and high-end toys into our store. Every item we sell is uniquely made. No copies, and a large array from all over the world.

North is actually kind of like Santa, but without all the jolly, saintly shit. He goes away for long stretches of time, and when he comes back, he's loaded down with a trunk full of goodies. Today is one of those days. He always saves the night before Christmas for his most exclusive items.

As a seasoned veteran of this store, I should know that tonight is hell night, but somehow it still takes me aback to hear him stand before us with his Gucci shirt pressed to perfection, arms crossed like the boss he is, handing out orders and expecting complete compliance...*or else*. There was actually a time I wanted to test the 'what else' to see if he was bluffing. But after watching ten of my fellow coworkers fleeing from him after they disobeyed orders...I'm good. I believe in the 'or else' as if it were Santa himself.

I'm setting up a display of twenty-four karat baby pacifiers (Ok, some things we sell are just freaking ridiculous, I'll admit.) in the window when I notice a shadow passing over from behind me. I turn my head to see if it's the paparazzi (we get a lot of that) or some protestor who wants us to donate all of these finds to a museum (get a lot of that too) but to my surprise it's him. *The* North Caspian. He's not one to be hanging around outside his shop (see above reasons) so I'm actually curious about what the hell he's up to as he stares at me with this unreadable expression across his chiseled perfect babyface.

He's dripping in black from head-to-toe which I find hilarious since it's the night before Christmas, one of the happiest holidays of the year and he basically dresses like the Grim Reaper. I mean, a really attractive version in a Gucci shirt and tie, but still.

North grimaces, and then he slides away from the window to enter the shop. I expect him to say something horrible about my display and bark out a long string of expletives, possibly even fire me on the spot, but he heads straight to his office upstairs without a word.

It's pretty much against everything in my being to go to him, he is *not* the kind of man you want to interrupt, or put yourself in front of, without warrant. It would be like purposely walking out into traffic and trying to take on a bus speeding my way at sixty-five miles per hour.

But it's also the season for giving and maybe I've choked down way too many sugar cookies and hot beverages sprinkled with pumpkin spice, but it appears that even the most evil and wicked people of the world should find joy on Christmas. Even if it means I have to step in front of a damn speeding bus. That's possibly on fire. Maybe some sharks swimming inside of the bus that's on fire speeding my way. Sweet Baby J, help me.

He doesn't answer when I knock the first time.

"Mr. Caspian..." I push the door open. Apparently for Christmas I want to be shark food.

North sits at his desk. It's a grand thing—mahogany wood with drawers that lock away all his secrets, shoved up against a large expansive window that overlooks the busy streets of New York, cloaked in white from the light fall of snow earlier. His dark hair and clothing, a ghostly silhouette to the backdrop of it all. He's like an onyx inkblot on a stark white page.

North's hands roam through his jet-black hair as if he's thinking of jumping out the window.

"I really need a hot dog," he mumbles.

"Excuse me, sir?"

He whips his head back and stares at me with the fire of fifty dragons. "What are you doing in here?"

"I knocked."

"I didn't answer. So, back to my question, what are you doing in my office without an invitation?"

"I was...worried about you, sir."

"You only need to worry about keeping your precious ass employed. Get back to work, Winterbourne."

I nod. He turns back to the window. "Um..." I toy with the doorknob. "Do you need me to get you anything, sir?" *Like a hotdog that has you feeling extra cranky.*

North is silent. His chair twitches back and forth like his legs want to say what his mouth refuses.

I try to gently suggest, "Something to eat, maybe?"

It takes several seconds before he answers me back. "I want a hotdog. All the fixings. From that cart just on the other side of the street."

I want to smile. But there's no such thing as smiling inside the gates of hell. I don't wait for money because I know he won't offer it up, so I just quietly duck out of his office and head for my coat. I'm buttoning up as Meg comes over to me in a huff. "You're allowed to go home?"

"I'm just getting Mr. Scrooge some lunch."

"Why not me?" she cries, flailing her arms in the air. Her long shimmery blonde hair is so light-colored it looks like snow falling around her head as she continues on her tirade.

I don't blame her. I'm quite happy to get to flee this circus for a while, despite the fact it's freezing cold outside. I guess Hell has its highs, too. I mean it is very toasty in here, no hat or gloves required. But also, out there? No pretentious baby pacifier displays to be built. Just good people doing good things, like selling good food at a low price. That's a bit of Heaven on Earth if you ask me. Joy to the freaking world ala weiners on a warm toasty bun for under two bucks.

And for some reason, North Caspian wants one.

Meg grabs her coat and hurries to shove it on. "I'll get him food. You stay and get my noon appointment commission sales. Buy your family something nice with the money."

I yank the crap outta her sleeve as she tries to book it to the door. "I don't want your noon. Your noon is worse than Caspian. I'm getting the wiener."

"I'm getting the wiener," she protests as we struggle.

By struggle I mean we are flat out having a miniature brawl in the middle of Wondrous Emporium where A-list celebrities and alike are trying to browse the best place to toss thousands of dollars on baby gifts.

"Girls," a firm voice calls from behind.

Meg and I stop instantly as if we're small children.

North has his hands in his pockets. His face is serious as he looks down at both of us and says, "You both can get my wiener."

I blink. Meg stares stupidly at him.

North nods. "Matter of fact, I'll sweeten the task. Whoever gets my wiener first gets to go home."

Now, I'm not saying that I'm proud of myself for shouting at the top of my lungs that Mason Lamoa—one of the hottest male celebs on the planet—is ten feet to our left browsing toy trains, which is also the farthest spot from the door, but *I am* saying that Meg is his biggest fan and there is nothing that I wouldn't do to get to leave purgatory all in the name of grabbing a cheap hot wiener.

CHAPTER 2

North

WHEN I WAS A BOY, Christmas was not very exciting. In fact, it was quite nonexistent in my childhood. To the outside world, I'm sure it seemed as if I had it all because my father was the owner of one of the most amazing stores for kids to find all kinds of trinkets and games, things to explore and grow your imagination. You could walk into Wondrous Emporium and sail to the moon on a rocket ship you built with your own two hands. On one aisle you could explore the depths of the sea, and just a blink away, a fifty-foot dinosaur fossil stood ready to destroy anything in its path. There were looking glasses from far away lands made from real gold. Maps found in bottles at the bottom of the ocean. Gold coins filled up old wooden crates.

And because of all of this, I was both the best known child at school and the loneliest. Most kids only wanted to be my friend because they wanted a shot at owning or playing with something from my father's store. And most of their moms wanted a shot at my father because of his riches and high dollar trinkets. My mother died when I was born. It had always been just the two of us, plus whatever nanny I had that year. They usually didn't stay long, since most of them found their way into my father's bed, and then soon after, the front door.

Once I turned into a teenager, I was roped into the family business and was forced to deal with the shop and all of its demands, including the clientele. At first I thought it was great, getting to sleep with super models and actresses and pretty much anyone who walked through the door needing something...but when all people want from you are material things, the magic wears off quickly. I felt reduced to nine-years-old again—the kid everyone wanted to hang out with all because his dad was cooler than he was.

Six years ago my father died and I was left everything in his will, including this horrible store and all of its ghosts. Every time the bell on the door chimes, I expect him to walk in and start barking orders at me. To remind me of everything I'm doing wrong. But instead, all I hear is my own voice echoing back at me as I yell at the people who now work for me in this place. They think it's some kind of joke and I kind of understand because that's how I felt for such a long time. But quitting now, just giving up on this place, that would feel like the final nail in my father's coffin. Like I failed him. Like I failed myself.

I stare out the window of my office and watch as all of New York moves so quickly, like everything in life is such a race to the finish line. They don't even know where they're going. They have no idea what happens next. And yet, they're in such a hurry to get there.

That's the joke, isn't it? Hurry up to get nowhere fast. This is nowhere. This is nothing. Shit, they look so damn happy.

A small child catches the last falling snowflakes on her tongue and she smiles like she found the secret key to unlock Heaven's gates. A man buying a hotdog from a cart walks away with such a bounce in his step, completely unphased by the fact that it's below freezing temps outside. He's just enjoying a shitty New York hotdog.

Ok, that's a bit of blasphemy, I'll admit. There's no such thing as a shitty New York hotdog. Even a shitty hot dog in New York is still better than the best hot dog anywhere else—but the point is, we are smack dab in the middle of a food mecca and he chooses to be out in the freezing cold just to enjoy something he could get any time of the year—and honestly, that man could have ducked into an eatery and grabbed a dog in the protection of four warm walls where he could sit down to enjoy his meal. But he picked a cart outside. He braved the brutal weather and hellish traffic of nonstop people and taxi cabs to grab *that* hot dog from *that* hot dog cart.

I want *that* fucking hot dog, too. That hot dog is a magical thing of happiness. I want it now.

Fuck, listen to me, I sound like my father, just fucking like him, except instead of hunting down buried treasures and exploring the nine wonders of the world (Yes, that number is the accurate one.) I'm sitting in the comfort of my toasty ultra-plush fucking office longing for a damn footlong while contemplating the purpose of my life.

And of course that's exactly when the hottest girl I've ever laid eyes on, Holly Winterbourne, catches me at my most vulnerable.

Did I happen to mention that she's my employee? And not just any kind of employee, but a damn good one. Holly's dedicated and meticulous. She's the kind of girl my father would have flown around the world on his private jet and given multiple orgasms to.

Holly's not just some person you work into the ground and force to hate the holidays. I could barely stop myself from ripping her from the display window as she stacked stupid fucking gold pacifers. I want to yell at her but not all of the cruel words that my father yelled at me. No. I want to yell at her in a way that reminds her that her life is worth so much more than dollar signs and trinkets. I want her to smile like that lady outside my office window as she watches her husband offer his hand so she can board the sled of the Clydesdale horse cart and go on a truly magical adventure through a tangible New York wonderland.

And even though I have ruined her holidays for the last five years, worked her like a dog, and never once treated her as if she were more valuable than the items in this shop, she still comes to care for me.

And that just breaks me down to my core. Like the good person she is, not a few minutes later, I'm treated to that damn hot dog I've longed for, complete with all the toppings and a drink and plenty of napkins and even some damn Tums because she is always on top of everything.

Today she's wearing a sweater that is so white and soft I'd imagine it feels better than the hyde of a rabbit even though she's cruelty free—but that's just the kind of magic she works. She makes everything better than it's intended to be—most days that means me. Yes, even though I'm this big of a mess, I'm still better than I'd be without her.

"Anything else, Mr. Caspian?" Her doe eyes lure me into a trance. The blue is so clear and light it's like looking into the ocean. I remember a trip to the Greek Islands with my father in Mykonos as a boy. The water was like looking into the reflection of Heaven, so clear and strikingly beautiful. That water has nothing on Holly fucking Winterbourne's eyes. She has the lips of a She Devil and the smile of a saint. A heart of gold and laughter that would make fairies the most plentiful creatures in the universe. Why do I torture her? Why do I keep her here? Because I guess I *am* like my father—I collect precious things and keep a price on their heads.

"Sir?" she tries again.

I snap from my thoughts and shake my head to free myself of the struggle. "This will be fine." Normal people say thank you.

Say it.

Tell her.

Two little words.

They won't make you less than you are, they'll make you more. Go ahead. "I... um."

She's already turned around and headed for the door. Holly pauses at my stuttering and raises her perfectly groomed brows. "Excuse me, Mr. Caspian? Did you say something, sir?"

Sir. She needs to stop calling me that. It's an instant erection.

"North . . ." I take a deep pull of air through my nose to center myself. "Just call me by my first name. I'm not my father." Why does that feel so cleansing? I roll the words around in my head once more, silently. I'm not my father. Damn, that feels quite good.

"North," she says it with a smile. Fuck, I still get hard. "I don't think I've ever had a boss who preferred to be called by his first name."

"Does it bother you?"

"Uh, no. No, not at all." She debates by the door. I try not to make my ogling so obvious but she shifts in a way that says motherfucker, you are way too obvious. But she also doesn't run away. Fuck knows there's plenty of work to be done. Does she want to be here? With me?

"Are you hungry?" I ask. "This is a lot of food for just one person. Two big wieners to swallow down."

"Uh...I told Meg I'd help her with her noon client."

"It's Tessica Salba," I say. "Meg can handle it."

"What about the window display? The other customers?"

"We are fully staffed today. Do you want my weiner or not?"

Her brows spike again.

I sigh heavily. "It's a joke. A really shitty one. Just take a seat, won't you?" I push out a chair beside mine with my foot. I don't watch her walk my way because it's all too much. Instead I pretend to read the paperwork on my desk, but truthfully, I'm hyper aware of what she's doing in my peripheral view.

She pulls off her coat to reveal that soft fucking white wanna-be bunny sweater. Her chest juts out as she wiggles her arm free and I take a deep, *deep* fucking breath to control myself.

"I have a confession," she says.

I watch as her legs cross before I look over, paying full attention to her face. "Please don't tell me you spit in my food."

"No. Of course not, sir."

I hold up my hand. "You never know."

"I was going to say..." She curls a section of her hair behind her ear. She has no earrings on. I'm stuck on that detail for a moment. "Sir?"

I blink. "North."

"Right. Sorry. Is everything ok?"

Ignoring her, I say, "You were saying you had a confession . . ."

"Yes. I don't eat weiners."

We both stare at each other for a moment.

Holly smiles. "Bad joke."

"Horrible joke."

"I'm a vegan," she admits. "At least I try to be."

"What does that mean exactly?"

"It means, I can't eat your wiener."

I laugh a bit. "We've established that."

She smiles bigger, a light blush forming on her cheeks.

And I'm hard as fuck as we talk about hot dogs. Fuck my universe.

"Well, if I'm truly making a confession, then I guess I'd have to admit to all of the Christmas cookies I ate that were made with real butter and eggs. I really fell off the vegan wagon super hard for a few weeks there."

"You naughty girl."

She laughs and I love that I can do that. A smile on her is so much better than the annoyance and hate that fills her features every time she looks my way. Even though I damn well deserve it for the torture I've put her through.

"Don't tell Santa," she whispers.

"Don't you know? Santa wishes he was cool enough to talk to a guy like me. I've got better toys than he does."

"This is true." But her eyes lose that playful light she had just a moment ago.

"Sorry." I glance away. "Bad joke."

"It's true, though."

"And also a shitty thing to say." I hesitate, looking away from her for a moment. "I don't really feel that way."

"This is an amazing place. You should be proud of it. Your family has put in so much work. So many years. It makes people really happy."

"Does it make you happy?" I blurt out the words before I even think about what I'm asking.

"I...uh..."

I smile reassuringly. "Don't worry. I understand that feeling too."

Holly's brows pull together. She inches a little closer to me in her seat. "It doesn't make *you* happy?"

I shrug my shoulders a bit. "It was my father's dream. This was his thing."

"Oh."

I stare out the window, through the white snow that begins to dust its breath across the glass again as it falls harder. People on the street turn into little ant-like dots worming their way through traffic to find shelter and warmth inside of busy specialty shops along the chaotic streets.

"Truth is," I begin, "when I was a kid, I used to hide in this place for hours. It was a lot different back then. The stuff my dad offered to people was for a different reason. It felt a little more hopeful. I feel like all we do is make a profit, but we don't really sell something. Does that make sense?"

"What did your dad stock the shelves with?" Holly asks.

"I don't know." I blow out a hard breath. "Things that made people believe in something bigger than themselves. Like he could bottle up an adventure and bring it to life. I've got you stacking gold-dipped pacifiers in the stupid window. What is that supposed to inspire?"

"Rage." She laughs. "It inspires rage."

"I'm sorry." I smile back. "It was such a dumb purchase."

"So why did you do it?" Holly asks. "Why don't you sell what inspires you?"

Because you're not for sale, I'd like to say. But that's cheesy. I won't go there. Plus, she's looking for an honest answer. Her eyes rest fully on me as I turn my chair slightly in her direction.

"I guess I don't really know what inspires me, yet." I swallow. "What would you sell?"

"Oh, me?" She blinks. "I'm the wrong person to ask."

"Why?"

"I'd just give everything away. Seriously. I'm the biggest sucker for a happily ever after."

"Really? I see you as a bit ruthless."

"Yes, of course."

"You have more sales than any other person that works here. You don't get to the top by being the nice girl."

"Maybe I'm just good at fetching wieners." She winks and it warms my chest by about a million degrees.

I yank at my tie. "I think there's a lot more to you than that, Miss Winterbourne."

"Holly. Since we're now on a first name basis."

"Holly." I let it roll around in my head. Imagine her under me and the name sighing from my lips as I fuck her senselessly.

As she rides me, taking every inch of my cock. Holly. Her hair twisting in my fist as she begs for me to come inside her.

Holly. Holly, Holly, Holly...

She breaks me from my fantasy as she turns things back to a less than spectacular subject. My solitude.

"Are you alone for Christmas, North?"

"I'm surrounded by chaos, in case you haven't noticed."

She grins with a roll of her eyes. "Not a smart way to get on Santa's good boy list."

"Holly," I say her name purposefully, " ...allow me to assure you, I have never been on the *good* boy's list."

"Somehow, I believe that."

"Somehow, you've stuck around for five years."

"Six," she corrects.

"Six." I nod and things go from playful to strained in a flash. "Damn. Has it really been that long?"

"Do you miss him?"

"My father? I don't know. He was a hard man to know. He wasn't around much, and when he was, his head was always somewhere else, thinking up new places to go exploring or what woman he'd conquer next."

Holly smiles and goes back to playful, with her playful little fingers tickling the back of my hand as she reaches out and says, "See? You're a little bit like him, after all."

"I don't conquer women."

Her brows don't believe me.

"I explore them."

That's when I'm treated to the best laughter of all.

Knock Knock...

Ugh.

"Yes?"

Meg pushes her little mousey face through the door. The girl is cute, but in a little sister kind of way. I have zero interest in going there. She quickly scans back and forth from me to Holly and then the hot dog that they were trying to fight to the death over earlier. "I'm going home."

"Have a Merry Christmas," I say and apparently it must not be something I have ever said before because I'm gawked at by two women as if I've grown multiple heads in their presence.

Holly blinks back to life, turning to Meg. "Merry Christmas, Meg."

She glances between the two of us. "Same to you all." Her eyes flash to Holly for a moment as if she's unsure about leaving her here with me all alone. Truthfully, we're not alone. There's an entire sales floor that needs our swift asses out there. Yes, even mine. Because like a damn idiot I just allowed my second top performer to go home on the busiest night for shopping in the entire world.

All because of a stinkin' hot dog and a shitty childhood.

Oh, and don't forget the hot girl.

"Well," Holly says, "I guess I better get back out there before everything turns to crap. Um...enjoy your food."

I nod at her and force myself to say the words, "Thank you."

And it's worth every minute of it because she smiles like it was a gift of grandeur. "You're welcome, North."

I turn back to my food and just as I'm about to dive in, what just happened hits me. I whip my chair around and call out to her.

Holly stops abruptly in the doorway with her big, crystal-blue doe eyes directly on mine.

"You brought me the hot dog," I accuse.

"Yes." Her face is a bit bewildered.

"I said whoever got the hot dog first could go home. So why is Meg leaving?"

Holly sighs softly. "She needed to leave more than I do. She has five kids at home. I'm just a single girl who needs to make rent." She smiles weakly at me. "I'm gonna hit the floor, unless there's something else, sir?"

I watch her for a moment. "I'll be sure to let Santa know about your little good deed."

"Thought you were too cool for school when it came to Santa?"

"Yeah, well," I shrug it off, "some people are worth looking less cool for, I suppose."

"You could send me home, too. You could send us all home, you know."

I nod. "Nice try. Get back out there and sell every last one of those golden pacifiers to every lame celebrity kid named Dream, Apple, Jimmy Choo-Choo Train, fucking Saber Tooth Timmy that comes into our store. Miss Holly Winterbourne—queen of ruthless sales."

She smiles with a laugh. "You've got it, North Caspian—king of New York wieners."

CHAPTER 3

Holly

I FEEL like my eyelids are glued together. I'm so tired. It's just after midnight when we finally turn the lock on the door and I can finally breathe a sigh of relief for the day officially coming to an end.

It's ironic, really. Because now it's also officially Christmas and if I were still a kid this is exactly how I'd feel on Christmas morning. I remember trying to pry my weak little eyes open as I dashed out to the tree to see what Santa left for me under there. Amazing what you'll make yourself do in the name of great gifts.

Now I just want to go home and crash in my bed for the next twenty-four hours.

I tidy up the front end of Wondrous, a long yawn escaping my mouth as I wonder silently who really would spend four grand on a puzzle? Miley Tenner. A-list influencer and beauty brand builder. That's who.

Imagine the issues that kid of hers is going to have. I mean look at North, my boss, a guy that was raised to work in the business his dad created and nurtured into success—he's a hot (super hot) mess with no ideas about what inspires him. He had to work for his empire and he's still a raging bull. Imagine a kid who's handed thousand-dollar puzzles as gifts.

Ugh.

On the upside, I'm glad I was able to give Meg the night off to be with her children. I know, I know...I said I wanted to leave purgatory at any cost, but what kind of crap person (and major hypocrite) would I be if I was at home getting smashed drunk while she was here being tortured by North while her kids missed their mom?

I'm ruthless, but to a point.

And that point is not keeping a mom away from her kids. Sorry.

Also, I made a pretty sweet commission tonight thanks to all the kids with really bad names. And a bigger thanks to their insanely rich and famous parents. I call it a win-win. Add North being playful with me in his office to that list and it's a triple crown victory.

Call me crazy, but I actually liked him for the first time in six years.

He was likable.

My boss.

North Caspian.

That's a bit of Christmas magic if I've ever witnessed any.

Typically, closing up shop is just cleaning up and locking the door. North never allows anyone to touch the money or deposits. He does all of that work himself. But, I do need to be patted down (no I'm not kidding) and have my purse checked for any stolen golden pacifiers or treasure maps, before I'm allowed to leave.

So, I head back to his office and knock on his door, one last time tonight. Or maybe I should say, for the first time today since it has passed the midnight hour. His door is left ajar to my surprise. Inside of his immaculate, exquisite, office it's grown dark, the stark white walls illuminated by a single lamp on his desk that casts his shadow on the wall to reflect him three times bigger than he actually is—a bit of a monster type of image.

"Need something?" He asks, his eyes not meeting mine.

"I'm ready to leave, sir. Um, North."

He's silent for a moment and then he calls me over with the tips of his fingers, still not looking at me.

I slowly walk toward him, my heart picking up the pace a bit as I inch closer for some reason. Maybe it's the dim lighting. Maybe it's because I'm so freaking tired, but I feel nervous.

I'm a little unhinged it being just the two of us alone, now.

North reaches across his desk and cups his hand over something, then shoves it slowly in my direction. When he pulls his hand away, there's a medium-sized white box underneath, wrapped beautifully with a bright red bow.

I assume someone forgot to bag it for a client and I'm going to be forced to go hand deliver it last minute. Instantly the tears and anger build inside my chest and threaten to burst out from me in a long string of expletives.

"Merry Christmas," he says low.

I blink away the tears he hasn't seen and try to steady my

voice—both the surprise and anger before I answer him. "Oh. This is for me?"

"Only if you'd like to have it, Holly." His shoulders shrug a bit.

Why's he so wrapped up in what's on his computer? I feel torn between tearing open the box and yelling at him to at least look at me.

Is this a joke? Is he for real?

Against my better judgment, I reach for the box. It's pretty heavy. After I pull away the ribbon, the lid lifts easily and I gasp a little bit as I peek inside.

It's not some cruel joke, thankfully.

A beautiful snow globe from his collection.

They're the only items in the store that are *not* for sale. A long snaking line of them string across North Caspian's office walls, proudly displayed on dark wooden shelves. There's now one spot empty that is home to a shadow.

"Oh, North, this is beautiful, but way too much. I can't accept this."

"Can I tell you something?"

I blink. "Of course you can."

He kicks the same chair out to me that I sat in earlier.

I try my best to be steady as I sink down beside him. He smells like luxury. Like the leather of a new car. Like an adventure. Like this whole damn wondrous place all at once.

He's pushed up the sleeves on his button-down and his tie is gone. North's hair is a wild nest on top of his head, like his fingers have been running a marathon through his locks all night. He gazes at me and it's the first time I've ever really noticed how long and gorgeous his lashes are that frame his smoldering eyes.

"I've never actually celebrated Christmas before," he admits, almost shyly. "I've always just watched it happen all around me."

"What do you mean? How can you not celebrate Christmas? It's the most incredible day of the whole year."

North shrugs a little, his face strained as he scrubs his hand back and forth across his jawline. "I've always stayed here after the store closed at midnight. I used to like the quietness. I liked staring out this window as the sun rose and remained this little grey neon light in the sky. I liked how empty the streets were."

"That sounds pretty depressing. No offense."

He grins a little. "It made me feel good actually. I liked that all of the hard work throughout the year meant something in the end."

I toy with the snow globe in my hands. "And this?"

North shoves away from his desk. "Consider that six years worth of thank-you's I've never said." He stares at me with a sincere expression in his eyes. "Thank you, Holly Winterbourne. And please accept my gift. It's my absolute favorite globe of the Caspian collection."

I'm stunned into silence.

"Don't look at me like that." He laughs. "I assure you I'm still the rotten bastard I've always been."

"Somehow . . ." I swallow hard. "I think I may have misjudged you."

North waves me off and gathers his coat, leaving his papers across the desk and then locks up the cash boxes in a large safe stuck inside a wall on the furthest end of his office.

"Ever been to The Baths?" he asks, shoving his long arms into his heavy wool coat.

"Of course I've taken baths. I do prefer showers, though."

He laughs a little and I squirm as he stares at me with those electric eyes and dazzling grin. "No, silly girl. The Baths is one of the most beautiful wonders of the world, surrounded by the sea, sand, and adventure."

I blush a little, feeling stupid for not knowing that. "Sounds like a great summer getaway. And no, I've never been there."

"It's a December getaway. A getaway from all this snow. That's where I'm spending Christmas. You should *getaway*, too."

I laugh. "Oh, but North...what would my boss think about something like that?"

He moves closer to me. "He thinks you'd look fucking spectacular in a bikini."

I smile. "And then he'd fire me when he's done 'exploring' me in that bikini, right?"

North stops shy of my feet. He glances down at me. "I'm actually firing you tonight."

"What? On freaking Christmas? Are you kidding?" Ugh. I knew better than to trust him. I'm about to hand him back his damn snow globe when he puts his hands on my shoulders.

"I'm closing the store. Next year we'll all be somewhere else, Holly. I hope to find the right place for myself. A place that inspires me to be a better person. A person that's more like you."

"Wow."

He smiles. "It was a very thought provoking weiner."

I groan and shove at his chest a little. Touching him makes my insides squirm. I fold my hand back over the snow globe. "I definitely won't miss your bad jokes."

North grins. "Walk you out?"

"For the last time." I sigh. "Wow. This actually feels a little bit sad."

"Not at all how you'd thought of quitting a million times, hm?"

I laugh and feel a bit embarrassed. Because I *have* thought of quitting a million times. All of which included North taking things like this very snow globe and shoving it right up his perfectly sculpted ass.

"I'm going to plead the fifth, Mr. Caspian."

We smile at each other and North flips off the light as we exit. The shop is also dark as we walk through the aisles for the last time. The air is bone-splitting cold as we step out into the midnight air.

I hug my arms around myself and try to breathe through my scarf to keep the cold air out of my lungs.

North locks the front door to the shop, and then takes a step back. Everything in the window boxes is still lit up and animated. I can only imagine him as a little boy standing here with all of his father's treasures whizzing around and yet North Caspian never got to celebrate a Christmas morning—how sad.

North tilts his head a little as he stares at the store. I can't imagine what he feels. My family life was pretty average, I guess. Both parents worked middle class jobs. Mom was a school teacher at my high school and my father was a basketball coach for the rival high school. But that was back home.

New York is not the place I ever thought I'd live in, growing up. My mother fainted, literally fainted, when I told her I was going to move here to attend college. After she came to, we had a battle over which is worse—tornado sirens or the possibility of being robbed on the subway. Rats vs not paying insane rent costs, and instead living free back home. Thankfully I was a good student and managed a scholarship to pay my way, because no matter how many killer points I made about epic rats throughout history (Master Splinter, Chuck E. Cheese, Rizzo from the Muppets, Speedy Gonzales, Ratatouille) she was not getting on board with my plan.

I visited the first year after I moved. Second year I called home. Third year we swapped texts. And this year...well, it hasn't played out yet.

North finally turns to me. "Are you taking a cab?" he asks.

"Oh, um, I can walk. I'm not too far from here." My teeth chatter as I pull back my scarf to block out the freezing air.

"Nonsense. I can take you. My car is waiting." He nods to the street.

There's a black SUV parked in the middle of the deserted road. So much for the city that never sleeps. Just look at the power Santa has. I laugh to myself. I want to say that to him, but I don't because it's way too cheesy. I'll leave the bad jokes up to him.

"Ok." I nod and he offers to carry the snow globe for me. I'm super thankful because it allows me to shove my frozen hands deep down into my coat pockets. The snow crunches loudly under my boots and he glances down. And then laughs a little.

"You make a lot of noise for such a tiny thing."

"I should make that my Instagram bio."

North nods. "Indeed." He opens the door for me and I eagerly climb into the warmth of the car.

My body shivers uncontrollably for a few minutes as I try to warm my hands and acclimate to the heat.

North appears unaffected by the chill of the air.

"You need a better winter coat," he says, unbuttoning his own as he makes himself more comfortable in the space next to mine. Other than sitting in his office, I don't think I've ever been this close to him before.

I keep my hands near my body because I fear touching him for some alien reason—as if I'll be sucked into a North Caspian sex vortex. I laugh to myself and shake the feeling away. It's only a ride.

"Are you leaving tonight?" I ask him, trying to keep my voice even.

North taps away on his phone, squinting his eyes a little as he tries to listen to me and work at the same time. "Yes. I just booked it now, actually." He narrows his eyes on me. "We do not remember days, we remember moments."

Oh my God.

He's looking at my Instagram bio.

My freaking Instagram *pictures*.

"That's private," I say, trying to grab his phone from his hands.

North grins, keeping a hold on his phone with ease. "Looks pretty public to me." His mouth forms a little 'o' as he studies the phone. "Well damn. You *do* look good in a bikini."

"North," I whine, covering my face. "This isn't happening."

"What?" He laughs. "You posted these things for any strange creeper on the internet to view but *I'm* not allowed?"

"I don't know those people. It's completely different."

"Exactly." He laughs again and then gazes at me. "You know what men probably do looking at these pictures of you?"

"Please don't go there, North."

He shrugs. "I'm just saying you're too beautiful to be giving it all away for free."

"Ah, the business side of North Caspian has arrived," I tease.

"No," he says, turning his full attention on me. North's voice softens a bit, lowering in register in a way that makes me squirm in my seat. "I'm just letting you know someone should cherish a girl like you. Someone you can create 'moments' with. The moments you want to have, like your bio says."

"How do you know I don't?"

He grins. "Because you have more pictures of your cat on social media than anything else."

"Leo is a really cool cat."

"Please tell me you named him after a Ninja Turtle."

"Definitely not after De-*crap*-io."

He cracks a grin. "I must confess, Miss Winterbourne, that I may have a crush on you."

I laugh and he smiles warmly.

With a heavy sigh North tucks his phone into his coat pocket. "There's a lovely little cafe up this way that stays open all night long. Unless you have someplace to be, I'd love your company, Holly."

"Only if you tell me what your bio says."

North shakes his head. "I don't give anything away for free."

"No social media whatsoever?"

"Just for the store. Nothing personal."

"Ok well, what would it say, if you had one?"

He thinks for a moment, tapping his finger over his clean shaven jaw. "Anything you can imagine can be real." North offers me his hand as the car comes to a slow and steady stop.

The ice crunches under the weight of the heavy SUV and I dread going back out into the cold, but I also don't want to be away from this man. It's such an odd feeling.

I've spent the better half of the last six years hating his very existence and now he's the person I want to be next to the most on Christmas. Maybe it's because his hand is strong and warm, matching his eyes and sincerity in his smile. It's a smile I've never seen during all the years I've worked for him.

He's somehow gone from being the Grim Reaper in Gucci to a saint in less than eight hours. I almost feel bad for judging him so harshly all this time. Who knew that a kid that grew up rich and privileged such as North Caspian would be the one missing out on Christmas morning. How epically tragic…right?

"Ready?" he asks.

I place my hand in his and nod with my own smile. It feels *so* good to touch him, to smile, and to laugh with him. I like how freaking North Caspian makes me feel—and I have no idea how to process this.

But I allow him to pop the door open and the cold air to assault us as we jump from the stunning luxury vehicle and race into a small but super cozy cafe.

North acts like a true gentleman once we're inside of the place. He offers to take my coat and hangs it limply over his arm as we find our own seats.

There isn't another soul in this place except for us and the staff. I actually feel incredibly shitty for making people work on a holiday such as this. North must notice because after he pulls out a seat for me and scoots it in, he takes up residency next to my ear and explains it all.

"I was told that they remain open so Santa won't go hungry."

I laugh a little. "Sounds legit."

He takes a seat next to me. "Actually, they stay open to make sure anyone on patrol can get a hot cup of coffee and a good home-cooked meal. Big time NYPD blood runs through this place."

"That's pretty sweet," I say. "Makes me feel a little less bad about being here."

"We'll leave a good tip, too." North smiles. "Order whatever you like. My treat." He nosedives into his menu and I kind of, oddly, enjoy this about him.

I've been on dates (Hell, is that what this is?) where the guy tries too hard to carry on a conversation and it becomes painfully apparent from the start that we're not a match.

Shit, listen to me.

I'm actually sizing him up.

I'm sizing up my boss like he's a head of cabbage in the grocery store, flopping him from side to side as I weigh him in my hands and decide if this guy is ripe for the picking. Oh God, what is happening to me?

I look down at my menu. Buttermilk biscuits with fried chicken and gravy are a main feature. French fries come as a side item. I keep rolling my eyes around the menu to find something less dead-animal-like. There's salad. That doesn't seem very Christmas-esque. Oh, well, one has cranberries. I guess that makes it a little more seasonal...ugh, sometimes it sucks being a vegan.

"Find anything?" North asks, closing his menu, and looking pretty satisfied by his choice.

"I think I'll just have some tea."

"No, you have to eat more than that," he argues. "Tea is not Christmas morning breakfast."

I laugh at him, but he looks completely serious. "Oh, um, it's just that there isn't a lot to choose from."

"I'm sure they can whip something up. What are you hungry for, Holly?"

And I have to stare at him because this is something that a person of his status would be able to say so easily—because he's used to getting his way and having anything he wants at anytime he wants it. Remember the hot dog just hours ago? Must be nice.

I shrug. "Pancakes would be nice...but they can be a little tricky to get them fluffy and not the consistency of a wet diaper."

"This is not exactly how I pictured the conversation flowing on our first date," he says, and then clears his throat. "I mean..."

"So you've had us in this scenario before, Mr. Caspian?"

He grins. "Oh, Miss Winterbourne...I've had quite a few scenarios dreamt up in my imagination."

I squeeze my thighs together to ward off the want he inspires deep inside me with his words. "If you can imagine it, you can have it. Isn't that what you say?"

He smiles a bit impishly. "I wasn't really thinking about it in such realistic terms. But it does remain true."

I brave staring at him, gazing into those dark haunting eyes of his.

The table is small and we're just an inch away from touching if we choose. I should feel weak, but there's something about sitting next to a man this powerful and confident that bleeds over and into me.

"What would North Caspian normally do to get a girl he wants?"

For a moment North is silent as a waitress drops off two cups of coffee and then flitters away.

"Every woman has been different," he says. "You would be," he pauses before continuing again, "much different. For a lot of reasons."

"Like?"

"Like," he takes a swallow of coffee and then wipes the brim of his mug with a scratchy white napkin, "you already know more about me than any other woman I've ever had, as a start."

Had. A woman he has had. Why does it sound so hot when he says it like that? As if the women in his life have been some kind of moment in time—like a nice designer handbag. Expensive, in style and wanted by millions, but only owned by a select few and then retired to a vault for the rest of its existence to remain in a collection of once valuable things.

More importantly, why do I want to so badly feel like a used, vintage Birkin bag right now? I have to cross my legs as I think of the possibilities of being 'had' by North Caspian.

"Is that good or bad?" I ask, grabbing for my coffee cup. Except I'm not as graceful as the hot Grim Reaper in Gucci, and it spills all the way down the front of my favorite white sweater.

"Can't dress me up and take me anywhere," I mumble to myself.

North only laughs. And then a napkin comes my way. From his hand. To my boobs. And he rubs my boobs with that hand and napkin as he tries to help clean my mess.

Holy Santa balls, Batman.

"Um...I think I can get it."

He grins a little, and then throws his hands up in the air. "I was only trying to help. This is not part of my plan, I promise."

I peek at him through my lashes as I continue to pat my sweater dry. "You have a plan, do you?"

North wipes his hands. "Just a joke." But his expression when he stares at me is not just a joke. It looks quite severe, actually.

I want to busy myself with coffee, but I'm nervous about dropping the rest on my pants and then that would lead to some serious trouble if he had hands on my...there.

And now I'm picturing his face between my quivering thighs, eyes connecting, while his mouth expertly eats me out until I come over and over.

I should have gone home. I should have left this at thank you for the gorgeous snow globe gift, six years of employment and a hefty amount of weiner jokes today. That would have made things complicated, but a lot less complicated than this.

North tilts his head a bit, measuring his words carefully before he goes for it, which only makes me even more nervous. "Tell me something, Holly. Have you ever, in the six years we've known each other, had a fantasy about me?"

"North," I warn.

He grins deliciously as he sets his mug down after taking a sip. "You can tell me. Your secret is safe."

I laugh, but it's a nervous laughter as I try to keep my cheeks from blushing. "I think letting you know what my fantasies are about is the most dangerous thing in the world, North."

He plays along. "Is that right?"

"Mhm. More dangerous than people texting while driving."

North leans in, full smile on his handsome face. "This should be so good. Curiosity piqued, Miss Winterbourne. Please do tell."

I swear it feels like the whole diner has shrunk in size as we sit here, sizing each other up, trying to get secrets from each other. "I'm not telling you."

"Oh, I think you will. Because I happen to know how to make the fluffiest vegan pancakes in the world."

Giggling like an idiot, I say, "I'm sure you do, but still not giving up the goods, Mr. Caspian."

"Ok, full disclosure? I really don't know how to cook fucking anything, but I do happen to have the best chef money can afford. I'm quite certain he can whip up a towering stack of vegan pancakes on demand. And whatever else your tender little heart of mercy desires."

I pretend to think, tapping my chin with my pink-tipped nail. "I would probably let you in on the details of these fantasies of mine if vegan crepes with vegan cream cheese and locally sourced strawberries were on the table."

North smiles with his eyes. "You could have asked for so much more, Winterbourne. You're supposed to be ruthless, remember?"

"Maybe I'm saving it as part of the fantasy itself."

Now he blushes, and oh my god it's adorable. "I think we should move this party twenty miles north of this cafe."

"I doubt your chef is going to be up for making crepes in the middle of the night, on Christmas, no less."

North frees his wallet from the pocket of his coat and tosses cash down on the table. Way more than the cost of our two barely-sipped coffees.

I try not to act like a little geek about it, but I've never seen a person be so quick to spend money so freely before. Well, I've never actually been talking on a friendly level to one, either.

Clients of Wondrous don't count.

"My chef is going where I'm going," he explains. "And I'd love for you to come too."

I swallow. Hard. "Are you making a joke?"

"No, certainly not, Holly." North offers his hand. "All you have to do is say yes."

I exhale hard as I try not to laugh, but his offer is so incredibly unlike anything that has ever happened in my life, I can't help myself. I feel like I'm dreaming. Like I'm falling down the rabbit hole and I don't know if anyone will be there to catch me when I fall.

Do I say yes? Do I take the plunge? Instagram is ridiculous but I did mean my words—I want moments. Really amazing moments. This feels like a big one.

Ugh.

Bad choice of words.

I glance at North, his dazzling raven-like eyes that will forever haunt me, and slip my hand atop his strong warm palm, interlacing our fingers.

"Yes."

CHAPTER 4

Holly

THE BATHS IS NOT like anything I've ever seen. It's something straight out of a travel magazine or cruise brochure. I'm not much of a traveler thanks to insufficient funds for things such as this, but in my mind I figured a beach is a beach is a beach and maybe there'd also be a nice hotel at the end of the day with a comfy bed and good room service.

Well, that was all before I went on a trip with North freaking Caspian and all his magical snow globe money. This place is so much more than 'just' a beach. Otherworldly.

Simply spectacular.

An adventure of a lifetime.

We spend most of our day in the warm sun (Gotta love that it is December. Freaking Christmas day.) climbing through a maze of caves and rocks along the beach like hidden treasures of the land. The rocks stand tall as giants and sometimes the spaces between them are so slim you have to turn sideways to slither through to the other side.

The water is so warm, clear and pristine, unlike anything back home in New York, not even Montauk can hold a glass to this Heaven on Earth, and that is the nicest beach town I've ever visited on vacation.

We have our own little set up complete with a gazebo that is draped in long, flowy-white linens and the most comfortable lounge chairs. A concierge is on hand for all the things we could possibly ever need or want. Drinks, snacks, sun tan lotion, extra towels.

North even had a special menu prepared for breakfast with, yes, you guessed it, the fluffiest vegan banana pancakes and strawberry topped crepes I have ever stuffed in my mouth.

He watches in delight as I hum and thank him a million times for such luxuries and thoughtfulness.

I try my best not to spy on him as he puts his mouth on the edge of his mug and tastes his coffee. There's something about the way he swallows. I can't quite do it justice by talking about it—it's something you have to see, but it floods my veins with warmth that should not exist from simply watching a person do such mundane, human things.

And if you think I'm heated by his morning coffee routine, then I shouldn't have to explain how walking around with him in low slung beach shorts showing off his incredible razor sharp abs all day makes me feel. What is it about that V between men's hip bones that sends a female brain into a complete puddle of goo?

Combo those bad boys with his helpfulness over the rocks and always putting his hand on my own hip to steady me as I climb and I'm a hot mess. I can't lie. I've never seen this side of

North. He's so carefree and swoony. He smiles. He actually smiles.

North Caspian knows how to have fun.

And he's uber generous.

"So," he says, swinging my hand as we walk down the beach nearing sunset. "What next?"

My stomach answers for me, growling loudly right on cue. "I think the beast wants to be fed."

North grins. "Relatable."

I feign disgust. "I knew this was all an elaborate scheme to 'explore' me in a bikini, North."

"Can't help that I was right," he says.

"About?"

His eyes slice in my direction as we walk side-by-side. "You look fucking amazing in a bikini."

"You knew that back in New York. You saw my Insta."

"In person is always such a different experience. A better one. Don't you think?"

I roll my eyes a little.

He holds tighter to my hand and I allow him to pull me a little closer to his side. His body is warm and fragranced by the salty air and sunscreen and whatever he was born with.

I love the combo.

I want to drink it in and never forget what it's like.

"I've had a very wonderful Christmas with you so far. Thank you again for such an amazing gift. I...I wish I had something great to give you, too. I feel really crappy that I don't."

"You gave me the gift of you," he says, seriously. "I've never had the pleasure of enjoying Christmas with someone before. That is pretty damn priceless. It has been equally as wonderful for me to be here with you, Miss Holly Winterbourne." North looks away to the ocean for a moment.

The sun's changing, turning into a fierce orange glow of fire that appears to double and then triple in size as it quickly sinks down, down, down. The sky could be a famous painting. It's so electric with swipes of sherbert rainbow colors.

"It's so beautiful here," I say. "I didn't know anything could be this beautiful."

North turns so he's stepping ahead of me, our fingers still laced together. "Also, relatable."

My heart swells a bit in my chest as he stares straight through me. I try to calm what's brewing inside me, but as he stops and gathers both of my hands into his I can't even begin to stop the jackhammering happening inside my rib cage.

"We could go on a lot of adventures together, Holly. Create a lot of real moments."

I swallow. "This feels like a moment."

North hums as he pulls me toward him. His fingers move to my hips and the feeling of his warm skin on mine creates goosebumps as he takes hold of me, cradling my hips with his hands. It sends off a firestorm of nerves and desire inside me.

"Give me your mouth," he demands. "I want to taste your kiss."

I reach up and twist my fingers into his hair as I pull his head down to me and allow him to take what he wants, tasting every last part of me as he savagely possesses my mouth with his hot tongue and expert kiss.

I quake in his arms, my legs trembling as he takes me tightly into his strong embrace allowing no space between our bodies.

Only North Caspian could take attention away from a

sunset so heavenly and divine. I forget all about the magic around us as he lifts me onto his hips and walks with our mouths still dancing, until we reach our very own private gazebo.

North carefully sits us down, me still in his lap, onto one of the lounge chairs. Without thinking, I grind into him out of sheer need. Sheer want.

His hard cock rubs against my aching clit as I moan into his mouth. He twists my hair in his fingers and tugs blissfully at the nape of my neck, exposing my pulse point to him. His teeth graze my skin before he sucks and kisses under my chin, and then all the way down to my collar bone.

Holy shit.

Is this really happening?

I'm soaking wet for my boss.

I'm practically dry humping North Caspian on the beach. And he's squeezing my barely covered tits and groaning as I swivel my hips into him, silently telling him to fuck me, ruthlessly.

Right here.

Right now.

And this is the exact moment that my stomach decides to voice its need for food again with a long, epic growl.

"Relatable." North chuckles against my mouth.

I'm still a panting frantic mess as I try to find my senses, pulling in long gulps of salty sea air.

"I can't believe we just did that." The words blurt from my mouth before I can slap my hand over my lips.

North clasps his hands around my wrists. "I can't believe we waited this long. What a waste of time."

"North." I giggle.

He appraises my face. "My treasure. A real treasure."

"North," I say with a sigh, and fall back to his lips for a haste kiss.

I can't quite tell you what we had for dinner because it's all quite a blur, to be honest. I'm sure it tasted great and was divine, but I was on another planet as it all happened, playing back the memory of him all over me.

Every detail of the way his skin felt against mine on the beach. The way he gazed at me with such heady eyes, needing me.

I sat through dinner completely wet, throbbing with desire for my boss. We drank champagne and at one point I must have ended up on his lap because now we're sitting at the dining table just like we did on the beach, lost in a scrumptious deep kiss.

I lick the bubbly champagne from his lips and he picks up the bottle in one hand and carries me off with the other, dotting kisses on my wet mouth as we head for the couch in one of the many living room areas. And what a room and couch it is. Our vacation rental is actually not a rental or plush hotel. No. It's a gorgeous home that North owns on the beachside, overlooking the incredible view.

The two-story villa appears almost ancient, like a maiden castle, but fitted with all of the modern magic you'd expect to find inside of a home of North Caspian's status.

After a meal fit for royalty, he treats me on a tour of his beautiful home, telling me all about his art collection, which is quite impressive, even by his standards. At the bottom of the stairwell is a large open space that leads to a great room, which is pretty bare in comparison to the rest of his house. It only takes me a minute to figure out why. The walls are made of glass and through the tall windows the moonlight filters in like an epic spotlight flooding the space with its magical glow.

In the milky casting of the moon North looks like a Greek god.

I can barely hold myself together from how gorgeous he is staring at me with those dark eyes of his, like I'm something great to him.

He holds out his hands and pulls me close to him.

I can't breathe.

He must sense it because he grins a little, and then tells me to relax in his deep husky voice, sending me into an even dizzier state of lust.

I've never in my life wanted a man like I want him and I know in my heart this is not something that will be wrapped up by the end of our trip here.

There's something greater between us. Something more magical.

I feel it in his touch when he puts his arms around me. Or when his hands land on my slender hips and he sways us gently to a rhythm he hums. I'm melting in his embrace and want nothing more than to pull his lips to mine.

Thankfully, we're on the same track and he dips his face closer to mine, teasing my mouth with his. At first he gives me gentle little pecks and then our kiss deepens into a whirlwind of clothes falling away, whispering secrets and laboring breaths.

"North," I moan into his open mouth.

"Just to be fair, Holly . . ." He laughs. "Oh fuck."

"What?"

He doesn't finish his sentence, instead he pulls me down with him to the plush carpet that honestly is more luxurious than any bed I've ever slept in. It feels as soft as cashmere under my skin, and the moonlight blankets over us as he frees himself of his button up shirt.

He skates his fingers up my thighs and draws my panties down my long legs, tossing them to the side before he hovers over me, coming to rest between my thighs.

I watch him in the moonlight and shiver at how beautiful he is. I know men don't like being called beautiful but that's how he looks. He's just like art from his collection and his touch is something new to me. Something I've never felt with a man before.

He's gentle and rough at the same time. I can't even explain it. It feels possessive and protective all at once. He loves on me with the most tender kisses on my neck, throat, collarbones, and even my hips. But, he also whispers dirty nothings in my ear and smacks my ass until I'm begging him to fuck me.

North doesn't hold back.

"God damn it," he says, laughing again. This time he pulls back.

"What's wrong?" I stare up at him. "Is someone watching us?" I glance out the window, but it's just me, North, and the moon.

"I thought I could do it, but I can't. Get up, come on."

"What?" I blink rapidly, confused by his words. Is he rejecting me? What the hell?

North reaches down and lifts me up into his muscular arms.

"Remind me to buy some faux fur rugs," he says, still chuckling. "For the vegan girl."

I scrunch up my nose until I realize we were just about to have sex on a rug made from real bear fur.

"North," I scold, gently. "Please say it's not true."

He grins a little. "It was a gift, if that makes it any better? I'll get rid of it, I promise."

"I do appreciate your thoughtfulness. Holy crap. This might be the most awkward *pre*-coital convo of my life?"

He chuckles. "How about fixing that?" He carries me off to his amazing bedroom, complete with a bed fit for a king. It's made of something that looks like pure gold. The four posts stand tall like daggers on each corner of his bed and the feeling of the cool sheets under my skin is just something otherworldly as he gently places me on the bed.

"All animal friendly." He grins. "Not a single creature was harmed making this bed. I promise you."

"Mmm," I purr at him. "Come here and hurt *me*."

North crawls to me. "I'm sure there is an amazingly bad joke I could tell you about beating up a pus— "

I pull his lips to mine and don't let his mouth ruin our moment with any more lame jokes, even though that's how we got here.

Damn hot dog jokes.

But I'm not thinking about that now. Right now, I'm lost in his expert kiss. How he pushes me down into his pile of pillows that I'm sure are not filled with goose feathers. I run my hands all over his strong back, along his spine until I grab a fistful of his thick silky-soft hair and make him groan my name.

"Baby," North growls. "I want you so damn bad, Holly."

"I'm yours."

He kisses me. "Say that shit again."

"North Caspian, I'm all *yours*."

"Well, merry fucking Christmas to me."

"Yes, joy to the world and all that good stuff, North. Now, please, just stuff my stocking."

He falls into my shoulder, laughing. "Please don't make jokes right now. I'm begging you."

"Ride me like a reindeer. Sleigh me with your candy cane. Put your jingle bells in my mouth. Eat my christmas cookie."

He pops up from my shoulder, his eyes bright with amusement, but also that bit of wickedness I know all too well. "Eat your cookie, huh?"

"Whatever gets you to make a move on this ho ho ho."

"You naughty little elf, Holly. Watch out or Santa is going to put his sack—" He laughs. "I can't even make that joke without hating myself. Please stop now."

"I'd like to get back to the cookie eating part."

He raises his brows with a sexy grin on his perfect lips. "Your wish, Miss Winterbourne, is my command."

North kisses a map down my legs, dotting hot stamps with his lips as he makes his way between my legs. He shoves my knees together and then my legs back, giving himself access to my pussy the way I like it best.

How does he know that?

I grip his forearms as he palms my bare breasts and kneads them so perfectly as his mouth tastes how wet I am for him.

His tongue works me like a pro, rolling around my clit and lapping at my center until I forget all about my bad jokes and only crave to have him inside me. He plunges a thick finger into me as he sucks on my aching clit, sending me over the edge.

I grasp his hair in my fists and tug as I scream out his name. It only makes him work harder and keep me locked in place, putting his strong fingers around my thighs and pinning me down so I can't escape the powerful orgasm that takes over my whole body. A white-hot fire floods through me like a summertime heatwave. My ears ring from how hard I come and I have to gulp at the air just to catch my breath. I've never experienced anything like it in my life. And that was only from his mouth and fingers.

I can't even imagine that huge cock between his legs and how he must know how to work it.

Will it even fit inside of me?

He's so thick and long.

I bite back making a joke to him about fucking me with his holiday Yule Log, even though it would be classic Holly. But he's sporting such a beautiful, massive hard-on I won't risk deflating it with a hideous lame joke.

Instead, I climb on top of him, pushing his shoulders until he is flat on his back and keep my eyes locked with his telling him silently that I'm about to rock his world.

And I think he knows it from how he grins, but still looks oddly vulnerable, for him anyway. It's a new thing I've learned to notice about North. He hides it well, but if you pay enough attention you can catch it.

I start at his neck and bite the tender skin behind his ear.

He growls and I grow wet for him all over again.

I love his sounds, his touch. How he grips my hips and kneads my skin with his fingertips. I nibble down his throat and chest. I lick all the way down his sexy abs until I'm at the tip of his hard dick, and I suck the precum away which makes him growl my name fiercely.

It spurs me on, making me grow brave enough to deep throat his cock, all the way to his balls. I suck him hard, giving him my best until he pulls me up to his lips, kissing me hard and stroking his hands through my hair with a loving touch. It's like he's thanking me with his kiss and touch.

"Mm," I moan into his mouth. "I love how you kiss me, North."

"How I kiss your mouth or your sweet pussy?"

"Both. I've never come like this. You make me crazy. It's like I can't get enough of you."

"Yeah?" He kisses me hard.

"Mm. Yes," I breathe into his mouth.

"Fucking good. You're mine now. Aren't you?" he asks, darting his tongue back into my mouth.

"Yes, North. I'm yours."

His free hand that isn't wrapped around the back of my neck plays between my legs, through my soaked lips until he's finger fucking me again, rolling my aching clit around with his thumb.

My thighs quiver as I feel like I could come again. I lean back and he devours my neck, then kisses down to my hard nipples and sucks adoringly on each side of me until I can't help myself, my fingers clawing at his neck and riding his middle finger until I come again. I wrap my hand around his cock and pump him, feeling him swell in my palm.

He flips us over and dives for my pussy, lapping at my aching core until I can't take it any longer and beg for him to fuck me.

"I thought about this so many times," he whispers over my wet lips. "Your body. Your lips. Fucking you. Making you come."

"You bad boy, North," I moan out, clawing at his back with my nails. "Thinking about fucking your employee."

"Holly, you feel so fucking good around me. That tight little pussy of yours. This sexy fucking body. Your kiss. Your lips. I'm so motherfucking gone for you." He puts my hands above my head and gazes down into my eyes. His hips slow and I have to remember to breathe. "I want to keep you with me. You're the one treasure I don't want to share with anyone."

"North," I sigh. "I want to stay with you, too."

He kisses my mouth. "Good." His hips pick up the pace, fucking me steadily like the monster in bed that he is.

I'm pressed down into the mattress with the weight of his body pinning me. I love how it feels to be imprisoned by him. To be owned. To be claimed in this way. He touches all the right parts of me as he fucks me harder, with purpose. I feel every truth inside of him as he moves, linking us up. The rise builds inside me, my body crying out for that one glorious movement that will send me over the edge. I pray for it and can't believe how much I need to have him, how good he feels. I am fucking my boss. The man I've hated for so long and now could not imagine living without.

His touch.

The way he looks at me.

He's such a different man than the one I thought I knew. He's a generous lover and pours into me with such care and ferocity.

I grip him tightly and allow him to take me over with everything he has, and fuck, he has a lot to offer.

"Holly," he growls, "come for me, baby. Come with me."

"Fuck." I clench around him as he drives into me, his slick skin gliding over my clit as he fucks me harder than I've ever been fucked in my life. I don't think anyone has ever hit my G-spot before, but North finds it just fine, sending me over the moon as my orgasm takes over me, sending a string of curse words flying from my lips.

He drinks them down as he kisses me, pausing for a moment as he comes hard.

We lie on the bed waiting to come back from the heavens, enjoying the feel of each other. He rolls me to my side and draws little pictures on my back with his fingertips, asking me to guess what they are. At one point he goes still and I think he has fallen asleep, but when I peek back at him, he's just glowing as he stares at me.

"I have never had a better Christmas," he whispers. "You're the best gift, Holly Winterbourne."

"I want to come back here every year for Christmas." I roll closer to him, tucking under our sheets and stealing the warmth of his body.

North kisses my forehead. "There's so many places to go, though. I want to show you the world. I want to go on amazing adventures with you."

"That sounds like a dream."

"Is that a yes?" He grins.

I gaze up at him. "Yes. I'd go anywhere with you."

"You hated me yesterday." He laughs. "It's amazing how fast life changes, isn't it?"

"I didn't know you yesterday," I argue. "But today I'm grateful that I do. And I want to just keep learning more. I want to know the real North Caspian."

His eyes squint a little. "Well, the real North Caspian has never dated a girl with strict convictions of animals being treated a certain way, so that's going to take some time to iron out. Although I'm totally down. I have no issues with it, just never really gave it the kind of thought I should have."

"Just promise me you've never been on one of those trips to kill elephants or lions as a trophy hunter."

"What?" He laughs. "Seriously?"

"Say the words, Caspian."

North smiles, curling my hair behind my ear. "I swear to God, or whatever you believe in, Holly, that I'd never even consider such a thing."

"Good."

"Still love me then?" He winces as soon as he says it. "Sorry, didn't mean it like that."

"It's ok." I tremble. "And yes, I still love you."

His dark eyes soften. "Holly . . ." he kisses me and his lips tell me everything, but he still confirms it. "I love you, too."

"Oh, North," I gently pull away. "But you have to promise me one thing."

"Anything," he whispers back.

"Promise me that you will never buy any real fur again in your life."

He breaks out into laughter. "I, North Caspian, swear to only buy faux fur from here on out. I am now a faux fur kind of man."

"Forever and ever," I add.

He gazes at me, his eyes shining. "Forever and ever."

EPILOGUE

North
   Four years later

I'VE SEEN SO many things in my life. I've been to almost every corner of the earth. I've met some of the most incredible people and been to the most exclusive spots known to man. I've lived a life of privilege and wonderment. I've been like a kid in a candy store most of my existence. But, I've never felt that I truly had a place of my own. I never knew what purpose felt like. I only knew how to serve the needs, dreams, and desires of other people. It wasn't until meeting Holly Winterbourne that all of that changed for me.

At first, becoming a lover, a partner to someone was the biggest part of that change. I had to learn not to be so selfish with my time and needs. I had to learn how to be sensitive to a woman who needed a man who could come down from the clouds and try to wrap my head around the things that meant everything to her. I didn't have to change me per se, I just had to evolve, to grow, to mature. That is the part I think a lot of men like me don't always understand. It's not about becoming *someone else* when you love a woman, it's about becoming a better version of yourself. She fell in love with me at my worst. She married me at my best. And now...now we have come full circle.

I stand at the front door and I'm not a man who gets nervous about much, if anything at all, but right now I'm practically trembling. It's been years since I have stood in this spot on Christmas. We have been hopping around the globe ever since we ran away together four years ago. We fell in love in the Virgin Islands. I married her in the Greek Isles. We created life in Rome. And I have kissed her under endless stars.

A square pane of glass is all that separates us from the beginning of our life together. The day I first saw her, I had to take an extra measured breath just to be sure she was real as I stared at the most beautiful woman I'd ever laid eyes on. In a shop full of trinkets and treasures, she somehow made herself stand out. She was not only so fucking good looking but she had a soul to match. She was kind to the worst clients we ever hosted. She kept her cool. She dealt with me and all my bullshit. And yet, four years later, this is where she wants to come back to for Christmas.

She has a box in her hands and she turns the key on the door. The sound of it unlocking feels like starting up a time machine. My chest feels more frozen than the fucking wind blowing across my face. I don't miss the snow and I damn sure don't miss this place.

But as soon as the door swings open, my world shifts again. Because this time I'm not seeing things through my eyes. I'm not hearing the wants and needs of bratty little fucking kids that beg for the most outrageous shit a kid could ever ask for. Instead, I'm mesmerized by a shop filled with the kinds of things my own eyes remember being dazzled by at Christmas, every time I'd swing that door wide and run into my father's store.

He yelled at me, of course he fucking did, but I still loved coming here. I loved finding all the new things. I loved trying to figure it all out. And that's what I see now as I watch our son, River, rush through the doorway and gasp at the inside of what was once my dreamland and nightmare all at once.

I haven't been back to the shop since I last locked the door. Holly runs everything now. I've sold off most of the things my father found. There's only a small collection of items I kept, like some of the snow globes. I always loved them. It was the one thing my father did right. He always remembered to give me something. Something that was just for me. And through the years I've learned to start forgiving him. To forgive myself. And to let go of what held a firm grip on my heart so I could reclaim it and give it to someone else. So that I could grow a heart big enough for her. And then for River.

Unlike my father, I couldn't give a shit if River explores the shop and ruins something he touches. These things are meant to be explored, that's the entire purpose of discovering something great. Otherwise, what's the point?

I make my way back to the place I used to love to hide the most.

As a kid, I liked sitting under the desk, at my father's feet as he made calls and unwrapped things, talking to himself about what it all meant.

As a man, I liked sitting in his chair, feeling powerful and pretending like that's all that fucking mattered in the whole fucking world. I liked lying to myself. Today the office looks much different, although there are a few things Holly has kept intact from my days of reigning here as king.

She kept the ledge that housed the snow globes. Except now the snow globes have been replaced with picture frames of our family. The snow globes I didn't keep we donated to a museum for children, with most of the other items from my father's collection. I wanted everyone to be able to enjoy the things that were discovered, not just the privileged few, and not just kids who were lucky enough to come from those kind of parents. Everyone should be able to see the magic. Everyone should be able to witness the wonders of this world, in all their epic, flawless forms.

I run my hands over the desk. She kept it the same too. "Now this brings back memories." I kind of laugh as I smile at her.

She grins as she moves closer. "I have no idea what you mean." Holly palms the wood and bends so her perfect round ass is pushed out.

I smack my hand lightly to her ass and grin back at her. "You're so fucking lucky we're not alone."

"You realize he's never going to leave that front room, right?" She grabs my tie and leans up on her toes, kissing me. "We're basically alone. As alone as two parents are lucky enough to get."

I wrap my arms around her waist. "You're all keyed up remembering how much of a prick I was to you here. I don't know if that's a good thing, love."

She laughs at me. "I'm all keyed up thinking about how much I wanted you to bend me over your desk and f-u-c-k me."

"You spelled it out," I chuckle at her. "You're such a mom, Holly."

"And you're a DILF and I want to FFFFFFF." I crack up at her making the "f" sound only.

"I love you, Holly Caspian," I say to her. "And I will F the S out of you as soon as we get home. I promise."

"Forever and ever?" She asks, wrapping her arms around my neck.

I try not to grin, but I can't fucking help it. It's too horrible of a joke. But I have to say it anyhow. "Forever and ever, with my New York footlong weiner."

She falls into me laughing.

I hate the fucking joke so much. It was corny and everything I never wanted to be, but that day, somehow in my office, she turned the hard shell of a man who would have gone more than two days without even thinking about vital necessities such as food or a soul into something that suddenly meant the world to me. So, little things like enjoying a moment in time, a damn hot dog from a street vendor, a snow globe I had not looked at in years out of fear of feeling something, and looking at someone—really looking into their eyes and seeing them, became the biggest moments of my life. Because the day those things changed, so did I. And I'm better for it.

Because of her.

So, do silly things. Don't be afraid to let a pretty girl in. Fall in love with her and then for the rest of your short time here on earth, spend it making memories, and even, really bad jokes. Because no one gets out alive, and everyone is given the same twenty-four hours in a day. It's not about what you collect in that time. It's not about who you dream of being. It's about who you will spend that time with. The time is a gift, and the people you choose to spend it with are the real treasures.

AND THEY ALL LIVED HAPPILY EVER AFTER.

THE END

Thank you for reading.

The fun isn't over yet, keep scrolling for a sneak peek of my romantic comedy PLAYBOY available NOW and FREE with KU!

>>>

PLAYBOY SNEAK PEEK

NOW A TOP 100 AMAZON BESTSELLER

From **USA Today** bestselling author Logan Chance comes a laugh-out-loud comedy centered around a

Doing this photoshoot with my best friend's little sister is about to get...hard.

They call me a playboy.

Sure, I like to have fun with the opposite sex, but hey, in my line of work, who wouldn't?

My name's Jonah and I work for Bunny Hunnies, a swimsuit magazine. Calling the shots, and taking pictures of gorgeous women is every man's fantasy, including mine.

That is, until Chelsea Sincock walks onto the set of one of my shoots.

I've known Chelsea since before she was this hot as hell vixen wearing nothing but a bikini.

What is she doing here?

Does her brother, Declan, know?

Did I mention he's my best friend?

This is going to be hard, I mean difficult, to work with her. And the more I gaze at her from behind the lens, the more I realize I'm in way over my head.

Click Here to start reading TODAY!

FAKE IT BABY ONE MORE TIME

Love Fake Romance? Do you light up whenever a new book releases about a fake engagement, a fake relationship, or a fake wedding romance story?
This fun & flirty Fake Romance Collection is available today and FREE with your kindle unlimited subscription. Three stories for the price of one, get ready to meet Vin, Graham, and Pollux...

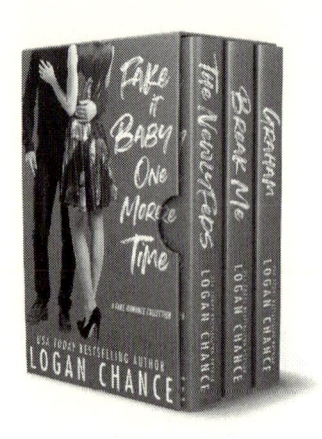

Click Here to start reading TODAY!

COLD HEARTED BALLER SNEAK PEEK

Read on for the first chapter of Cold Hearted Baller, Book One in the Cold Hearted Series.

I have three superstitions I live by:
1. No dating all season.
2. Don't jinx a no-hitter while one's in progress.
3. Be cold-hearted. If you find something you think about more than baseball, destroy it.

Calliope Thomas is one of those things. Ever since she left a bad review on the Max Energy Drink I endorse, I haven't been able to stop thinking about her. Obviously, when she said she hoped I had a losing season, I had to meet her and get her to take the words back.

Now, she's making me do insane things. Like, obsess over the color of her panties or if I can make her blush. Read superstition one—I don't do this sort of thing.

I play ball, not chase after a woman I barely know.

But, I am, and she wants nothing to do with me.
She thinks I'm the devil.
And I have to say she makes me want to sin.

I'm becoming a borderline stalker.
And to make matters worse she's affecting my game.
I can't pitch.
I can't hit.
I can't focus.
Something needs to give, and it won't be me.

CHAPTER ONE
CALLIOPE

My veins are going to explode. I scan the list of ingredients in the Max Energy drink I consumed this morning, checking to see if drugs are listed. They aren't.

With a move I imagine is worthy of Maxwell Hunter, the star pitcher who endorses it, I wind my arm back and rocket the sleek silver can across the conference room of Mayhem Marketing. It thunks against the cream-colored wall and lands with a thump inside the small trash can.

"Yesss," I exclaim as the door opens.

"They're ready for you, Calliope," Rita, assistant to the man who's going to hire me to cater all of his marketing company's functions, informs me with a furrowed brow.

He hasn't actually agreed to hire me yet, but he will, because according to the energy drink 'It's winning in a can.'

"Let's do this, Rita," I nearly squeal, ping-ponging around the room where I'll be serving the King and his court various items I've created. "I'm going to win them over with my baking skills."

CHAPTER ONE

"You ok?" she asks, at half the speed I seem to be talking.

I give her two very animated thumbs up, feeling like my arms are going to shoot off to the ceiling.

"Yes." I smooth my hands down the long length of my hair, from root to bottom. The usually heavy brown locks feel like they're standing on end. I need to calm down, but I can't. I feel electrified. Times one hundred.

She moves to the corner of the room as Tobias Longwood, grey-haired owner of Mayhem Marketing, enters, followed by two men in suits. My heart rate accelerates to an unnatural rhythm. I'm not sure if it's the energy drink or the fact I've been dreaming about this opportunity for such a long time. If I can land this account, I'll finally have the extra money to expand my cafe. Thanks to Max Energy, that thought makes me extra excited.

"Miss Thomas, hello," Tobias greets me. "Thanks for coming."

"Nice to meet you," I respond a little too loud over the pulse in my ears, giving his outstretched hand several vigorous pumps.

His brow furrows just like Rita's did, and I try to dial it down a notch, but my dial is broken.

It can't be normal that my lips tingle when I smile as Tobias introduces me to the two execs who will help decide my fate about whether or not I'll be hired.

While the people I'm here to impress take a seat at the rectangular table, I chatter, uncontrollably, about my creations and with jittery hands remove the rich chocolate cake adorned with the Mayhem logo from its box.

"Looks delicious," Tobias compliments me as I move closer at warp speed.

CHAPTER ONE

My feet walk faster than my heels can keep up, and instead of placing my showpiece in the center of the table, the cake somehow teeters amidst a chorus of gasps to end up a ganache mess... right in Tobias' lap. All three layers.

"I'm so sorry," I apologize, staring at the broken lump on his groin.

"Are you on drugs?" he asks with a pinched face, looking down at the red Mayhem logo smeared on his pristine white shirt.

"No," I deny, "I can explain." My eyes dart at a rapid pace to the shocked expressions on the other faces seated at the table.

"You get one shot here. That was yours. Thank you for coming in, Miss Thomas."

"It was an energy drink—Max Energy—by that famous baseball player," I tell him, because like he said, this is my one shot. "Listen, whoever marketed that as success in a can should be fired."

As he removes a lump of cake from his soiled trousers into the garbage can Rita retrieved, he informs me, "We designed that campaign."

The room is silent as I pack my things and go. All of my dreams follow me out the door. I'm too high on Max Energy to be depressed.

I have no one to blame but myself. And Maxwell Hunter, the man behind the drink.

When I get home, I drop my purse on the kitchen counter and beeline straight for the fridge. On the top shelf, next to the milk, sit the remaining cans of Max Energy. I tilt one of the tall cylinders and read the tiny black font:

Max Energy will give you that extra you need to reach your goals. It's winning in a can.

Share your success.

Leave a review.

The words taunt me before I toss it in the trash. The four cans left in my fridge follow it into the garbage before I move over to my laptop on the island in my kitchen. I type in the web address to the Nile site listed on the can and search for Max Energy, clicking on the tiny thumbnail, and then, scrolling through all the five-star reviews.

Delicious! I finished a project for work that earned me a bonus.

Homerun. Finally, put together the bookshelf I'd been dreading.

Review after review raves about this drink.

7 stars!

I'd give it 100 if I could! I've never tasted anything like this or had so much energy. You will love it!

Seven out of five?

I can barely refrain from commenting to ReviewQueen that her rating is impossible. You can *not* give more than you have.

I click on 'My Review' and select one star. Annoyance flows through my veins and spills out from my fingertips as I type.

Let me share my story with you. It doesn't have a happy ending, just like the book I had stayed up all night reading didn't. I was tired the next morning, and my coworker had given me these from her PR package, so I thought, 'Sure, I'll try it.' I drank one before the most important meeting of my life. Big mistake.

This is not success in a can. Don't drink the kool-aid, people. Or actually, do. Maybe you won't bounce off the walls and lose your dream client. Thanks, Max. Thank you for my failure. I hope you have a losing season.

And then, I press the submit button. Take that, Maxwell Hunter.

CLICK HERE to continue reading!!

LOGAN CHANCE

Logan Chance is a USA Today, Top 20 Amazon, KDP All-Star, and KDP All-Star UK bestselling author with a quick wit and penchant for the simple things in life: Star Wars, music, and smart girls who love to read. He was nominated best debut author for the Goodreads Choice Awards in 2016. His works can be classified as Dramedies (Drama+Comedies), featuring a ton of laughs and many swoon worthy, heartfelt moments.

Keep in touch with Logan.
Join The Logang
Get a special gift from Logan!
Hang out with Logan on Facebook

Want more sexy fun romantic reads?
Sign up for Logan's List and receive a copy of RENDEZVOUS, a steamy spring fling novella.
CLICK HERE to claim your book.

Don't be shy, follow Logan on all platforms:

ALSO BY LOGAN CHANCE

Cold Hearted Series

COLD HEARTED BALLER

COLD HEARTED BASTARD

The Playboy Series

PLAYBOY

HEARTBREAKER

STUCK

LOVE DOCTOR

Mafia Romance

THE DECEIT DUET

TAKEN

WE ALL FALL DOWN

THE NEWLYFEDS, A Romantic Comedy

The Me Series

DATE ME

STUDY ME

SAVE ME

BREAK ME

The Boss Duet

LIKE A BOSS

LOVE A BOSS

Made in the USA
Coppell, TX
31 October 2021